FLASH BANG

MEGHAN

NEW YORK TIMES BESTSELLING AUTHOR

MARCH

Visit my website at www.meghanmarch.com

CONTENTS

ABOUT FLASH BANG

Rowan Callahan is a career-climbing attorney focused on her future. But vicious—and false—rumors are destroying her professional life. That all ceases to matter when a plane crashes in downtown Chicago and the entire city goes dark, and she realizes she's just witnessed the kick-off to the apocalypse. Armed with a backpack of supplies, she leaves Chicago, intent on resetting her skewed priorities and seeking shelter at the family farm with her father and sister.

She's injured and running for her life when she stumbles directly in the crosshairs of two men who just might be her salvation . . . and her greatest temptation.

CHAPTER ONE

September—Chicago.

A plane fell from the sky.

It was quite possibly the only interruption that could have dragged Rowan out of the epic pity party she was throwing herself. It was the kind of pity party one threw when a carefully planned life and decades of hard work were demolished by a complete and utter shit storm. And not demolition by a run-of-the-mill shit storm. A shit mudslide, followed by a category five shit hurricane. Rowan doubted anything other than the plane, the fifty-story building it toppled and the hundreds of lives that had been violently and tragically cut short could have pushed the thoughts of the lying asshole and blackballing bitch who owned his sad sack from her mind.

Rowan had to swallow back the bile that rose when what she'd just seen started to sink in. The loss of life ... *What the hell just happened?*

The symphony of honking horns that filled the Chicago

streets died abruptly, right in time with the falling plane. For a single moment, the lunchtime crowds on North Wacker Drive completely stilled.

A beat of silence.

Then chaos erupted.

"We're under attack!" a woman screamed. She was only three feet away from Ro, and her screech nearly ruptured an eardrum. *Terrorists. Okay. That makes sense. Doesn't it?*

"Run!" a large man in a suit shouted as flames burst from the collapsing building.

Traffic stood still. The familiar sound of idling engines and car radios was eerily absent. Rowan's gaze darted around frantically. The traffic lights and DO NOT WALK signs were dark. There were no fire truck sirens screaming toward the building that was quickly becoming a fully involved inferno. No ambulances were rushing to the scene to try to save potential survivors.

A greasy feeling of panic pooled in Ro's stomach. Loud popping noises punctured through the sounds of chaos as the glass globes of the nearby light poles shattered before bursting into flames.

Without taking her eyes from the disaster playing out before her, Ro rooted around in her bag for her cell phone. Her panic spiked when she pressed the button and swiped her finger across the darkened screen. Nothing. It had been nearly fully charged when she'd unplugged it from the charger on her desk only twenty minutes ago. Ro's continued furious pressing of buttons did nothing to bring it to life.

Her brain snapped into focus. *No way. It's not possible.*

A firefighter crashed into her bistro table as he ran toward the burning building. Her uncapped bottle of iced tea toppled, spilling onto her lap. The splash of cold liquid freed Rowan from her temporary paralysis, just as three other firefighters ran past. *Thank God help is on the way.* In that moment, she made her decision. She reached down to yank off her pumps, swapped them for the ballet flats in her bag, and started to run.

CHAPTER TWO

The sidewalks were crammed with frantic people, and Ro veered into the road, running down the middle of two lanes of frozen cars. Dodging the doors that were flung open, she sprinted the five blocks to her condo, forcing down the bubbling fear that threatened to strangle her. Her building was still standing, and there was no sign of smoke or flames. Residents crowded the sidewalk in front of the building, some were yelling, but most looked completely bewildered. Ro shoved back the instinct to try to explain what she thought might be happening. They would all think she was crazy. *As crazy as I sometimes thought dad was.* She darted around the crowd and threw open the lobby door and headed for the stairs. Seven flights later, she bolted down the hall and jammed her keys into the lock.

Even though she knew her condo was going to be silent, it still felt unnatural. There was no hum from the fridge, and the displays on the microwave and stove were black. There was no annoying blink of 12:00.

As was typical when Rowan was alone, she started talking to the empty rooms.

"This isn't happening." She dropped her bag at the door and headed into the bedroom. "He couldn't have been right. It's just not possible. It should have been the opposite of possible."

She tore off her light gray suit jacket and blouse, dropping them on the unmade bed. The tangled sheets were evidence of her sleepless night. It was unbelievable how the things that had kept Rowan up for all hours could instantly seem so inconsequential. Especially when she thought about the insane tragedy she had just witnessed. She could only begin to imagine how the people at Ground Zero had felt on that fateful September day. Sick with helplessness. Suffocated by fear. Ro leaned against the wall, sagging into it for support. She needed to stay calm. She needed to focus.

In the positive column—maybe the only item in the positive column—if her father's Vietnam vet slash doomsday-prepper on steroids predictions had actually come to pass, the dick-tastic Charles, his strap-on wearing mistress of evil, and the utter disaster they'd made of Rowan's professional life had just ceased to matter.

Ro pushed off the wall and headed to her dresser. The bottom drawer yielded a few well-worn pairs of jeans and old t-shirts she kept for sleeping in. Tossing them on the bed, she headed for the walk-in closet, flipping the light switch as she entered. No lights flicked on. Obviously. But the habit was too ingrained to stop.

The lack of lights triggered another bout of talking to herself. "I just can't believe this is happening." Ro knew, rationally, that she could be completely wrong. Probably was wrong. But something in her gut had her believing the worst. It was like a Magic 8 ball from middle school: *All signs point to yes.* Too bad her gut had kept eerily silent about Charles. Ro forced the thought away. *Not important anymore.*

Moving farther into the dark closet, Ro shoved aside the

rows of sophisticated suits and the tasteful blouses she'd so carefully selected to make up her work wardrobe. No slut gear for her, despite what her recently acquired reputation at the firm would suggest. *So ridiculously unimportant now.* Within seconds, she had her hands on her salvation. A camouflage MOLLE backpack. Dad's Army surplus special. This particular backpack was one she'd grudgingly dragged from dorm rooms to apartments before finally shoving it into the corner of her closet in the swanky condo she'd been oh-so-proud of until she realized just how superficial she'd become.

She hefted the bag from the closet and dropped it on the bed. She unzipped the main compartment and surveyed the contents. MREs, bottled water, first aid supplies, a flint and steel, lighters, Ka-Bar, compass, flashlight, batteries, hiking water filter, single person tent, emergency blanket, toothbrush, toothpaste, and a host of other random survival gear. And a *taser*, for the love of Christ. Dad must have added that during his only visit to the city last summer. Hell, knowing him, he'd probably swapped out most of the contents with fresh supplies. Her dad was strange and amazing that way. Anything to make sure his girls were safe. Even if they thought he was a few pieces short of a full puzzle some days. Returning to the closet, she felt around until she laid her hands on her only pair of hiking boots, tucked away in the back of her shoe rack, and then pulled a sparsely-used black Helly Hansen rain coat from a hook on the back of the closet door. Ro tossed the coat on the bed next to the backpack and grabbed a hooded sweatshirt, handful of socks and underwear, and added it to the pile of jeans and t-shirts on the bed. She dressed in a pair of jeans and a black t-shirt, then rolled the remaining clothes into small bundles and shoved everything that would fit in the backpack before sitting on the bed to pull on a thick pair of socks and the boots. From her position on the end of the bed, she could see directly out the window to the building frenzy on the streets below. Small fires were starting to spread and would soon probably rage out of control without the luxury of fire trucks. Would the hydrants even work? Mobs of people shoved their way in and out of the stores, carrying everything they could hold. *Good to know it took less than ten minutes for the looting to begin.*

Gunshots punched through the commotion, and Ro knew she was making the right decision. She hefted the back-pack over her shoulders and started for the condo door, knowing she wouldn't be coming back. It was a sad testament to her life that she had no problem walking away from everything. The only person she would have dragged out of the city was her assistant, Amber. But Amber was visiting her mother in Idaho. Which was probably for the best. Tears started to well up in Ro's eyes when she realized she probably wouldn't ever see her again. Because she'd spent nearly every waking hour at work, Amber had been her only real friend. Except for the few weeks when she'd "dated" Charles, Ro didn't socialize. She didn't have a group of girl pals she met up with for drinks. She only had acquaintances from work. And if they went out, they talked about work. And they'd been quick to drop her like a bad habit when the rumors started swirling. Ro silently wished them all the best of luck. She couldn't hold it against them. Everything she'd spent the last ten years of her life working for had become essentially meaningless in a single, insane moment in time and so had the slights and grudges. It was time to let it go and unbury that country girl Ro had covered with layers of silk, suit, and polish. It was time to get the hell out of Chicago.

CHAPTER THREE

Six days later—Somewhere in Michigan.

Rowan's heart beat erratically. The stitch in her side pinched viciously, and her lungs burned from exertion.

She darted into a thick stand of bushy pine trees, hoping she'd lost them. And if she hadn't, Ro prayed the trees and the thickening darkness would at least make her difficult to spot.

Dropping her backpack, she fisted her hands on her hips and attempted to catch her breath. Damn, running sucked balls. Especially running for your life. Because Ro was pretty sure that was what she was doing. She studied the woods, watching for any hint of movement, ready to grab her bag and run again, but all she could see was the dim outline of trees. It was easy to forget how fast darkness fell in the woods. She focused, but heard nothing but the sounds of the forest bedding down for nightfall. Regardless, she wasn't going to be getting any sleep tonight.

The events of the last hour, much like the last six days, had been surreal.

Avoiding towns and people as much as possible on her trek home seemed like the best choice on a short list of shitty alternatives. She'd stayed just off the roads, kept to herself, and ventured even farther afield to set up her makeshift camp each night. Sleeping with one eye open was hell on the REM cycle. Exhaustion seemed to double the weight of her pack and make every mile longer than the last.

The evening had started much the same as the last six had—Rowan walked until she wanted to cry at the thought of taking another step, and then started assessing her options for the night. She'd been in Michigan for a few days, and houses were becoming fewer and farther between. She figured she had to be within a few days from home, depending on whether she could continue the pace she'd set. And that was debatable.

With thoughts of home distracting her, Ro ventured deeper into the woods than she'd planned. Then she heard the scream. Not a *help I'm a damsel in distress* type scream, but a wild and desperate keening sound that was wholly primal fear and cornered animal. The kind of scream that sounded like someone was fighting for her life ... or dying. The kind of scream that a sane woman, on her own and six days into what might truly be The Apocalypse, ran away from. Not toward.

But that scream ... even though it was irrational, Ro pictured her sister. When the second scream pierced the tranquility of the woods at sunset, Ro couldn't help but move furtively toward the sound until she spotted what appeared to be the redneck trailer-hood in the middle of the woods. Four mobile homes, so rusted it was impossible to tell what color they might have been during their younger days, formed a square. Most of the windows were boarded shut, and one had a roof-type structure built over it that extended beyond the trailer to a workshop area. A long stack of neatly piled firewood ran behind the workshop and trailer. Ro ducked behind the pile and peeked over the top. Animal skins were stretched on frames, and a fresh carcass sat on a workbench, waiting to be butchered. Flies buzzed around the blood that pooled on the tabletop. Dead doe eyes stared back at Rowan. And then she saw her.

The kick of adrenaline that sent her running toward danger drained out of Ro like water cupped in the palm of her hand, leaving icy shivers of fear in its wake.

A man with greasy, gray and red streaked hair and a shaggy beard dragged a woman by her hair out of the trailer directly across from Ro and pulled her off the ground to her knees. His gut hung over the dark pants he wore, and his faded red plaid flannel shirt split between the buttons to contain his bulk. The screen door slammed against the rusted exterior as two other men burst out, one clutching his unzipped crotch with both hands, heading toward Red and the hysterical woman who was clawing at the hand he had twisted in her brownish blonde hair.

"Listen to me, you stupid cunt," Red said, pulling a wicked buck knife from the sheath at his belt. He tugged her hair back and pressed the knife to her throat. The woman stopped struggling. "I will gut you like a fucking pig if you make another sound." Her cries dropped to whimpers.

"Fuck that, Pa. I'm going to cut that bitch! She almost bit my fucking cock off!" This was from the crotch-cradler. Ro cringed. He sounded seriously evil. The man behind him shoved him aside.

"That fucking cunt ain't worth the food it takes to keep her alive. I say we bury her and find us a more … accommo-datin' female." He spit a long stream of tobacco juice at the kneeling woman.

She looked pitiful—brown liquid dripping down her cheek, her clothes torn, and her eyes wild and terrified. The feelings of helplessness that had been swirling through Ro since that plane went down multiplied. She wished for a gun. Or an RPG. Or a freaking Black Hawk helicopter. Anything to eliminate these disgusting men from the face of the planet.

Red leaned closer to the woman and started to speak. Unable to make out what he was saying, Ro edged around the end of the woodpile, just beyond the roof covering the workshop. *Bad decision.* Her backpack strap caught on a piece of kindling and started a firewood avalanche. All three heads swung toward the sound. Their eyes widened. Red released the woman's hair, and she collapsed onto the dirt.

"Get her!"

Saying a quick prayer for the woman, Ro bolted. *I can't help her if I'm dead.* Ro promised herself she'd find a way to help her. As soon as she made sure she wasn't their next victim.

Fast-forward to the present.

Breathing starting to slow, Ro crouched, flipped open her compass, and flicked on her penlight. She needed to head northeast. After getting her bearings, Ro snapped off the light and leaned up against one of the trees for a blissful moment of rest and listened for any hint of her pursuers.

A stick snapped in the darkness.

The image of Red's wicked hunting knife flashed through Ro's mind, and the evil words of the creepy trio had her shouldering her backpack and springing into motion.

Unable to see through the utter blackness that had settled over the woods, and too scared of drawing attention to her position to use her light, Ro just ran. Hands out, crashing through brush and swerving between the trees, she tried to block the branches, but they scraped across her face. The needles on the pine trees felt like porcupine quills when they made contact with her hands and cheeks. She ignored the sting and focused on putting as much ground between them as she could. Ro hoped their bulk would inhibit their ability to run long distances, but she didn't slow down. The creepy trio might have endurance down to a science if they were used to living off the land.

The roar of her pulse made it nearly impossible to hear, but she thought she heard a man's voice behind her. She risked a quick backward glance. If she saw red flannel and scraggly gray and red hair, she'd lose her shit.

Nothing.

She couldn't see a damn thing.

A quick rush of relief, and then a burn tore through her ankle as she pitched forward. Ro threw her hands out to catch herself just before her face made contact with the ground.

Ro squeezed her eyes shut and bit the inside of her cheek. The coppery tang of blood filled her mouth, but it kept her from yelling.

Good Jesus, that hurt like a son of a bitch. The sharp pain in her ankle had the MRE she'd eaten for lunch threatening to reappear.

The simple reality of the situation hit her like an open-handed slap to the face. If she couldn't run, she was screwed. If she couldn't walk, she was screwed.

Brilliant, Ro. Ten points for stating the obvious.

She pushed away the image of the creepy trio coming up behind her and forced herself to her knees. A twinge shot through her right wrist. *Even better.* Must have strained it catching her fall. Apparently Ro needed '90s-style rollerblade wrist guards for a walk in the woods.

Working as quickly and quietly as she could, Ro dropped onto her right hip and kept her left ankle off the ground. Shrugging the pack off her shoulders, she dragged it around beside her. There was an ace bandage and an instant ice pack in the first aid kit. Trying to keep her movements silent,

Ro unzipped the backpack and pulled out the smaller red bag that contained first aid supplies. She paused just before squashing the instant ice pack between her palms to start the chemical reaction. Was she supposed to take off her hiking boot and wrap the ice around her ankle before shoving it back into the boot and then trying to walk on it? Or was she better off leaving it tied up tightly in the high, leather hiking boot? At times like this it was clear that med school would have been a much better investment than law school. Ro rubbed her face with both palms in frustration, before realizing her hands were covered in dirt from catching herself as she fell. *And now so was her face.* Ro tried to take a few deep, calming breaths, and didn't know whether to laugh or cry. *Dead tired, running from crazy, scary, possibly murdering rednecks, and likely suffering from a sprained ankle. What a fucking disaster.* She'd been so proud of herself for making it this far. Rather than lose her ever-loving mind, Ro opted for the mental pep talk: *Maybe it's not that bad. Just a slight sprain. I could just pull some brush around me for cover, lay low for the night, and hope like hell the creepy trio gives up looking for me. And be on my way well before they could possibly find me in the morning.* Good Lord, that sounded like a whole lot of hope, and Ro much preferred to deal in realities.

Brush rustled. Ro froze. *Oh fuck. They're here.* Ro waited, heart pounding, to hear another sound that would indicate the presence of another person. Nothing. A gust of wind barreled down through the woods. The leaves clattered, and the trees swayed. Ro couldn't discern any other unusual noises. *Come on nature … throw me a bone here.* Her eyes darted right and left, trying to make out anything in the darkness, holding the rest of herself completely still. And then she felt a presence behind her. She went for the Ka-Bar strapped to her belt. But before she could reach it, a large hand clamped over her mouth.

CHAPTER FOUR

Fire watch was the most boring fucking job of all time. Before the events of the last week, Graham hadn't kept watch in years. Just one more reason it was good to be in charge. No shit jobs. But after the grid went down, every man living at Castle Creek Whitetail Ranch pulled his weight on fire watch. No exceptions. Which meant Graham was back on rotation. With ten men, and three or four on watch at all times, no one got a pass on that shit. It wasn't easy to patrol the ten-foot perimeter fence that surrounded the 660 acres of woods, hills, fields, creeks, and living compound that made up one of the most exclusive, if rustic, whitetail deer hunting outfits in the state. With the security system they had set up and a few other tricks, they were pretty well locked down. But Graham knew they couldn't afford to take chances. Especially six days into the biggest goat fuck anyone had ever seen in the good ol' US of A. Inhabitants of third world countries might be accustomed to going without power and running water, but that was because they were either (a) too poor to have power and running water in the first place or (b) they'd had the shit bombed out of their homes. The average U.S. citizen was soft. Not used to going without the luxuries that had become so common and forgettable. Sure, everyone had watched the towers fall on 9/11, but from the safety of their living rooms, on big screen color TVs. Graham could imagine the chaos that had broken out in the last six days across the country—if, in fact, the whole country was affected by what he and his team were pretty damn certain had been an electromagnetic pulse, or EMP. The cause of the giant burst of electromagnetic energy that had knocked out the electrical grid and damaged unprotected electronics was still up for debate, though. It could have been a nuke detonated high above US airspace, or a solar flare that finally didn't miss. The ham radio that Ty kept screwing around with stayed mostly silent. There'd only been a few transmissions in the last week, giving the term 'radio silence' a whole new meaning. Each one of those transmissions had confirmed what they feared: no functioning electrical grid reported anywhere.

Every fire watch rotation that Graham had taken during the last week had been uneventful, but tonight's watch was shaping up to be a little more exciting. A signal had pinged in the command post, indicating that a sensor on the outermost perimeter, fifty yards outside the fence line, had been tripped. Command had radioed the men on watch, and everyone was on alert. Graham had climbed into a tree stand that doubled as an observation post to try to get a better look at what was going down outside the fence.

Graham trained the night vision scope of his M4 carbine rifle on the break in the trees where he could hear snapping branches and crunching leaves. Whoever had tripped the perimeter sensor and headed toward the fence wasn't even attempting to be stealthy about it. Someone was plowing through the woods like a gut shot deer. Either the person was an idiot or he had no clue he was running straight toward a fence that stretched for a square mile.

A body burst through the tree line just beyond the fence. Graham sighted in his shot, rested his finger on the trigger. A ponytail. *Shit.* Female. Sliding his finger away from the trigger, Graham kept her in his crosshairs. Spending any amount of time in the Sandbox taught you that women sure as hell weren't all innocent. He'd seen more than one with a bomb strapped to her chest, hoping to take out as many American troops as possible. They also made good bait for a trap. This one wasn't paying attention to where her feet were landing and went down hard. She didn't get up.

Graham scanned the tree line behind her. No sign of anyone else.

"Got a live one about twenty yards out from the southwest perimeter fence," Graham reported to the team through his radio. "Possibly injured. I'm holding position."

Graham watched as she maneuvered herself onto her ass, clearly trying not to jar her left ankle. "Scratch possibly. Female is definitely injured."

"Say again? We got a chick running around out there tonight?" Jonah's voice shot back through Graham's earpiece.

"Female. Either that or a smallish man with tits and a ponytail," Graham said.

Graham's finger eased back over the trigger when he saw her drag her backpack around. Was she going for a weapon? She pulled out a smaller bag … of first aid supplies. Okay. So she was either bait for some sort of trap or legitimately injured and in need of assistance.

"Outermost southwest perimeter sensor just lit up again. Same sensor as before. We've got more incoming. You copy?" Jamie, his teammate stationed in the command post, reported.

It could be a coincidence, the second part of the trap, or it could be the reason the woman was running through the pitch black woods like a bat out of hell. Graham sure as shit didn't believe in coincidences.

"Copy that. I'm going to retrieve the female. Can someone get over here to cover me?" Graham asked. Usually, rescuing damsels in distress was more Zach's M.O., but Graham figured now was as good a time as any to wear the sucker sign. He might be a dick most of the time, but the woman had been running for all she was worth when she took that header. It was a risk, but a calculated one. He could always shoot her later if it turned out to be trap.

"You sure about that, G-man?" Jonah asked through the radio. "She could be bait or a poacher."

"Not a fucking idiot," Graham replied. "It's my call, and I'm making it. Cover me like you've got a pair if you're so worried about it. I'll be inside the walls in fifteen or less. Get someone out here to take my post."

Graham climbed down the spikes protruding from the tree and headed for a barely perceptible gate that was built into the fence line.

Rescue mission or clusterfuck. Graham figured it could go either way at this point. Good thing he could handle either.

CHAPTER FIVE

The hand that clamped over her mouth cut off Rowan's scream and air supply. A really, really big hand. It covered half her face. Then the hand's owner spoke low in her ear.

"I'm going to pick you up, and you will not give me any shit, and you will not struggle. When I move my hand, you will not scream. Get me, woman?"

The voice was deep and so close; Ro felt his words more than heard them. The hand not covering her mouth was slipping the Ka-Bar from the sheath on her belt. She was now officially incapacitated and without a weapon.

Apparently he wanted some indication that she did in fact "get him," because he pulled her head to the side to make eye contact. Even though she was pretty damn sure he wasn't Red, based on the fresh pine scent emanating from him, seeing dark eyes and a face smeared with camouflage paint was a relief. Momentarily. Because then he spoke again.

"I said, get me, woman?" he repeated, sounding annoyed. And scary. "When I take my hand off your mouth, you're going to keep it shut like a good little girl. We clear?"

Ro wasn't sure how he expected her to answer when she couldn't even *breathe.* He shook her, as if trying to get her attention. Like he didn't already have it.

"Are we clear?" His low rumble had turned into a growl.

Ro didn't *get him,* and she wasn't *clear.* As far as she knew, this guy could be worse than the creepy trio. After the six-day march on Ro's personal trail of tears, the scene she'd witnessed less than an hour ago, the pain shooting from her ankle, and the asshole currently barking orders at her, Ro hit her limit. Her survival instincts were screaming at her to do something to get free. So she decided to go for the backward head butt. WWE Smack Down-style. Classy-like.

Something in her movements must have telegraphed her intent, because before her head could connect with his nose, the hand across her mouth tightened, and his other hand palmed the back of her head, pulling in the opposite direction of the hand over her mouth.

"I could snap your neck in less than a motherfucking second. I don't have time to fuck around. We're moving." Without waiting for a response, he tossed her up over his shoulder like a bag of feed. From her upside down perch, Ro saw him snag her backpack and throw one strap over his other shoulder. He paused for a moment before trotting in the same direction Ro had been running before she'd taken a header into the forest floor.

Apparently Conan the Barbarian, as Ro had dubbed him, liked to manhandle women. God only knew what he had in mind for her. *Why am I not fighting back? Am I going to make this easy for him?* Ro considered trying to drive her elbow through his back and then recalled his threat about snapping her neck.

Fuck it. How much worse could things really get? After all, she'd just added being kidnapped to her list of life experiences.

She elbowed him in the back as hard as she could. His muscles felt like slabs of concrete. He didn't even pause his easy jog when she landed her strike. Not even a hard exhale. The helpless feelings began to mount. The second time she was determined to make sure he'd feel it. She rammed her elbow between his shoulder blades and thought she heard a grunt.

Ro was congratulating herself on a least scoring a hit when a large hand came down on her ass in a hard *smack*.

Conan had just spanked her! *Oh, hell no.* Rather than being subdued, Ro's temper flared white-hot. No one had spanked Ro since her beverage container of choice was a sippy-cup. And Conan the Barbarian with the camo-painted face was not getting away with it. Ro wished for the acrylic claws the Mistress of Evil had for nails. The ones she'd trailed down Ro's cheek in that über creepy way that made Ro struggle not to projectile vomit. The memory made Ro shiver. *Focus on now. I am not helpless. Not then and not now.* So Ro did the next best thing she could think of. She bit him.

———

"Motherfucker!" Graham wanted to rage, but the word came out as a low growl. Operational security required silence. The bitch and her bony elbows and vampire canines weren't going to fuck up Graham's simple mission.

He smacked her round little ass again, harder this time. She squeaked and jabbed his back with one of those pointy little elbows. At least she couldn't yell with her teeth embedded in his back. That had actually kind of hurt. Not that Graham would ever admit it. He probably should have been more pissed about the bite mark that he was going to be sporting, but he found it a little hard to condemn the girl when she was probably scared out of her damn mind, and

20

her instincts were ricocheting between fight and flight. It didn't take much combat experience to become intimately familiar with the human instinct to survive. How many combat virgins had Graham seen run at the first sounds of live fire? Or duck when they heard mortar rounds whistling into camp? Too many to count.

But still, Graham wasn't a fan of teeth marks on his back. Fingernail scratches sustained during a marathon three-way? Perfectly acceptable. But teeth marks while fully clothed he could do without. Thoughts firmly in the gutter, as usual, Graham's cock twitched. Little fucker didn't know or care whether now was the appropriate time to stand up and take notice. Graham slipped back through the gate and turned to make sure it was latched.

He started a brisk jog toward the walled compound that housed their living quarters, which was located about forty acres in from the southwest corner of the spread. Her struggles ceased in favor of gripping Graham's back to hold on. Graham still had no idea why she'd ended up near his fence, but he was damn curious to find out.

CHAPTER SIX

From her upside down vantage point across Conan's back, Ro watched another man close, bolt, and bar a small porthole-like door in a giant steel wall topped with razor wire. It closed silently, but it might as well have slammed like a cell door. Panic rose as Conan strode farther into the camp.

Ro renewed her struggles. And she didn't keep quiet this time either.

"Put me down! Let me go! Umpf—" Ro's words were cut off as her still-stinging ass landed on a picnic table bench.

Conan got in her face. "You're in no position to be giving orders. And until you answer my questions, you aren't going anywhere except where I put you."

Ro opened her mouth to let out a scathing reply, but snapped it shut when she realized she could see the angles and planes of his painted face in the glow of artificial light. She hadn't seen any working lights in the last week and was shocked to see one now. It was amazing how quickly things she used to take for granted became oddities. But back to the face in front of hers. He had lowered himself into a crouch in front of her. He looked like G.I. Joe come to life. But even bigger than the Channing Tatum version. His face was covered in smears of brown, black, and gray, and a black long-sleeve t-shirt stretched tightly over linebacker-esque shoulders. He looked as if he was easily twice Ro's size. The bulging muscles and defined pecs briefly distracted her, but the rifle held casually in his grip, barrel pointed in her general vicinity, caught and held her attention. An M4, the smaller, more compact version of the M16, if she remembered her dad's lessons clearly. Her eyes darted between his face and the gun, trying to figure out her best course of action if he decided to unload the thirty round magazine in her direction. *Nothing. There wasn't a damn thing she'd be able to do if he decided to use her for target practice.* And the look on his face wasn't inspiring any confidence that he wasn't intending to do just that. His piercing dark eyes cataloged every detail of her appearance. Thinking it was best to present as small a target as possible, Ro wrapped her arms around herself and shrank back until the edge of the picnic table dug into her spine.

Under the camo paint, his dark brows furrowed, as if he was confused by her actions. He followed her eyes to the gun and lifted his dark gaze to hers.

One brow arched sardonically when he said, "You do know that I'm not planning to shoot you." Ro couldn't help mentally tacking on a "yet" to the end of his sentence.

She decided it was time to unearth her lady balls and stop acting like a scared little girl. Decision made … Ro couldn't stop her snark.

"No, as a matter of fact, I was not aware that you weren't going to shoot me when you've got the barrel of a gun less than twelve inches from my face. And after you mentioned snapping my neck, I've developed the impression that my continuing to breathe isn't exactly a priority of yours." Ro held his stare, unwilling to show any more weakness or fear by breaking first.

Wasn't there some animal you were supposed to stare down to show you're not afraid? Or was that what you were not supposed to do? Yet another instance where law school failed to teach her practical skills. Like how to stare down a giant, camo-painted man who comfortably held an assault rifle as if it was a part of his daily uniform. A man with too-long, dark brown hair that curled over his ears and the base of his neck, making him look unbelievably sexy.

Wait. What?

Ro must have hit her head when she'd fallen. That was the only logical explanation for the errant thought.

Standing, he propped the gun against a four-by-four beam that supported the porch covering the area surrounding the picnic table. He lowered the barrel and resumed his crouching position in front of her.

"Point taken."

He looked like he was about to say something else when a tall, nearly as broad, man with longish golden brown hair sat down right next to her on the bench as if they were long lost friends.

"Don't worry, doll. He's all bark. He won't bite unless you ask for it. Probably." His drawl was as smooth and potent as Tennessee sippin' whiskey. He stuck out his hand. "I'm Zach. Zachariah Sawyer."

Ro automatically stuck out her hand to shake his. The habit was too ingrained to stop. *Because that's what you do when someone offers a hand. Shake it. Even if you're in an end of the world nightmare scenario and the man offering his hand is beyond gorgeous.*

Good Lord. Where was she?

But instead of shaking her hand, he kissed it. In a move that Ro was certain no man outside of the 19th century could pull off without looking like a complete tool. And yet,

24

he made it look sexy. And feel sexy. Heat began to swirl low in her belly. *Seriously, body. Timing more than a little inappropriate.*

His eyes reminded Ro of whiskey, too. Golden amber and flaring with what appeared to be interest; as if he knew the effect he was having on her body. An irritated throat clearing broke the moment.

"Sawyer, if you're finished eye-fucking the shit out of her, I'd like to ask her a few questions."

Zach tossed Conan a bandana and rested his arm on the picnic table behind Rowan's shoulders.

"Clean the paint off your face, G, and calm down. I'm just getting acquainted."

Turning his gaze back on her, he asked, "What's your name, doll?"

Ro scooted down the bench to put some space between them and grasped her lady balls tight in an attempt to sound tough. "It sure as shit isn't doll. Could you back up off me?"

Conan laughed, or at least that's what Ro made of his gravelly rumble.

Conan was using the bandana to wipe the paint off his face as if he'd done it a million times. *Who were these guys?*

The face that came clean underneath was unexpected. A broad forehead, sharply carved cheekbones and a strong, squared-off jaw, covered in dark stubble. If she'd seen him dressed in a suit, passing her on the streets of Chicago, Ro might have spontaneously orgasmed. *Seriously, who were these guys?*

"What's your name, girl? And why were you alone and running through the woods like you were being chased by the devil himself?" Conan asked.

The statement wasn't far off the mark, and the images of the beaten woman, knife at her throat, came rushing back. Ro shifted, jostling her ankle, which had started to throb like crazy. She squeezed her eyes shut and tried to suppress the images and the pain. The shame of forgetting about the woman for even a moment burned sharper than the pain in her ankle.

"It's Rowan. Not girl, not doll, not anything else. Except maybe Ro, if you're not a total asshole. I was running through the woods in the middle of the night, by myself, because I didn't have a choice. It was either that or end up the backwoods bride of three creepy, inbred rednecks. Or dead." Ro wasn't convinced dead was the worse option of the two.

"Care to elaborate?" Conan asked, both eyebrows arching this time.

Ro couldn't think of a good reason not to explain further and told them what she had witnessed. Guilt for not doing something, *anything*, filled Ro. Hot tears pricked her lids. "I just left her there and ran."

Zach slid down the picnic table bench, and his big arm came around Rowan in a comforting gesture. For some reason, this time she didn't pull away.

"It's okay, Ro. What could little ol' you do against three grown men? You did the best thing you could possibly do." Ro looked at him, completely confused by his words.

Zach smiled at her and clarified, "You came straight to us."

The girl, *Rowan*, looked at him, and then Graham, and then back to him, before asking, "Who are you? And where the hell am I?" Her earlier attitude seemed to have drained away, leaving her sounding young and lost. She glanced around her, and in the pale glow of solar lights, Zach could see her trying to make out her surroundings.

He was about to answer her questions when Graham spoke.

"You'll get your answers when we're satisfied with yours. Your story sounds like complete bullshit to me."

Her attitude flared back to life. Zach wasn't sure what Graham's angle was. It sounded like she'd almost had an unfortunate meeting with their inbred neighbors. For years, Jonah had been telling the rest of the team about the family that lived a few miles from their fence line. With no obvious form of income, Jonah suspected they were deeply involved in the rural meth trade.

"You think my story is bullshit? Then go out there and fucking get her. Go be all Rambo badass commando, and you'll see that I'm *not fucking lying*."

Okay, someone had issues with being called a liar. *Interesting*. But Graham was a total hardass. It was embedded in the man's DNA. It was what had made him a great leader of their Force Recon team for six years. But Graham was solidly in the camp of seeing before believing. Zach had zero facts to base his conclusion on, but his gut said she was telling the truth. She looked pretty busted up over the fact that she'd left some stranger behind when she didn't have a chance in hell of being able to go up against three armed men. That type of reaction didn't seem like it would be easily faked. But Zach knew damn well that Graham wasn't going to leave the security of the ranch to chance. This interrogation was just beginning.

"G," Zach said firmly, giving Graham a hard look. "The questions can wait." It wasn't often that Zach countermanded Graham's orders, considering it used to be insubordination, but the girl was still freaked and obviously in pain, if the way she cringed every time she moved was any indication.

Graham clearly interpreted Zach's *back the fuck off look*

27

and returned one that said *this goes bad, it's on you.* But Graham backed off and took a seat on the bench of the picnic table that was parallel to the one where he and Rowan sat.

"You hurt, sugar?" Zach left the bench to go to his knees in front of her, lifting her ankle carefully. She flinched.

"I don't think it's broken. At least, I really hope not." She sounded like she was panicking at the thought.

Zach heard Graham speak into his radio, "Beau, need you at the mess ASAP."

"Copy that. On my way," Beau, the group's SARC—Special Amphibious Reconnaissance Corpsman—replied within seconds. As a Navy medic, Beau was the only non-Marine on their team. But since he'd actually gone to med school before joining the Navy and had saved most of their asses at least once, they didn't hold it against him.

Graham stood and gave Zach a long, hard look. "Don't move her until I get back."

Ro watched as the two men shared a look that carried an entire conversation. Both nodded before Conan stalked off.

Ro was relieved he was gone. Except for a few brief moments, his intensity had completely unnerved her. She looked at the man kneeling in the dirt before her. He was almost as big as Conan, but didn't emit those *I'm-a-badass-mofo-and-you-better-watch-yourself* vibes that Conan did. He still looked like a badass mofo, but somehow he was more approachable. Strange, that.

"We'll get you all fixed up, darlin'. Don't you worry 'bout a thing," he said, smiling up at her. *Definitely more approachable.*

"I'm not the one you should be worrying about. That other woman ..." Ro paused, replaying the scene she had witnessed in her mind. "You need to get her away from them. You don't understand, they were ... *disgusting* ... and the way they were treating her ..." She shook her head, stomach twisting at the memory.

Zach gripped her calf with his big hand.

"Babe, put it out of your mind for now. We'll handle it." Ro was well aware he was trying to soothe her, calm her down, because it must have seemed like she was gearing up for a freak out. Accurate assumption.

"Seriously—"

Zach cut her off, and this time his tone was stern. "Listen to me. There wasn't a thing you could have done, and you're lucky your pretty little ass made it here in one piece and without holes."

"But—"

"Damn, woman, you wanna argue with me. Just let it be. Let's worry about Rowan right now."

Apparently Zach wasn't as approachable as she thought. Ro's spirits fell, along with her hope that the commandos would rush in and save the day. Because that would be too much like a friggin' movie. Men weren't like that in real life.

Ro settled back against the picnic table and looked away from Zach. What little she could see of her surroundings had her forgetting her disappointment with individuals of the penis variety. The glow of the solar lights was muted, definitely not bright enough to be seen beyond the walls, and the giant branches of the towering oaks and white pines formed a canopy overhead. Ro could make out rustic, wood-sided buildings scattered around. The thump of a bag hitting the ground in front of her brought her attention back to the man—check that, now men—in front of her.

Piercing blue eyes assessed her from beneath black brows. His black hair was cut ruthlessly short, not shaggy like

Conan and Zach's. He didn't smile, which made his knife-edged cheekbones stand out even more.

He met Ro's gaze for only a minute before shifting his attention to Zach.

"What you need, Sawyer?" He sounded annoyed. Like he'd been in the middle of watching his team in overtime and had been interrupted. Except there were no games, no teams, and no overtime happening right now. Ro was pretty damn sure of that. What could she really have interrupted? His spank session? He didn't need to look so put out by her. She was the one brought here against her will. Ro's attitude fired into overdrive. As if Zach sensed her building tension, he squeezed her calf before he stood and stepped to her side.

"Beau, meet Rowan. Rowan, Beau." Beau nodded at her, looking completely uninterested in her presence. "Rowan here twisted her ankle, and I'd appreciate it if you'd check her out."

Beau didn't respond; he just squatted before her without ceremony.

Without looking up at her, he asked, "Which leg?"

"Left." Ro shrank back when he reached for her ankle.

"Babe, it's okay. Beau will fix you right up," Zach said.

"He looks like he'd just as soon amputate over handing me an ice pack," Ro replied.

At that, Beau finally cracked a smile.

"I do have a handy saw for amputations, but I think I'll leave it stashed tonight." He looked up at Ro. "It's going to hurt like a bitch getting this boot off. I'll try to go easy, but there's not much I can do about it."

Ro had figured that. She nodded as he got down to the business of unlacing her boot, gritting her teeth as bolts of pain shot through her ankle. She gripped the edge of the picnic table and closed her eyes. She tried to think of her sister and her dad. Waiting at home for her. A warm hand

30

covered her left hand and squeezed. She didn't open her eyes, but grabbed it like a lifeline and squeezed back when the pain kicked up another notch.

Cold air hit her sweaty sock. Finally. Her boot was off. And then the sock. Ro let out a slow breath and opened her eyes, first looking down at Beau grasping her ankle, and then over to where her hand was clasped by another large, callused one. But that hand didn't belong to Zach like she'd assumed. It was ... Conan. He'd appeared soundlessly, and for some reason ... offered her comfort? Ro was shocked. Amazed. Freaked out? She didn't even know. She pulled her hand back, trying not to look at him.

"What's the verdict?" Conan asked, actually sounding like he gave a shit. Which was strange, considering he'd threatened to kill her upon meeting her. She would've thought he'd gotten off on torturing people.

Ro sucked in a sharp breath and cringed as Beau manipulated her ankle. Conan's hand grabbed hers again, and the shooting pains tapered off.

"I don't think it's broken. Could be a hairline fracture, but it's hard to say without an X-ray. Which we obviously don't have. Probably a bad sprain. Either way, she's going to need to stay off it for at least a few days to start, but probably longer. Unfortunately, I have three pairs of crutches—old school wooden ones, built for guys our size. They're not very adjustable and would be way too fucking big for her," he told Conan, as though she wasn't present.

"Hey, I'm right here and would appreciate you giving *me* the diagnosis, thanks."

Beau looked at Ro condescendingly and said, "Okay, *Rowan,* your ankle is sprained. Don't walk on it for at least a few days to a week. Keep ice on it for fifteen minutes at a time, and keep it elevated and wrapped up. Got it?"

Ro couldn't help feeling like she'd just thrown a bit of a

temper tantrum and deserved his annoyed glare. He'd never done anything to her to merit her throwing him attitude, but now that throwing attitude had moved back into her repertoire, it was instinctive.

"She won't be going anywhere. So, that's not a problem. You'll wrap it up for her and grab her an ice pack." That wasn't posed as a question. It was definitely an order. And then Ro played his words over in her head. Um, yeah. That *was* a problem.

"Um, thanks, Conan, but I'll just take the wrap and the ice. If you have a place I could crash for the night, I'm sure I'll be all set in the morning. I've got somewhere to be."

Zach let out a strangled laugh-cough. "I think that's probably the most accurate nickname anyone's ever given him. Gonna have to share that one with the team."

Conan was silent, and she had to assume he was not as impressed by her creative naming skills. Her suspicions were confirmed when he said to Zach, "I know where you sleep."

She could feel Conan's intense stare drilling into her. When she didn't look up at him, his hand shot out and tilted her chin up.

"You got somewhere to be? How 'bout you share that with us."

When Ro didn't reply immediately, she swore she saw the muscle in his jaw twitch. Ro yanked her head away from his grip and looked at Beau, about to ask him for that ice pack, when the hand that grabbed her jaw turned her face back to meet a snapping brown gaze.

"Look, woman. You are in my house, and you will answer my questions. All of them. Get me?"

About to launch into a snit to end all angry snits, another hand on her shoulder stopped Ro. This one belonged to Zach.

"How'd you like to clean up? Get some of that mess off

you? I'm not sure if there's an inch of you not covered in dirt."

Ro checked the snit. A chance to get clean trumped throwing another tantrum. Priorities and all.

She tried not to sound too excited when she answered, "That would be great. Even some water and maybe some paper towel would be fine."

"Oh, honey, we can do better than that. You can take a proper shower, if you'd like."

Shower? Um, yes please.

"That would be awesome." Because six days of wet wipe baths left a whole lot to be desired. Ro figured she had to be pretty ripe, in addition to dirt-covered.

"She can't stand to take a shower, dumbass. What're you thinking?" Beau said.

Undeterred, Zach responded, "So we'll get her a chair. She can sit and shower. I mean, I know she needs to get her foot up, but that can wait ten minutes while she cleans up, right? I'll give her a hand."

A grunt had Zach looking toward Conan. "You need to report for fire watch. Now."

"I don't have watch tonight."

"You do now. I had to ... redeploy some assets, and you're taking Alex's shift."

From the mulish set of his jaw, Ro could tell that Zach wanted to argue, but for some reason he didn't. He just tapped her cheek with two fingers and said, "Later, doll. Enjoy the shower."

Ro was so excited about the shower she didn't even bother to ream him for calling her doll.

CHAPTER SEVEN

Ro's excitement turned into uncertainly in a hurry. She *really* wasn't sure about this. Well, she was damn sure she wanted a shower. But the fact that Conan was carrying her, bride-on-wedding-night-style, across the threshold of a rough-hewn wood-sided building was ... unsettling. First the handholding, and now the picking her up and carrying her places. And when he picked her up, it was like she weighed nothing. Ro wasn't a stick figure; she struggled to stay in a size eight, and definitely toted around ten extra pounds she could stand to lose, but Conan didn't seem to notice.

He flipped a light switch inside the building, and it worked! He sat her on a wooden bench in a room that looked, but didn't smell, like a high school locker room. Complete with a shower room set off to the right with showerheads attached to the walls. No curtains, no stalls, no dividers. Ro would have dwelled on this design flaw a little more, but she was still marveling at the fact that the light switch *actually worked*. Where the hell was she anyway? Neither Zach nor Conan had answered her earlier question. Ro resolved to figure it out. Right after she showered.

Conan headed back to the door.

"Stay put."

He walked out of the building, pulling the door shut behind him. Ro took in the yellow and white tiled interior. There was a long counter top studded with sinks every few feet. A mirror, hazy and spotted around the edges, ran the length of the counter. The big lockers lining two walls of the room had cage-like doors, so she could make out the contents. It looked like they were mostly filled with clothes in the colors of the camouflage rainbow—all black, green, brown, gray, tan, or actual camo print. Except for one locker, which looked like it held ... *pink bath toys?*

A stack of white towels sat piled in the locker nearest the shower room, which was separated from the main room only by an ankle-high tiled barrier. The entrance to the shower area was at least eight feet wide. Definitely no privacy. At all.

The door opened, and Conan stepped back inside carrying a brown metal folding chair. He walked to the shower area and set it up under the showerhead that was nearest to the entrance.

How exactly was this going to work?

Without saying a word, Conan squatted at her feet and unlaced the one boot she was still wearing before pulling it off, along with the sock.

Ro was stunned that he was undressing her like a child. "I can do that. It's fine."

"You'll want to lose the hoody," he said, as if she hadn't spoken. Ro pulled it over her head, but left on the t-shirt underneath. She was not stripping down in front of him. Better to make that crystal-freaking-clear right now.

"Um, you can go now. I can take it from here."

Conan didn't respond, but swung her up into his arms again and stepped over the divider into the shower room and sat her on the folding chair.

"Strip and toss me your clothes. You should be able to reach the shower knob from there."

Ignoring his order, Ro replied, "I said I can take it from here. You can go now."

"Toss me your clothes. You don't have anything I haven't already seen a hundred times before."

Nice.

"Seriously—"

"Strip. Or I'll do it for you."

"Turn around."

"Fine."

Ro looked behind her to see if he complied. He had. She unbuttoned and unzipped her jeans and wriggled them off. She tossed them into the locker room. Followed by her shirt. Ro reached to unhook her bra, but then stopped. Did she really want to be tossing her underwear at Conan like he was some rock star and she was a desperate groupie? Not really. *Not at all.*

As if he could read her mind, Conan said, "Just toss your fucking underwear, woman. I don't have all night to fuck around with you."

"Then just go!" Ro shot back.

"God, you are a frustrating piece. Just fucking strip. It's not a big deal. I'm sure you've been naked in front of plenty of guys."

Asshole. That comment stung, given Ro's recently acquired reputation as a raging slut, but even that couldn't dull her desire for a shower. So she went with the mature option and unhooked her bra and threw it at his head. He grabbed it off his shoulder and tossed it over to the bench. She pulled her underwear off and tossed them on the floor.

"I can take care of those. Now, could you please just go?"

"Just turn on the water, woman. I'm not going to look."

Ro grasped the knob and twisted it too hot. She couldn't

contain the squeak that came out when the first spray of cold water hit her. To his credit, Conan didn't budge.

"It'll warm up fast. Try to make it snappy. We don't like to waste the hot water."

True to his word, the water warmed up, and Ro had to adjust the temperature to avoid being scalded.

Trying not to moan like a porn star, Ro pulled out her hair tie and leaned into the spray to get her hair wet. It. Felt. So. Good.

"How do you even have hot water? And lights that work? I haven't seen lights anywhere else," Ro asked.

"We were more prepared than most. Got a good system set up. Alternative sources of power. Have our own wells." His words cut off. Like he just realized he was sharing with the enemy.

"You do know I'm not here to try to infiltrate your little camp, right? I didn't even know it was here. And you're the one who brought me here, against my will, I might add."

"That's what bait would say."

"Whatever." Ro wasn't about to spend the time she could be enjoying her shower arguing with Conan. He'd probably shut off the hot water because she was taking too long, so Ro got down to business.

Hair wet, and the metal chair getting slippery and sort of uncomfortable, Ro realized she didn't have any soap. She saw the dispenser on the wall. Bingo. Eau de commando couldn't be that bad. At worst it would smell like that scent-masking soap her dad used to use during hunting season that made him smell like dirt. But the dispenser was a little too high for her to reach from her seated position. Ro slid forward on the chair and put her weight on her right foot and reached out for the lever on the dispenser. Jackpot. Liquid soap filled her hand. She went to sit back down, but her wet ass slipped right off the slick metal seat, sending the chair skidding back across the shower floor. Ro tried to catch herself, and couldn't stop from putting her left foot down, the weight causing pain to shoot through her ankle. She started to fall backward, a girly shriek coming from her mouth. She braced herself for the pain that was about to be shooting up her tailbone, but before she made contact with the tile floor, a pair of strong arms wrapped around her wet, completely naked body, catching her just underneath her breasts. Ro let out another shriek, this time in surprise.

"I got you. Hold still." Ro froze, realizing that she'd started wriggling out of his grasp, which did nothing to get her free, but instead caused his hand to shift. It now covered her left breast. Like full-on, hand over boob.

Graham couldn't help that his dick was now rock hard. He had the girl's tit in his hand. And she didn't have a bad rack. Actually, she felt pretty fucking good, all slippery and wet, and definitely bigger than a handful. Which was saying something given the size of his hands.

When he'd heard the chair scrape across the floor, Graham had known exactly what was happening. What he didn't know was whether it was heaven-sent or hell-bound. He couldn't stop himself from turning around at the sound. When he saw her falling, that deliciously rounded, heart-shaped ass heading for the shower floor, he'd reacted. Simple as that. Which brought him to now, with her tit spilling out of his palm, and the rest of the slippery, wiggling woman in his arms.

"I got you. Hold still." If she didn't quit moving, she was going to have her naked ass pressed up against his hard on. She froze.

"Finally, she listens," Graham said, more to himself than

to her. "Okay, sweetheart, I'm going to sit you down." Graham hooked the chair with his foot and dragged it back toward the spray that was soaking them both. Chair back into position, he lowered her into it. Graham was just barely able to restrain himself from squeezing that luscious handful. Man, she was stacked. And they were one hundred percent real. He'd bet the ranch on it.

That train of thought was not helping his erection deflate. Predictably, she didn't turn when he stepped out of the shower room. Unpredictably, she also didn't say anything.

"Don't reach for the soap; I'll bring you some." Graham would've kicked himself for not thinking of grabbing her a bar of soap and some shampoo before, especially if she'd hurt herself falling, but he couldn't bring himself to regret it at that moment. First off, she'd been stripping and tossing her clothes to him like his own personal striptease. Even if he didn't get to watch, he had a damn good imagination. And secondly, it was pretty obvious—he got his hands all over a wet, naked woman. Nothing to regret there. With only two female residents on the ranch—Allison, who was married to Jonah, and Grace, their five year old daughter—there was no action happening for him or the eight other unattached guys who called the place home. If they'd had advanced notice of the apocalypse, maybe they all would have considered attempting real relationships rather than just hook ups. Although that was debatable.

Graham snagged a bottle of Allison's homemade shampoo and a bar of soap out of the locker filled with Grace's bath toys. Neither Grace nor Allison would mind. Graham headed back to the shower, trying not to stare at the girl as she wrapped her arms around herself, covering all of the goods.

"Here." Graham called upon what little shred of gentlemanly nature he possessed and looked away from her when he got close enough to hand off the soap. "Take it."

Feeling her grab the soap, Graham barely resisted the urge to turn his head. He forced himself to head back to the locker room. He thought he heard a quiet "Thanks," but he wasn't sure.

"Just holler when you're done. I'll hand you a towel, and you can dry off."

This time he definitely heard the clipped, "Thank you."

Graham sat down on the bench and waited. And tried not to recall exactly how fucking perfect she'd felt in his arms.

Ro could only imagine what shade of red her face must be. Without a mirror, it was hard to judge whether she was tomato red or fire engine red. Seriously. *Holy. Balls*. Ro tried to push aside the feeling of Conan's hand cupping her breast. *Sweet baby Jesus*.

This was bad. As in, not good. Very bad. Because while she should hate the guy who'd manhandled her and pissed her off with every word he spoke, she could only think about how good his callused palm had felt as it grazed her nipple. Which, Exhibit A, was still hard. Ro forced herself to calm down and study the bottle she held in her hand. It was clear, and the contents were a creamy white. Sort of like semen. She flipped open the cap and squeezed it into her hand and tried not to picture stroking Conan's cock until he came in her hand. Ro froze and forcibly shoved the thought from her head. *Seriously? One boob grab and she was fantasizing about giving him a hand job? Bad, Ro. Very, very bad*. Maybe she really was a slut at heart. *No*. She just had a very active imagination.

Mental tongue-lashing over, Ro lathered her hair. The

scent of lavender infused the steam. The shampoo was better than the ridiculously expensive crap Ro bought at the ridiculously expensive salon she had frequented in Chicago. Where she'd never go again. Which was most likely out of business and probably had already been looted. Okay, that was incredibly depressing and got her mind off sex. With Conan. Almost.

Recalling that she should be hurrying this up because she didn't want to use up all the hot water they were generously sharing with her, Ro moved through the rest of her shower at warp speed. The lightly scented bar of soap felt amazing on her body and face. Thank God for laser hair removal, or Ro's underarms and legs would be looking a little shaggy by now. And going for the full Brazilian had seemed to be a bold choice at the time, because what if someday she wanted a landing strip? But Ro was definitely appreciating her decision now. She gently soaped up and rinsed her sprained ankle before rinsing the suds out of her hair. Surprisingly, whatever was in that shampoo had left it fairly tangle-free and smooth. Which was no easy feat given Ro's long and unruly curls. After shutting off the water she just had to let Conan know she was done so she could cover her naked self with a towel. And get dry.

Ro tried to sound unaffected, and somewhat polite, when she called out, "Could you toss me a towel, please?" No reason to act like she'd been raised without some manners. It was amazing how much her mood had improved after she'd gotten a little (unintentional) action and was able to indulge in a hot shower with good smelling soap and shampoo. The simple things in life, indeed.

"Here." A towel brushed up against Ro's arm. She looked at Conan, to see if he was checking out her nakedness, but no, he was looking away. Arguably like a gentleman. Or something.

Ro grabbed the towel. "Thanks."

"When you're done drying off, wrap yourself up in the towel, and I'll carry you out so you can get dressed."

Ummm.

Conan must have seriously overestimated the size of the towel, because although it wasn't one of those teeny tiny gym towels, it wasn't a whole lot bigger. But Ro complied, drying off, because honestly, she was starting to get cold, even in the steam-filled shower room. She wrapped the towel around her body and tried to sit on the edge of the seat to avoid soaking it with the water pooling in the middle.

"I'm good."

Conan stepped into the shower room. He'd stripped off his wet shirt. *Gulp*. He was ripped. Cut. Defined. Fucking. Hot. The tattoo of combat boots and a rifle that peeked around the right side of his chiseled abs would have been straight up lickable, except it looked like it was a memorial tattoo. Nothing like death to take her mind off the heat gathering between her legs.

Ro looked up to find Conan's eyes on her. Her body. Not her face. And even Ro could tell he liked what he saw. His dark brown eyes flared to life with heat and interest.

He swung her up into his arms again, bridal style, but the towel wasn't quite long enough to cover her generously rounded ass. Ro shivered as she felt both cheeks make contact with the inside of his muscle-corded forearm before she slid and the arm caught her under the knees. He paused, as if cataloging all of the places her naked skin was touching his. Or maybe that was just Ro.

Conan moved more slowly than she would have expected out of the shower room and back into the main locker room. His movements were equally slow as he set her down on the bench, his gaze leaving trails of heat in its wake as it raked down her cleavage, pausing for a moment on the bit of towel stuffed between her breasts to anchor it.

Ro knew she had a decent rack. The double Ds got plenty of attention from the boys. Always had. Most of it not the kind of attention Ro wanted. But Conan seemed to like them. A lot, if the trouble he had breaking his stare was any indication. Ro could feel her nipples hardening further. Was that even possible? She dragged her mind out of the gutter and tried to get back to practical thinking. *Lock it down, Ro.*

She cleared her throat and asked, "Could you hand me my clothes?" She tried her best to sound unaffected, but wasn't sure she'd actually pulled it off.

Conan finally tore his eyes away from her cleavage.

"You sure you want to put dirty clothes back on? It's your call, but …"

"It's not like I have a lot of options. You have my bag, and even if you didn't, my clothes are all just varying shades of nasty at this point." Ro tried not to sound ungrateful. Because she was grateful for the shower, really. But putting on dirty clothes after said shower kind of sucked.

"Look, just borrow some tonight. They won't fit, but at least they'll be clean. We can see about getting your clothes washed tomorrow." He hesitated, as if actually waiting for her to respond this time.

"Okay. I guess that will work. Thanks. I appreciate it. The shower and everything."

Graham nodded once and turned away from her to a locker door that read "G-MAN" in black marker on duct tape and pulled out a black t-shirt, gray hoody, gray sweat-pants, and white socks.

"Here. You need help getting dressed?" He paused. "Shit, you don't have underwear."

"No problem," Ro said, "I'll just go commando. That's what I do anyway when I'm too busy to remember to send out my …" Conan stared at her, and Ro went silent. She couldn't believe she'd just shared that little tidbit. She just needed to shut up. Maybe forever. "Thanks again, though. I can handle it from here."

Graham grabbed a dry shirt for himself and then turned toward the shower room so his back was to the girl. He had just about talked himself down from his hard on when she dropped the bomb about going commando. Jesus. Now all he could think about was the fact that her naked pussy was going to be rubbing all over his sweatpants. And her tits were going to be braless under his shirt. Graham was doubly glad that he'd opted to give her his clothes rather than Alex's, the smallest of the crew. And by small, he meant the fewest inches over six feet. Graham didn't even want to think about why that made him happy. He just needed her to hurry up and get dressed so he could bring her to the clinic, have Beau wrap her ankle up, and find an ice pack for her so he could go take care of his raging hard on. He was a man with priorities.

He heard the clothes rustling and tried not to think about it. But it was impossible. Graham forcibly turned his thoughts to the three men he had out in the field at that very moment. Graham told himself that he had only sent the team out to confirm the girl's story. To see if she was lying about how she ended up less than a hundred yards from their fence line. But he'd already decided she was more than likely telling the truth. She was way too … open … or something … to actually be a good actress. Or she was a fucking phenomenal actress and Graham was still thinking with his dick. But Graham was pretty confident. His instincts about people had always been better than

44

average, and his six tours, four as a Recon team leader, had only sharpened them. He might act like he didn't give a fuck what anyone thought, but Graham liked to think he had a decent handle on what people around him were thinking. Which brought him back to the real reason for sending out the team: if there was another woman not far from his backyard whose life was seriously in danger and had probably already been irrevocably damaged, Graham couldn't ignore it … and Zach sure as hell would never let him. He knew he couldn't save everyone, or he'd have eleven other men living on the ranch and not just nine. If he could save a life, it would at least be something. Penance, he supposed.

Graham's attention shifted abruptly when he heard her say, "I'm all set."

Graham turned and froze. The impact of her fresh-faced beauty was startling. She looked young, and without dirt smeared on her face, he could appreciate her smooth, ivory skin and wide dark eyes. Her dark hair was long, and Graham could tell that it would dry into a wild tumble of curls. All but drowning in his clothes, he couldn't help but picture her naked. In his bed. She'd rolled up the sleeves of the hoody multiple times, but they still hung over her hands. She must have rolled the waistband of the sweats down, but the crotch still hung too low. Damn. She was straight up beautiful. He tried not to mentally gloat about the fact that he'd seen her naked and Zach hadn't. Regardless of their preference for sharing, they'd always been competitive with women.

"You good to go?" Graham asked. She responded with only a nod this time, then opened her mouth to speak, but closed it again.

"What?"

"Could you hand me my clothes? I know you said something about laundry, but I'm not going to be here long enough for that."

And there it was. The stacked and gorgeous woman, whose curves had fired his blood and whose attitude and grit had intrigued him, had no intention of sticking around. Not since his mother had walked out on him at seven years old had Graham allowed himself to get attached to a woman. And he sure as hell wouldn't start now. Besides, it wasn't attachment, he reasoned. She was injured, and for all intents and purposes, helpless. And even if she weren't injured, they could not and would not send her back out into the fray alone. It was just dumb luck that he wanted her. Naked. In his bed. And if she was up for it, between him and Zach. It was just a side benefit of the situation they found themselves in. Might as well make the most of it. Nope, Graham decided, she wasn't going anywhere any time soon.

How to explain her new reality without pissing her off to an incredible degree? Probably not possible. So Graham fell back on his standard M.O.—he ignored her question.

He plucked her off the bench, and when she protested, he said, "Worry about it in the morning."

Ro was still sputtering when Conan shouldered the door to the locker room open and stepped out into the night. He strode across the camp, heading for a narrow building that had a solar light glowing next to the door.

He paused. "Open it, would you?"

Ro complied, grasping and turning the knob. Conan used his foot to push the door open and stepped inside the surprisingly well-lit room containing three sturdy-looking cots covered in crisp white sheets.

This was clearly the infirmary or clinic or whatever they

called it. IV poles stood waiting for use next to the cots, and a steel instrument tray was pushed into the corner. Ro tried not to speculate about what kinds of injuries they expected to deal with that merited surgical tools.

A full complement of kitchen cabinets and countertops, complete with deep triple sinks, wrapped around two walls of the room. A closed door was visible in the far right corner. Beau sat in a leather executive chair, his boots propped up on a desk pushed up against the front wall. He put down the book he was reading when they walked in. Wait, was that *World War Z*? Ironic.

Dropping his boots to the floor, Beau appeared to be studying Ro in Conan's arms. Ro assumed it was out of character for Conan to be carrying women all over hell and back. Which was surprising, given his recent penchant for it.

"Drop her on the cot. I'll wrap her up and get you an ice pack. Where you putting her tonight?"

Ro was wondering that as well. Although, all she really cared was that there was a bed. Sleeping on the ground this last week, even with her sleeping bag, had sucked. She'd gotten soft over the years. Roughing it for a week without indoor plumbing or an air mattress used to be a regular occurrence in the Callahan family.

Conan sat her down on the cot closest to the door and moved to lean up against the counter, ignoring Beau's question. Beau rolled the chair to a cupboard and grabbed an ace bandage and rolled over to the cot. He didn't comment on her borrowed clothes as he surveyed her swollen ankle. An ugly bluish-black bruise had formed, stretching from her heel around to the top of her foot.

"I know you think I'm full of shit, but if you start walking on this too soon, you're going to do more damage." Beau said this as though he knew she was going to argue with him.

"How long? Really."

He studied her ankle. "Hard to know exactly, but you'd be better waiting a week rather than a day."

"Two days."

Conan chose that moment to join the conversation. "This isn't a negotiation. You want to be hurt worse?"

"You can't tell me that if you or one of your commandos sprained an ankle, you'd have him on bed rest for a week. That's ridiculous."

Conan inclined his head. "Fair point. But we've got crutches here that fit us and any of my *commandos* would be on desk duty until Beau gave him the all clear. Especially now. In case you haven't noticed, little girl, everything's changed, and it's going to keep changing, and not for the better. You need to get smart ... and quick."

"You condescending *asshole*. You think I don't know that everything's changed? While you've been hiding here in your little fortress, I've been out there," Ro pointed toward the outside, "and I've seen it firsthand. I know it's going to get a hell of a lot worse before it gets better. Do you think I don't realize that? Do you think that maybe I have a damn good reason to be in a hurry to get where I'm going, and that's why I'm trying to get there as quickly as I can? People are confused right now, and scared, and hoping someone's coming to save them. It's not going to be too much longer before everyone gets desperate and violent, and it'll be survival of the fittest, or survival of the best armed and most ruthless. You better believe I'm going to be tucked away safe when that happens." She looked toward the wall, not wanting to meet Conan or Beau's eyes after her speech.

Conan pushed off the counter and stood before her. He tilted her chin up, forcing her to look at him. Beau kept wrapping her ankle.

"At least we can agree on one thing: you need to stay safe and in one piece." His tone was implacable. "You might not agree with my methods, but at least we'll agree on the result."

Ro tugged her chin out of his grip and crossed her arms. "Whatever. I'll stay tonight and regroup in the morning."

Stubborn woman. That's what she was. A stubborn ass woman. After Beau had wrapped her ankle and handed her an ice pack, Graham didn't waste any time scooping her up and carrying her to the cabin he shared with Zach and depositing her on his bed. He could have put her on the couch, or even in Zach's bed, but the possessive part of him wouldn't let him put her anywhere but his bed. *Jesus.* If he didn't rein himself in, he'd be pissing on her like a dog marking his territory. And that wasn't a kink he understood.

"Please tell me this isn't your bed."

"No can do, sweetheart. It's this or the ground." Graham felt a twinge of guilt for lying, but it had been a long fucking day, and he wasn't up for another argument with her. He had three men out in the field, and his dick needed some atten-tion. And he didn't think he'd be successful in convincing her to take care of it. Though the thought had his cock twitching.

He lit the oil lamp that sat on the nightstand while he waited for her to explode.

"Look, Conan—"

Graham couldn't help the chuckle that came out. He knew he hadn't given her his name. He wasn't big on offering information, let alone personal details. He supposed Conan was marginally better than calling him asshole.

"It's Graham, not Conan. Graham Buchanan."

"What, no rank and serial number?"

"Not anymore, sweetheart." Graham liked her sassy attitude. This one could definitely hold his interest past morning. And she'd certainly already charmed Zach. But Zach was a sucker for all pretty women.

"I thought once a Marine, always a Marine?"

Graham's gaze snapped to her face. Had he been wrong? Had she really been bait? Fuck. He needed to know once and for all.

He leveled his *don't you fucking lie to me* stare at her. "I'm going to ask you one time, and you better tell me the whole fucking truth or you won't be leaving this room … who sent you?"

She met his stare head on. "What are you talking about? No. One. Sent. Me. Are you dense?"

"Then how do you know I served in the Corps?" Graham's voice had taken on the deadly quiet tone he generally reserved for interrogations. But that didn't seem to stem her attitude.

"Are you serious? It's obvious you're military … or were. Everything from the camo paint to the M4 to sending guys out for fire watch to the way you make your bed! And I didn't know you were a Marine. It's just something my dad always says. You know, 'There are no former Marines?' So back the fuck off." Graham could almost feel her grinding her teeth as she said the last words.

He opened his mouth to speak when his radio squawked.

"The boys are coming in fast. They've got a fourth. Being carried in by Cam. G-man, you copy?"

Graham grabbed the radio but locked eyes on Rowan when he responded, "Roger that. Male or female?" He'd taken out the earpiece after his accidental soaking and turned up the volume, so she was hearing the report, too.

"Female."

The word got her attention, and comprehension seemed to dawn. Her mouth dropped open. Speechless. Graham would bet a decent amount of money that it didn't happen often. He also felt a warm rush of triumph—she wasn't bait. Which meant that his instincts weren't going to shit, and even better, she was fair game.

Still staring at her, he replied, "Roger that. I'm on my way."

He clipped the radio to his belt, looked at Rowan, and did something he rarely did—apologize.

"I'm sorry. I have reasons, but I won't make excuses. You good to bed down for the night?"

She looked stunned. "Yeah, I'm good. Did you ..." she trailed off. Apparently when she was stunned, she couldn't form complete sentences. But Graham knew exactly what she was asking.

"Yeah, I did."

CHAPTER EIGHT

Graham left a speechless Rowan in his cabin and headed toward the command post. Jonah, the only married member of the team, would be waiting for him. Graham looked down at his watch; it was closing in on oh-one-hundred. Jonah had a bed with a warm, willing woman waiting for him, but tonight, so did Graham. Well, she was warm, at least. Willing was a stretch at this point.

Graham made his way to the concrete structure they'd built to house the command post and the armory. It was centrally located and was one of the few buildings that weren't already on the premises when he'd inherited the ranch from his uncle.

Sure enough, Jonah was standing outside the door waiting for Graham.

"Perfect timing, G. They're just coming in the west bolt hole."

"If she's in the shape I suspect, then she needs to go straight to Beau to get checked out," Graham replied.

"Already radioed him."

Three of the men—Alex, Jamie, and Cam—moved

soundlessly into the compound. Alex and Jamie broke off and headed toward Graham and Jonah while Cam, woman in arms, headed toward the clinic.

Alex and Jamie were grim-faced when they stopped in front of Graham and Jonah. Graham didn't speak, just waited for the report. Jamie slung his M4 over his shoulder and pulled a bandana out of his pocket and started to wipe the paint off his face. Alex white-knuckled his rifle. Neither spoke for a long moment, and then Jamie, normally the happy-go-lucky one of the group said, "G, you know we've seen some fucked up shit in our day, but I've never felt so good about killing someone as I did tonight. I don't know exactly what they did to that girl, but she's practically catatonic."

"How many?"

"Two."

"That all of them?" Graham needed to know if they needed to be ready for someone seeking revenge.

Alex answered, "I don't think so. There were four trailers. Seems like there should have been more."

"You torch the trailers?"

Jamie nodded. "We lit those fuckers up like the Fourth of July."

Alex was still shaking his head, as if picturing what they'd seen.

"They had her chained up like an animal, not that she could probably move anyway. She's in a bad way, man. I don't know if she's going to make it. She was covered in blood and mud and God only knows what else. She looked like she'd been beaten almost to death. But if I had to guess, the physical injuries might be the easier ones to heal."

Graham nodded. For all the shit they'd done and seen, violence against women bothered them the most. Zach especially, and with good reason. The human psyche was a fragile thing, and there was no telling if she'd be able to pull herself through it.

"You get a name from her?" Graham asked.

Jamie shook his head. "Lia, I think. She didn't say much. Just went limp as soon as Cam picked her up and told her she was safe."

Ro waited until she heard the door latch before she slid to the edge of the bed. If they'd rescued that woman, Ro was damn sure going to see her, and no one could stop her. Not that she would actually ask for permission. She knew Conan —Graham—would've shut her down hard if she'd gotten over her shock quickly enough to ask before he'd left.

The clinic wasn't that far across the camp. She could hobble there. It might not be pretty or quick, but she could make it. Right?

Ro hopped out of the cabin on one foot, using the wall for support. Once she made it outside, the distance between the trees seemed to multiply. Her right quad was burning from bearing the brunt of her weight and the awkward hops. Ro leaned up against a thick oak, pausing to catch her breath before hopping forward again. So ... the clinic was a little farther away than she'd thought, and her balance was suffering with her fatigue. Stumbling, she put the full force of her weight on her injured ankle to catch herself, sending hot streaks of pain shooting up her leg. *Holy shit, that hurt like a mother. Not doing that again.*

After what seemed like an hour, Ro leaned up against the wood-sided wall of the clinic and could make out Beau's black hair and another man through the window. Thank fuck it wasn't Graham. Somehow she knew he'd make her regret this little jaunt. She pulled the door open and hobbled inside.

Beau was rolling around on his stool, grabbing supplies, and Ro could make out a blanket-covered form with a mass of brownish hair on the pillow. She couldn't be sure of the actual color, as the brown seemed to be mostly from dirt. At least Ro hoped it was dirt. The woman's face was a swollen mass of overlapping, multi-colored bruises; she looked like she was wearing a Halloween mask. A man with buzzed light brown hair was standing over her. Ro swallowed back the rising bile. She just hoped that her interruption of the creepy trio had saved the woman from further abuse.

"Fuck me running. Are you serious right now?" Beau was looking at Ro with disbelief. "How the hell did you get here? And don't tell me you walked."

His snapping blue eyes dared Rowan to lie to him ... or maybe they were daring her to tell the truth.

"I—" Ro started to explain—something, somehow—when two large hands wrapped around her waist from behind and yanked her off her feet. Before she could make a sound—or complain about being manhandled—a deep voice filled her ear.

"I'd like an answer to that same damn question, woman."

Ro could feel his hot breath on her ear and against her neck. He was holding her suspended, his hands nearly spanning her waist. And Ro didn't have a tiny waist.

Before her thoughts could head fully into the gutter, he spoke again, "I'm pretty damn sure I left you in my bed not fifteen minutes ago and told you to bed down for the night."

Ro squirmed in his hold. "Seriously? You didn't see this coming? You honestly thought you could tell me to stay put and I would? Especially after what you told me?"

As Rowan's voice started to get louder, the man with the high and tight buzz cut stalked over.

"Keep your voice down. Or do you want to wake her up and scare the shit out of her?"

Ro looked down, chastened. "I'm sorry. He just ... pisses me off. I don't know. I'm sorry."

"Tell me you didn't walk over here yourself," Graham said in a low, quiet, and quite frankly, scary as hell tone.

Ro figured he meant that rhetorically, and didn't bother answering.

"I swear—" Graham started, but Beau interrupted.

"This isn't the place to be having this discussion."

"I just wanted to see—" Rowan began to speak, but shut her mouth when Graham threw her over his shoulder, caveman-style.

"Now you've seen. And we're leaving."

Turning her face away from his black shirt, Ro could see the amused smirks on the faces of Beau and the other men. Assholes. Every last one of them.

CHAPTER NINE

Rowan struggled against Graham's hold as soon as they were outside, which added fuel to the fire that was Graham's temper. He'd always thought of himself as relatively even-tempered, but this girl somehow knew exactly how to rile him up.

"I oughta beat your ass for that stunt, woman. What the fuck were you thinking? How the hell did you get from my cabin to the clinic? Fly? Wait—don't answer. I don't want to know, because then I *will* beat your ass so red you won't be able to sit for a week."

She stopped struggling. Smart girl. Graham strode through the dark, up to the door of his cabin, and wrenched it open. "Now let's try this again." He stalked through the front room, into the bedroom, and dropped her, not as carefully as before, onto the bed. "You ... stay put. Sleep. Get me?"

Graham didn't know what pissed him off more—that she'd disobeyed a direct order, which didn't happen often to him, that she'd probably injured herself more by hobbling over to the clinic on her own, or that Ro's face had been as white as the sheet covering the injured woman when she'd caught sight of her bruised and battered face. Graham had never wanted to wrap someone up and protect her from all of the bad shit in the world before, but he was becoming acquainted with the feeling. Rowan didn't need to see that. If the little bit he'd learned of her character already was any indication, she was going to beat herself up for not mounting a rescue effort herself.

Graham leaned over Rowan on the bed, where she was now propped up on the pillows. His bed. His pillows. Graham braced himself with an arm on either side of her body and spoke quietly.

"I know what you think you were doing, but you shouldn't have. You hurting yourself worse won't help her any. You need to worry about Rowan." When he finished speaking, his face was only inches away from hers. He could feel her breathing, which had quickened. In the yellow flicker of the oil lamp, her pupils were dilated and Graham's gaze was drawn to her tongue as it darted out to swipe across her bottom lip. He groaned and started to pull away. His movements were halted when Rowan's hands tangled in his hair and dragged his head down to her mouth.

Rowan didn't know what kind of craziness had possessed her, but in that moment, she had to kiss him. She had to have his lips on hers, if only to block out reality for a minute. As wrong as it seemed, his caveman-like actions, his protectiveness, and his quiet words, had her body softening and readying itself for him.

And although Ro might have started out in control of the kiss, he didn't let her keep it. One of the hands that he'd used to brace himself had moved to cradle her face, angling her so he could cover her mouth more fully with his. He slanted his lips as his tongue sought entry. He slid his knee between her legs, and his hard thigh rubbed against her center, sending flares of pleasure though her, making her gasp. When she opened, he conquered. Tongues tangling and body clenching, Ro dug her nails into his scalp. Graham growled, pulling her up and into him. Then a throat cleared, Graham jerked away, and she was grasping at air.

"You don't usually start without me, G," Zach said, leaning against the doorframe, arms crossed.

Ro froze. The breath in her lungs caught, and she was choking on his words.

"I didn't tell you that you could start without me," the seductive voice drawled from across the room.

"Not again." Ro didn't realize that she'd whispered the words out loud until the gazes of both men fix on her.

Zach moved toward her first, reaching his hand out, but Ro scuttled back to the headboard, out of his reach.

"Don't touch me." Her voice quavered. She needed to pull herself together. They weren't Charles and Evelyn. Trying for a more even tone, she said, "Just back off for a minute, okay?"

Zach dropped his hand and stepped back. Something was all sorts of wrong here. Rowan was pale and shaking. Just minutes ago he'd watched her latch onto Graham and hold on for dear life. It'd be one thing if she wanted Zach to leave, but Graham, too? That didn't make any sense.

Speaking quietly to her, like he would to a spooked horse, Zach said, "It's all right. I'm backing off now. No one is going to hurt you here."

"It's not that ... Just give me a minute," she said, already sounding a little steadier.

Zach glanced at Graham, but Graham looked just as confused by her one-eighty.

"What's wrong, sweetheart? You weren't scared of me before. And you didn't look too scared of Graham just now. What's going on in that pretty head of yours?"

"It's nothing. Just a bad memory." She looked up and met Zach's gaze. "I'm not a slut. I don't know if I'm wearing a sign that's only visible to guys that says: 'Loves long walks on the beach and gang bangs.' But I'm really not like that."

Graham spoke up. "We don't think you're a slut. Or into gang bangs. Zach was just joking around. He's a jackass. Ignore him."

That statement pissed Zach off, but now wasn't the time to argue. He hadn't been joking around. He liked this girl. Liked her spunk and her attitude. And Graham clearly liked her too, as was evident from the way he was letting her hump his leg when Zach entered the room. Zach and Graham had been sharing women since that crazy night they graduated boot. Hell, they'd picked up a woman at the bar together just a few weeks before the grid went down. It worked for them. Graham didn't have to actually speak to the women, and Zach charmed them while capitalizing on Graham's dark and dangerous vibe that never failed at luring them in. Most women said it was the most intense sexual experience they'd ever had. It wasn't like Zach didn't bag chicks on his own. But he wasn't entirely certain Graham did. Which made what he had walked in on all the more surprising. And honestly, it had made him happy as hell. Graham had never formed an emotional bond with any woman they'd been with. Ever. Zach supposed that being abandoned in a cheap motel room by your mother as a kid might stunt your ability to form emotional connections with women. But apparently not with this one. This girl, who'd been dropped into their lap only hours ago, seemed to have already gotten under Graham's skin. Which worked for Zach, because even before the world went to hell, Zach had wanted a woman. A woman who he and Graham would permanently share. Zach knew Graham had been aware of his desire, but never verbally acknowledged it and certainly never displayed this level of interest in any of their hookups. But this girl could change everything. She could be the one who finally got Graham to give an actual relationship a chance. Hell, they were all envious of what Jonah had with Allison. And the little rugrat they were raising. Zach wanted that for himself, and he wanted to share it with his best friend. But Zach had yet to find a woman who could entice Graham into a relationship. Until Rowan. And that was why Graham's comment pissed him off.

Zach gave Graham the look his comment deserved. Fucking asshole.

If his plan had a chance in hell of working, he needed to understand what had set Rowan off. So he would take a risk and hope he didn't freak her out again. He moved closer and sat on the end of the bed. When she looked at him and didn't jerk away, a flare of hope warmed him.

"Why would we think that, sweetheart?"

"Because of what you said." Her voice was strong and sure now.

"And you said *not again.*" Zach didn't like the ideas that were swirling in his head. "Did someone ... hurt you? Or make you do something you didn't want to do?"

Zach saw Graham move closer and was shocked when he sat down on the bed next to where Rowan was sitting against the headboard, arms wrapped around her knees. He was more shocked when Graham reached for her and pulled her close to him.

Oh yeah, G was already in deep with this one, whether he'd admit it or not.

"You give me a name, and I will make sure he dies slowly," Graham said.

"That's not necessary, really. I think karma will take care of Charles and Evelyn."

"Wait. What?"

"Charles ... and Evelyn?" Zach asked.

"Look, it was a seriously fucked up situation. And before the shit hit the fan with the rest of the world, that situation was basically responsible for destroying my life. What you said just brought back something I'd rather forget."

Ro couldn't believe she was telling them this. Actually, she couldn't believe Zach's words had triggered that much of a reaction in her. They had just been so close to the same words that Evelyn, the Mistress of Evil—as Rowan had begun to refer to her—had uttered as she walked into the bedroom where Ro and Charles were about to make love. Except that wasn't what it was for Charles Leonard Ashford III. Despite the old money name and pedigree, he'd only been a pawn. Evelyn had been the spider, and Rowan had been the fly. Charles had just been the bait in a fucked up trap.

It had all started one night at a closing dinner. Rowan had been leaving the restaurant, when a partner had asked if she wanted to share a cab. She'd thought it was odd he was even at the dinner, because she didn't recall him working on the deal. But as a second year associate, Ro wasn't about to say no. He'd been charming and flirtatious when he'd tossed the cabbie some bills and asked him to wait so he could walk Ro the thirty feet from the curb to her building. Rowan had thought the move strange, but didn't dwell on it. A few days later, he'd dropped by her office and brought her a latte and stayed to chat. The next evening, while working even later than normal, he'd stopped and asked her out for a late dinner. Ro had been flattered. They didn't work in the same practice area—with Rowan a corporate associate and Charles a litigation partner—so Ro didn't think it would raise too many eyebrows. The firm didn't forbid dating co-workers, just frowned on it when you reported directly to the person you were dating.

Charles was attractive, in a three-piece suit kind of way. He was tall, with a runner's physique, expensively cut blond hair, and pale blue eyes. And she had thought, naively, that he was interested in her. Although, she supposed, he probably had been at least somewhat interested in her. She hadn't imagined the bulge in his Brooks Brothers suit pants when he'd walked her to the door of her building after dinner and kissed her for the first time. She hadn't imagined the desire in his eyes when, after several more late night dinners, he'd finally talked her into coming home with him. And he had definitely been interested when he'd thrust himself against her while they were tangled up in his bed, about to have sex. And that erection hadn't deflated when Evelyn stood in the doorway, naked, but for the black strap-on harness and giant black cock jutting out from it. Ro shivered at the memory. As far as unpleasant surprises went, that was a doozy.

Graham squeezed her hand.

"Sorry, I just ... I had a rather unpleasant surprise once. The closest I've ever come to a three-way, and you could probably say that it scarred me for life."

Graham's grip tightened. Before he could speak or jump to anymore conclusions, Ro quickly said, "It's okay; it wasn't like I was raped or anything. I just got a little too up close and personal with the pointy end of a strap-on that was connected to a rather evil woman—Evelyn—who used a sorry excuse for a man—Charles—to get me into her bed so they could both fuck me. When I declined, rather vehemently, she didn't take it well. She decided to destroy my career, which at that point, was pretty much my entire life and the culmination of everything I'd been working for since high school. To make matters worse, I wasn't the first associate they'd run that game on. Like I said, unpleasant surprise, but I definitely won't be making that mistake again."

Ro was surprised at how easily that came out. Granted, it was the extra-abbreviated Cliffs Notes version, but it was more than she'd told anyone else. So much had happened in the last week that it made Evelyn and Charles's little game seem so trivial.

What still bothered her, however, was how easily she had fallen for it and how, even though her life had been work, and her co-workers had been more acquaintances than friends, not a single one of them had stood by her when Evelyn destroyed her reputation at the firm. Evelyn had claimed that Ro had tried to steal her fiancé, even though Rowan had no idea if she and Charles had actually been engaged. And if that wasn't a bad enough rumor to start, Evelyn followed it up by telling everyone that when Charles told Rowan he wasn't interested, Rowan had planned to blackmail him to get ahead at work. Which made no fucking sense! The rumors spread fast and hot, like wildfire during a drought. Rowan couldn't walk from the elevator to her office without looks of disgust. She had refused to cower, because she'd done nothing wrong … except be stupid enough to think that Charles's interest was legit. Evelyn had demanded she be fired immediately, and the managing partner hadn't yet announced her fate. Before the plane crashed, she'd been fairly certain that day was going to end with her carrying a file box of her things out of the building, escorted by security.

Ugh. Whatever. It was over and done with, and she was never going back. Not that there was anything to go back to anyway. Not a lot of legal work was getting done without any working electronics. People had way bigger problems to deal with right now. Like survival.

When she finally looked up, she realized she had somehow ended up in Graham's lap, and Zach was standing right next to the bed, his mouth gaping open.

"You want to share a few more details?" Zach asked.

"Umm ... not really. I think I covered all of the high points," Ro said.

"Sweetheart, you can't just drop a bomb like that and expect us to nod like we understand. That's a new one for both of us ..."

Ro smiled. "You and me both. But it's over and done with. I'm sorry for freaking out."

"What if we swore there'd be no strap-ons in sight? Would the idea of a three-way really be that horrible?" Zach asked.

Ro's gaze shot to Zach and then swung around to stare at Graham. "I thought you said he was joking? You two ... wait ... are you ...? Good God, I really have no gaydar."

"No. We're not gay," Graham replied. "We just have a kink. And, at that moment, Zach was joking. He knew you weren't ready to climb in bed with us. Trust me, that's not something we spring on women. We're all about full disclosure up front."

"So you're saying ... I mean ... what?" Ro couldn't form a coherent sentence. The idea of being between these two men —in the bed she was currently sitting on—had her heart thumping like a drunken tap-dancing leprechaun on St. Patrick's Day.

Zach squatted in front of her, the same way he had when she'd been plopped onto the bench of the picnic table a few hours ago. God, was that only a few hours ago? It seemed like it had been days ago, at least.

"Ro, baby, I didn't mean to spring it on you like that. You don't need to get all worked up about it, but it's good that you know. Because I think I can safely say that we're both attracted as all hell to you. And if you'd let us, we'd—" Ro reached out and put her hand over his mouth, cutting off his words.

"Please. Just ... not right now. I can't even process ... I just ... I don't know," Ro stuttered, and then paused to take a deep breath and tried again, shaking her head. "I can't deal with this right now. I'm not staying, and I'm not looking for a one-night stand, even if you throw out that old line about this being the last night on Earth. So just, I don't know, let me go to bed, and we'll forget we had this conversation. I mean, seriously, please forget everything I told you. It definitely wasn't my finest moment." Ro removed her hand from Zach's mouth, and he didn't speak. She looked to Graham, and he stayed silent as well. If he looked disappointed, that wasn't Ro's problem, or so she told herself. Both men studied her before they gave her a nod, standing and leaving the room without another word.

CHAPTER TEN

Graham strode out of the bedroom and straight out of the cabin into the night. Hell, at this rate, he'd be pulling an all-nighter instead of sleeping.

He dropped into one of the chairs on the covered porch that fronted the cabin, and rested his elbows on his knees. He rubbed his face roughly, trying to figure out what the fuck just happened.

Zach slumped into the chair next to his.

"Well, that was unexpected."

"Understatement of the fucking century, man. What the fuck were you thinking, anyway? Springing that shit on her like that? You used to be smooth. Lost your magic touch." Graham almost groaned when he thought about how fast that situation had deteriorated. Goat fuck two-point-oh.

"Yeah, not my best moment. But seriously, did you ever expect a reaction like that? Or a story like that? I mean, good God. What the fuck?"

"True, but still. Messed up beyond belief. And when I was just starting to get a taste of her."

"Sweet?"

"Like you wouldn't believe."

"You want more?"

"Like you wouldn't believe."

"You want to keep her?"

Graham looked at him before admitting quietly, "Like you wouldn't believe."

"How are we going to make it happen?"

"Fuck if I know. Before, I thought we just had to worry about her being dead set on lighting out of here as soon as humanly possible, but now we've got this other shit to deal with, too. And you wonder why I've never been keen to get involved with anyone."

"But she's sweet."

"Hell yes. Not that you'd know." Graham couldn't help but rub it in.

"Oh, I'll get mine. Don't you worry, old man."

"Fuck you."

"Sorry, man, don't swing that way."

"Fuck off, jackass. I'm going to get a shower, and then I'm crashing. It's been a long fucking day."

"I'm gonna grab some rack time. I'll keep an eye on our girl. Make sure she doesn't go for another midnight rendezvous." Zach was laughing at him now. But Graham didn't punch him because he was too busy liking the way 'our girl' sounded.

"Heard about that already?"

"Everyone has. Not sure how many of them will still respect you in the morning when they know a little slip of a girl won't even follow your orders."

Graham didn't bother telling him to fuck off again before he headed to the showers. He was pretty sure Zach knew he was thinking it.

Hell, Graham thought to himself, *he probably knows I'm going to jack off in the shower.* At least that was Graham's plan if the showers were empty. After getting a taste of Rowan and having her grinding her hot little pussy against his thigh, Graham's dick was aching for relief, and after what she'd told them, there was no way he was satisfying himself with her curvy little body tonight. He stalked to the shower building and ducked inside.

Empty.

Thank God.

He sat to untie his boots before stripping out of his shirt, cargo pants, socks, and boxer briefs. He turned on the water, and when the initial frigid blast had passed, he stretched his arms out to press his hands against the tile wall on either side of the showerhead, and let his head drop forward, and his eyes closed. As the spray streamed down his body, the tension of the last few hours washed over him. First, Rowan, and then the mystery woman because of Rowan, and then Rowan again. God, she was already complicating his life. And now that he'd tasted her, he feared he was getting attached. Recipe for disaster. But it'd be perfect while it lasted.

He grasped his cock in his fist as he pictured Rowan's tempting mouth. She'd been so sweet when she'd finally opened for him. After he'd gotten an eyeful of all that creamy, soft skin in the shower, and had his hands on that amazing rack, all he'd wanted to do was corner her under the spray, push her to her knees, and grip the back of her head while he fed his cock into her hot mouth. And that was before he'd even gotten a taste of her. He would have urged her to take him deeper, to suck harder and swallow him down. Graham groaned as he stroked his cock, gripping it hard. He pictured that dark mass of curls falling across her face as she took him deep, until he bumped the back of her throat. The image of her looking up at him from beneath those dark lashes had his balls drawing up to the base of his cock. He could imagine the look in her dark brown eyes as he fucked her mouth and emptied himself down her throat. The sparks of need shot down his spine, and his balls ached. Two more strokes ... and Graham let go, groaning as he came.

Bracing himself with one hand against the cold tile wall, Graham let the warm water run over him, washing away his fantasy, but leaving him still hard. With the image of Ro on her knees before him embedded in his brain, he'd be hard for a while.

He finished up his shower and shut off the water before walking out of the shower room to snag a towel out of the end locker. He rubbed himself dry, grabbed the shirt he'd changed into after Ro's shower mishap had soaked his last one, and then pulled out clean gray boxer briefs, black sweatpants, and socks. The clean laundry was courtesy of Allison, and he needed to thank her again for all that she did for them. Jonah's wife looked after their whole motley crew, and she was an angel for doing it.

Graham dressed as he contemplated the next hurdle— how to let Rowan know she wasn't going anywhere in the morning, and if they could help it, anytime for the foreseeable future. She was going to be furious. Graham couldn't help but smile at the thought of seeing her all riled up again. Damn, she was beautiful when she was pissed.

CHAPTER ELEVEN

Rowan awoke slowly, feeling a large source of heat at her back. A large, human source of heat. One that had a thick arm wrapped around her stomach and the hard ridge of an erection pressed between her ass cheeks. She assumed it was Graham, but the fact that she wasn't entirely sure made her slut radar spring to life again. Whatever. He was the one who put her in his bed. He just hadn't mentioned they'd be sharing. But it was early, and she was going to roll with it. She tried to move away, but the arm tightened around her.

"Where do you think you're going?" Graham's voice rumbled from behind her, sounding scratchy with sleep.

Okay. One mystery solved. On to the next.

"Why are you in bed with me?"

"You're in my bed. Where else would I be? I sure as hell wasn't sleeping on the couch or bunking with Zach."

"I could have slept on the couch."

"I wanted you in my bed."

"Oh."

"Yeah. Oh." Graham smoothed her hair. It must have been all up in his face.

"Could you, I don't know, maybe let me go? I really need to use the facilities."

"I like you here. I wouldn't have pegged you for the cuddling type, but I'd have been wrong."

"I can't be held accountable for whatever I did while I was unconscious." Ro tried to wiggle away, but all she succeeded in doing was rubbing her ass repeatedly over his dick.

"Sweetheart. You might want to stop squirming so much, or we're going to be getting to know each other a whole hell of a lot better in a few seconds."

Ro froze. And then elbowed him in the gut. *Hard.* Graham cursed.

"Jesus, woman, your elbows are lethal. What was that for?"

"I have to pee, and you need to keep it in your pants."

Graham released her, and Ro slid to the edge of the bed, only to be stopped by his hand on her arm.

"You aren't getting out of this bed without help. So just hold it for two seconds. You don't even know where the bathroom is."

Fair point, but Ro wasn't about to admit that.

"Where is it? I can hop there. I hopped all the way to the clinic last night. It's not that big of a deal."

Ro was yanked back onto the bed, and Graham was on top of her in an instant.

"I wouldn't be bringing that up if I were you. Not unless you want me to turn your ass red for that stunt."

"Duly noted, now get off me before you squash my bladder."

Graham rolled off her and swept her up into his arms. *Again.* But Ro figured she was lucky he wasn't tossing her over his shoulder.

He walked to a door on the right side of the room that

Ro hadn't yet noticed. He knocked on it, but when there was no answer, he opened it and carefully lowered her to the floor. She steadied herself with a hand on the counter and asked, "Where does the other door go?" Ro nodded to the door on the opposite side of the bathroom.

"Zach's room."

"He lives here, too?"

"We've lived together for a long time. It made sense to do the same here. We've all doubled up in the cabins."

"Okay, thanks. You can go."

"Holler when you're done. Don't even think about trying to walk on that ankle, woman."

Ro huffed, and he left.

She quickly took care of business in what appeared to be a composting toilet. *What hadn't they thought of?* She hurried to pull her sweats up, not thrilled about the idea of Zach barging in and seeing her on the toilet. Not a sexy pose.

Wait. Why did she care if Zach thought she was sexy? She tried to tell herself that the errant thought was an anomaly, but she didn't like to lie, especially not first thing in the morning. It set the wrong tone for the day.

Ro hopped toward the door and opened it, finding Graham waiting on the other side.

As he leaned down to pick her up again, he said, "You don't listen real well, do you?"

"Oh, I listen. I just still do whatever the hell I want. Thought you'd figured that out by now."

She was a sassy one, Zach thought, as he met Graham and Rowan in the front room.

"You sick of being carried around yet?" he asked.

"I don't do meek and helpless very well," she replied, smiling.

"How about a ride instead?" he offered, making the motions to show that he meant a piggyback ride.

Zach caught Graham's glare, but focused on Rowan instead.

"Ummm ... sure. Might as well mix it up."

Zach figured she'd go for it, if for no other reason than to needle Graham. He crouched down in front of where Graham held her in his arms and felt her climb on. Graham didn't say a word in protest, just made sure she was settled before he let her go. Graham was a good man; one of the very best he'd ever known. And even Graham had to realize Rowan needed to be comfortable with both of them if she were to ever get on board with the plan that was collectively percolating in their brains.

"Hold on tight, sugar. Let's go get some grub." She gripped him around the shoulders and neck tighter and wrapped her legs around his waist. He turned to throw a triumphant look at Graham, but Graham was just shaking his head, as if to say, *you tricky son of a bitch*. Which would be well deserved, because Zach was a tricky SOB.

As they headed out of the cabin, he pointed out some of the various buildings to her.

"Over there is the bathhouse, which you saw last night." He gestured off to the right. "And beyond that, closer to the outside wall, is the greenhouse and the livestock barn."

He could feel Rowan craning her head for a better look. "We can check it out after breakfast, if you'd like."

She didn't respond. "You nodding back there? I can't hear your head rattle."

"That'd be fine. What kind of livestock do you keep?"

"A small herd of dairy goats and chickens, mainly. There are a few pigs in a pen just outside the walls, but those won't be around much longer. It's almost butchering time. And then there's the deer."

"Deer?"

"We've got about eighty total. We were just gearing up for hunting season when the grid went down. Another few days and we would have had hunting parties bunking here, too."

"Hunting season? That doesn't start until October first. Right?" Ro asked.

Zach slowed and turned his head so he could see her. "This is a whitetail deer ranch, sweetheart. We breed 'em. They hunt 'em. And we sell assorted deer products to places like Cabela's and Gander Mountain."

He could see the comprehension dawning in her expressive brown eyes, followed by confusion. "That explains the fence, but this place looks like Rambo's summer camp, not a hoity-toity place for rich guys to stand around and shoot a deer without having to work at it."

Graham paused beside them.

"That's not really our style. My uncle prided himself on offering prize bucks in challenging hunts. We've continued the tradition. The people who come here, they come expecting to *hunt*. Not to sightsee and shoot their allotted deer. And we only allow bow hunting. No rifles."

Ro's surprise was clear. Her lush mouth had dropped open into a tempting little O that he wanted to do very bad things to. It wasn't lost on Zach that Graham's stare was just as stuck on her pouty lips.

"Ask your questions, doll," Zach said.

"Okay, so you said something about your uncle? Does he live here, too?"

The lust in Graham's eyes died a quick death. Even after five years, Jerry's passing was still a subject Graham avoided. Zach didn't blame him. Jerry had been the only family

Graham had ever been able to count on. Hell, besides Graham and the team, Jerry had been the only person that Zach had been able to count on after he'd enlisted. But that was an even darker subject that he didn't want to contemplate if he could avoid it.

Zach took pity on Graham and stepped in to answer the question. "Graham's Uncle Jerry has been gone about five years now. We all miss him. He'd let us crash here when we were on leave. Put us to work."

Ro nodded, as though she was processing that information.

"And the Rambo summer camp look? I can't picture rich guys coming to rough it here."

Zach smiled. "We cater to the serious hunters. Not the executives out for a weekend jaunt. The people we draw are more concerned about the quality of our bucks and our terrain."

Graham finally joined the conversation again. "And this place was a summer camp at one time. It went out of business in the late '60s or early '70s because it wasn't on a lake and couldn't offer watersports like so many others. Uncle Jerry bought it in the late '70s and slowly bought up all the land around it that he could and converted it into a whitetail hunting preserve."

"That's kind of incredible. Did you spend a lot of time here growing up?"

Zach could tell Graham was uncomfortable with the question, but surprisingly, he answered anyway.

"Ten years. Right up until I enlisted."

"Oh, I didn't realize your parents lived here, too."

Zach cringed.

"My parents were out of the picture by then. It was just Jerry and me."

Ro's questions ceased, and an awkward silence descended.

They'd been standing in front of the mess hall for the last five minutes while Rowan asked her questions and scoped out the place. Time to move on.

"Let's get you some food," Zach said, reaching for the door.

Rowan took in the three large rectangular wooden dining tables, each surrounded by eight chairs, inside the large room. The plank wood floors looked old, but clean. At one end of the room was a large service window that opened into the kitchen area with a wide counter extending out into the dining room. Right now it looked like it functioned as a buffet for the hot breakfast food. The steam and smells emanating from the platters set off a round of growling in Ro's stomach.

Zach heard it, or maybe felt it, first. "Here, sugar, take a seat." He pulled out a chair and squatted down so she could slide onto it.

"Thanks for the ride," she said with a sincere smile. Zach was easy to like, and the fact that he was gorgeous and saved her from the awkward silence following her nosy questions didn't hurt.

Ro forced herself to look away from his twinkling amber eyes and take in her fellow companions seated at the table.

Three men, all large and wearing long-sleeve thermal shirts and cargo pants in various earth tones, and then one little blonde angel dressed in jeans and a pink sweatshirt that had a giant, purple, glittery flower in the middle. Her pigtails were accented with matching pink ribbons. The largest man at the table, sporting a completely shaved head and light mocha-colored skin, sat next to the little girl and occasionally cut her pancakes into smaller pieces when she tried to shove a giant chunk into her mouth. He would have easily been the most intimidating man in the room, except for maybe Graham, but the look of complete adoration in his eyes when he looked at the little girl effectively derailed the scary vibe. Beau was seated across from the little girl, and a man who Rowan hadn't seen before sat at the foot of the table. Even seated, Ro could tell that he was also tall and broad, with shoulders fit for a linebacker and looked like he could crush the chair he was sitting in. He had shaggy hair that was more copper than brown and stunning green eyes that were currently making a careful study of her.

Rowan opened her mouth to introduce herself, but Graham beat her to it.

"This is Rowan; she's a guest. You've already met Beau. Next to him is Travis, and across from Travis are Jonah and Grace. What do you want to eat? There are pancakes, eggs, sausage, bacon, and hash browns, if Allison is going with the usual today."

Ro looked up at Graham in semi-shock. That might have been the longest string of words she'd heard come out of his mouth yet.

A female voice called from the window in the kitchen, "There's also toast and blackberry preserves."

Rowan looked toward the sound of the voice and saw a woman around her age, dressed in what looked to be a homespun blue dress with a white apron. It reminded Ro of what Amish women wore and seemed out of place among the commandos.

From the seat he had pulled up between her and Beau, Zach faux whispered, "That's Allison. She's married to that brute across from you, although none of us can figure out why. And that sweet little girl covered in syrup is Grace. Why she's not terrified of Jonah, we aren't sure."

The maligned Jonah threw a piece of bacon at Zach. Zach caught it in flight and popped it into his mouth.

Jonah rolled his eyes and gave Ro a manly chin jerk. "Nice to meet you. I understand you had a bit of a rough trip on the way here."

Ro looked down to the table and the plate of scrambled eggs, bacon, sausage, and pancakes that was shoved in front of her. A mug of coffee followed. She looked at Graham questioningly, as he seated himself at the head of the table, just to her left. He just shrugged. "Eat. You need it."

Opting not to argue with him, she answered Jonah. "It wasn't a picnic, but I did all right."

Beau spoke up. "How's your ankle feeling this morning?"

Ro tentatively rotated it in a circle under the table.

"Actually, it feels pretty good. I don't think it was as bad as it looked last night."

Graham interrupted, "We'll let Beau decide that after breakfast."

Whatever, Ro thought as she dug into her food. It was delicious. The eggs were light and fluffy, the bacon crispy, and the pancakes tasted like her mom's homemade buttermilk recipe, which Ro hadn't had since her mom passed away when she was a kid. She blinked back the tears that misted at the memory.

"So," Travis began, "where ya headed?"

Ro could swear she heard Graham mumble, "Great fucking question." She ignored him and focused on Travis.

"Home."

"Care to elaborate? And did you really come all the way from Chicago on foot?"

"I'm a little off my bearings, but my family's farm shouldn't be too much farther northeast of here. My dad and sister will be waiting on me. And yeah, I left Chicago pretty quickly after whatever happened, happened."

Jonah looked up from where he was still helping Grace eat her pancakes. "How did you know to get out of the city that fast? Figuring the distance, walking, you must have left the day the EMP took out the grid, or at least by the day after."

"So it was an electromagnetic pulse? I wondered."

Jonah nodded, eyes narrowing.

"I left the city the day it happened."

"Most people wouldn't have left that fast. Or known what the hell an EMP was." He paused, and his assessment made Ro feel self-conscious. "I've seen your bag." He gestured to the corner of the mess hall. Ro looked and was relieved to see her pack on the floor. "You had everything you'd need for the trip in your kit. How'd that come about?"

"As much as I'd like the answer to that question, Rowan needs to eat while her food is still hot," Graham decreed.

For once, Ro was actually grateful for Graham's high-handed behavior and took a huge bite. She didn't really want to explain. After she chewed and swallowed, she asked the question that had been nagging her since she'd arrived, "How do you still have working electronics when no one else does?"

"Just eat, woman," Graham ordered.

Ro let the question go, for the moment, but only because she was starving. She ignored the stares of the other men as she worked on tucking away her giant breakfast. *Whatever, boys. A girl's gotta eat.*

After she was finished, she pushed away from the table and went to stand, momentarily forgetting about her ankle. Surprisingly, the two seconds she put weight on it before Graham shoved her back down onto the chair, she felt only a twinge of pain.

"What the hell are you doing?"

"Calm down, Conan. I'm fine."

The other men at the table bit back grins at her nickname for Graham. She hadn't actually meant to let that slip out.

Beau intervened before she and Graham could square off and verbally spar.

"Let me take a look at it." He turned her chair so he could crouch in front of her and peeled off her sock. He unwrapped the bandage and manipulated her ankle. The bruising was still there, but the swelling was almost completely gone.

"It actually looks a hell of a lot better. Definitely better than I expected. You sprain your ankle fairly often?" he asked, looking up at Ro.

"Yeah, it happens. I've broken both of them, and I'm not sure they've ever been totally right since. I bounce back pretty quickly though. I figured more than a day or two off it would be completely unnecessary. I can probably walk on it today and be fine."

"Doll, how about you let the good doctor here make that determination," Zach said. "So, Beau, what's the verdict?"

Ro waited with great anticipation as Beau continued to manipulate her ankle. "Does that hurt?"

There was a twinge, okay, maybe a *slice*, of pain, but nothing Ro couldn't handle. "Feels fine."

"Don't lie to him," Graham said, dropping a heavy hand on her shoulder. "You won't like the consequences."

"It's *fine*. Barely a twinge. Don't get your panties in a twist," Ro shot back. She didn't take well to threats.

"Beau?"

"I'd suggest staying off it for the rest of the day today, at the very least. And preferably tomorrow, too. You might as well give it a chance to heal up right this time. Especially if you're planning on walking on it eight hours a day like you've probably been doing."

More like ten or twelve hours a day, Rowan thought.

"She's not going anywhere," Graham decreed. Rowan's temper flared like a Roman candle.

"Excuse me? I'm headed out today, whether you like it or not. I don't have time to screw around. I need to be somewhere, and I've got people waiting on me, and whether I stay or go is not your call." Ro had put her family last on her list of priorities too many times during the last decade. They were first on her list now, and any desire to stay— regardless of the reason—had to be ruthlessly shoved to the bottom.

"How exactly do you think you're getting out of here? Not a single person here is going to open the gate for you. You're going to stay put until you're healed up completely and I figure out what the hell to do with you."

Zach spoke up then, as if sensing that Graham's words were just pissing Rowan off more. Which would be an accurate assumption. "Sweetheart, it's not safe for you to be out on the road alone. I know you made it this far, but we can't in good conscience let you leave by yourself. We'd be throwing you to the wolves."

"I'll be fine. And regardless, I'm not your problem. I'm not far from where I'm going. It'll only take me another day, maybe two, to get home."

"I don't care if you're only crossing the street, you're not going anywhere. And that's final." Graham reached down to pluck Rowan off the chair, but she shoved his shoulders back.

"I don't know how things usually work around here, and I don't really care, but this whole *what I say goes* attitude you've got going on doesn't work for me. So just let me grab my pack and I'll be on my way. You won't need to trouble yourself with me again."

Graham cursed, spun, and left the mess hall, slamming the door behind him.

"I think Mr. Graham is mad, Daddy," Grace said to Jonah. "I think he doesn't want Miss Rowan to go because he likes her like you like Mommy."

Ro dropped her head into her hands. From the mouth of babes and all.

Zach lifted her chin and dropped a quick, and completely surprising, kiss on her lips. "Been wanting to do that since I saw you covered in mud. I'll talk to Graham. We'll figure something out."

Zach left the mess hall and spotted Graham heading for the command post. He jogged to catch up.

"That could have gone better."

Graham shot him an annoyed look. "No shit."

"You got a plan besides telling her she ain't leaving?"

"I'm still working on that."

"Because she seems pretty damn determined to get on her way. I want her to stay as much as you do, but we can't force her."

"Says who?"

"Seriously, G. Don't you want a willing woman in your bed?"

"As long as she's in my bed, I don't much care."

Zach knew posturing when he saw it, especially in his best friend.

"There's got to be some middle ground here." And Zach was determined to find it. After all, he wanted her to stay, but even more, he wanted her to *want* to stay.

"You think she'll figure a way out of the camp?"

"Not a chance in hell," Graham said confidently.

"She's a firecracker, all right. Might surprise you."

"Everything that woman does surprises me. Can you imagine her setting out without any protection to *walk* home? Over a hundred miles?" Graham shook his head. "Unfucking believable."

"You have fire watch this morning?"

"Shit. I have a shift in the command post." Graham looked down at his watch. "Which started five minutes ago."

Graham took off for his post, and Zach called after him, "You ever been late before, G?"

Graham shot up his middle finger before he disappeared into the building.

Rowan waited at the table until the other men gave her apologetic looks and left to go about their business. Jonah took Grace into the kitchen to sit with Allison, and he helped her clean up breakfast and set the leftovers aside for those who hadn't yet made it in for breakfast.

Room empty, and the others occupied, Rowan spied her backpack in the front corner. She stood, gingerly putting weight on her ankle. Only a twinge, okay, more than a twinge, but still, she was satisfied that she could walk. At least a little. Thankfully, both of her boots were sitting next to her bag. She dragged the bag to the nearest chair and attempted to fit her wrapped ankle into the hiking boot. Not happening. She pulled her sock off and unwrapped the ace bandage and shoved it in the bag and then pulled the boot on and laced it. Standing, she took a few tentative steps. The pressure from the boot definitely helped. She wouldn't get ten hours in today, but she'd get a few. She shouldered the pack and slipped out of the mess hall.

Outside, Ro ducked around the side of the building and

took a look around. The whole area seemed to be enclosed in the shape of a hexagon. The twelve-foot corrugated steel walls topped with wicked looking razor wire were impressive. Very twenty-first century, barbarian stronghold chic. And not what she'd expect from a simple, rustic hunting retreat. She surveyed her surroundings and racked her brain to figure the best way to get the hell out. Graham was undoubtedly right that none of his guys were going to be opening the door for her to leave.

A few of the giant oaks that shaded the interior of the compound had platforms built into the high branches, forming covered camouflaged lookout posts that probably gave a good view outside the walls. If she hadn't known to look for them, she wouldn't have even noticed they were there. It was possible someone was using one for watch. She didn't see anyone, but it didn't mean someone wasn't there. On the far side of the compound, she could see the goats Zach mentioned munching away at the grass growing in a wire-fenced pen. A lean-to type barn provided shelter from the elements, and a large chicken coop sat off to the right of the goat pen. Rowan couldn't count how many chickens fluttered around, but she estimated a few dozen. What looked to be some type of vertical garden, with plants growing out of pallet-like wooden shelves and metal mesh arches flourished not far from the livestock. A greenhouse about thirty feet long ran alongside the vertical garden. And a decent size stream ran across one corner of the camp, snaking under the walls to make its way in and out.

Bingo.

If she tried to scale the wall somehow and make her way over the razor wire, she'd end up sliced to ribbons, but the stream had definite potential. She just needed it to be a few feet deep, and she could swim right under the wall and out of Graham's little kingdom. She didn't look forward to starting her hike soaking wet, but it was better than bleeding from razor wire. She didn't allow herself to consider the possibility of staying. Family first. That had become her mantra. And one added bonus: she'd be proving Graham wrong. Something Ro figured didn't happen very often. *Humility. Learn it, Conan.* Checking the trees again for lookouts and coming up clear, as far as she could tell, Ro made her decision and hefted her bag. She hobbled toward the stream and the wall it flowed under, careful to keep as much weight off her now-burning ankle as possible. A pine tree offered decent cover, so Ro dropped her bag and started to unlace her boots. Might as well keep as much of her stuff dry as possible. She peeled off her socks and then stripped off the borrowed sweatpants and hoody. She kept the t-shirt on because otherwise she'd be skinny-dipping. She tied her hiking boots onto her backpack and shoved the clothes inside. She heaved the pack upward as hard as she could, watching it sail over the razor wire. The thump on the other side meant she was committed. Ro studied the stream. She really, really hoped it was deep enough.

Ro took a steadying breath and looked around the branches of the pine to make sure no one had noticed her. Not seeing anyone paying attention to her or her impromptu strip show, Ro stepped barefoot into the stream, shivering at the icy cold and—hell, yes!—hip-deep water. She slipped on the rock bottom and winced as a jagged edge gouged into the side of her right foot. Another tentative step toward the wall and Ro almost lost her balance on the moss-covered rocks. She felt a sharp stab of pain as her ankle rolled and swallowed her curse. Fuck it, she was determined. Taking a deep breath, Ro slid beneath the surface and pulled herself under the wall.

CHAPTER TWELVE

Graham's radio squawked. "G-man, I think your pretty little chick has flown the coop."

Graham jerked his head away from the wiring diagram he'd been studying and reached for his radio. "Say again?"

"I've got a bead on a half-naked girl just outside the wall pretending to be a mermaid."

"What the fuck are you talking about?" Graham roared into his radio.

Zach burst into the command post.

"Ro's gone. I went to take a leak and she wasn't in the mess hall when I came back. She's not in the cabin. She's not in the bathhouse."

Graham gripped the desk to keep from throwing his radio across the room.

"G-man, I suggest you get outside the wall right fucking now."

Graham glared at Zach and shoved to his feet.

"Go get a fucking towel. And get someone to cover my shift."

"No way in hell, huh?"

Graham didn't reply as he shoved the door open and headed for the bolt hole.

He reached the stream on the outside of the wall just as Rowan was trying to pull herself out and onto the bank. He stopped next to her bag and watched as she stood, eyes closed, wiping the water from her face. The wet black t-shirt was like a second skin, outlining her generous breasts and the nipples jutting out from the cold water. The fabric stuck to her stomach, and Graham's fury evaporated as he realized that she was nearly naked, and her movements flashed him a peek at her completely bare pussy. His cock twitched, and it was all he could do to stop himself from dropping to his knees to lick every drop of water from her skin. Instead, he reached for Rowan. She blinked, eyes widening as she caught sight of him, but Graham had her settled over his shoulder before she had a chance to open her mouth.

"Hey! Put me d—" Rowan's words became a screech as Graham's heavy hand came down, smacking her on her cold, wet, and very naked ass.

"What—" Another *smack* connected.

"Stop—" *Smack.*

Ro gave up on trying to talk and began to struggle instead.

"What did I tell you about following orders, little girl? And what part of *'You aren't going anywhere'* did you misunderstand?" she heard Graham say over his shoulder. "Although," he said, "I can't say I haven't wanted you soaking wet and ready for me."

Speechless at the abrupt change in the direction of Graham's thoughts, Ro didn't respond.

Graham's hand smoothed over her ass and damn near brushed her girly parts.

Before Ro could come up with any type of suitable reply, Graham's hand stilled and flipped her off his shoulder and re-situated her in his arms. Thankful that her ass was no longer bared to the world, and whoever must have spotted her attempted escape, she stayed silent.

Graham carried her along the wall to the front entrance, which swung open as they approached.

Zach met them with a towel as Ro's teeth started to chatter.

"She's going to need more than a towel," Zach observed.

"Back to the showers, I imagine."

Zach lifted her foot. "Back to Beau first, I think."

Rivulets of crimson dripped down the side of Ro's right foot.

"Goddammit, Ro," Graham said. "You are going to stay put this time, even if I have to tie you down myself."

He hefted her higher in his arms and headed toward the clinic, radioing Beau on his way.

CHAPTER THIRTEEN

Beau had once again okay-ed the shower, leaving her ankle unwrapped and covering her stitches, which had hurt like a mother without local anesthetic. Graham had glowered at her the whole time, squeezing her hand tighter each time she flinched as the needle cut into her skin. At least she had only needed six. Any more and she might have lost a hand. Zach held her other hand, and rather than squeeze, he'd spent the entire time rubbing his thumb back and forth across the back of it and playing with her fingers.

This time both Graham and Zach waited just beyond the shower room for her to finish, holding up the tiled walls like sentinels standing guard. Ro shut off the water and reached for the towel that Zach held out. He didn't even pretend to look away as he handed it to her. She was pretty sure they'd both taken more than one glance at her during her shower. Just the thought of them watching her had heated her more effectively than the hot water. She didn't give herself the luxury of enjoying the shower too long, though. She was focused on hiding her hardening nipples and trying not to clench her thighs to assuage the building ache.

"Done?" Graham asked.

Ro nodded, pushing herself from the seat. Before her feet made contact with the floor, she found herself in Zach's arms, Graham right behind him.

"Forgetting something, doll?" Zach asked.

Ro's short bark of laughter bounced off the tiled walls. "I guess so."

Zach sat her on the bench and Graham held out a t-shirt. Gratefully, Ro slipped it over her head and shoved her arms through the sleeves.

Then he crouched at her feet, holding open a pair of gray sweatpants.

"Leg."

Ro complied, sticking first one leg and then the other into the warm cotton pants. Being dressed like a child was new. And then she realized her lack of panties meant Graham had a front row seat to check out her goodies.

"Hey!" She scooted the pants up her legs and glared at Graham.

"Babe, I saw every naked inch of your pussy while you were dripping wet and climbing out of the creek."

Ro's gaze shot to Zach, who looked intrigued.

"Did ya now?" Zach drawled.

Ro's cheeks burned.

"Do you have to be such a dick?"

"Baby, you have no idea."

Ro decided studying the floor was the better alternative, but Graham's hand shot out, lifting her chin.

"We need to talk."

"I'm really not interested in anything you have to say."

"You sure 'bout that?"

"Pretty damn sure."

"What if I offered you an armed escort home?"

Ro's gaze darted from Graham to Zach, who looked a bit confused.

"Are you serious?" she asked.

"Completely," Graham replied.

"What's the catch?"

"You nix the escape attempts for a few days and let yourself heal up."

Ro considered the offer. It would mean a slight delay in her plans, but she'd be giving herself a chance to recuperate, and she wouldn't have to face whatever craziness was outside these walls by herself. That was a hell of an incentive. And being smart about this didn't mean she was putting her family last.

She looked from one man to the other and started to nod.

Then Graham added, "And you're in our bed until we leave."

CHAPTER FOURTEEN

"What the fuck, man?" Zach held it together until he and Graham had dropped a strangely silent Rowan back in their cabin. She'd probably never speak to them again after Graham's ultimatum. As soon as they were out of earshot, he shoved Graham back against the side of a cinderblock storage shed painted a deep forest green. "You're going to force her to sleep with us? What the fuck is wrong with you? I'm no fucking rapist. Didn't think you were either."

Graham pushed off the wall and shoved Zach back. "Calm the fuck down. It's not like that."

Zach rubbed his face with both hands before lacing his fingers together and gripping the back of his neck. "Oh really? Then what the fuck is it like? Because I *like* this girl. She could be the one. And you want to extort our way into bed with her?"

Graham leaned back against the building. Zach shook his head in disbelief at Graham's casual pose.

"Did you see how she reacted to the idea before?" Graham asked.

"Yeah, she freaked the fuck out." Zach started pacing.

"That might have been her initial reaction, but if you were paying attention, she was intrigued. Curious."

"What's your point, man? Because I seriously think you fucked this one up. I mean ... after the experience she had ..."

"This gives her the right motivation to let go of all that and give it—hell, us—a try."

"By forcing her?"

"No one is forcing her to do anything. She says no, then it ends there."

Zach stopped his pacing and waited until Graham met his gaze. "If she even *thinks* no, then it ends there."

Graham nodded. "Just wait and see. Give her a little time to mull over the idea. What do we have to lose? You want her. I want her. We only have a few days to make it happen. If we can't tie her to us, she walks away forever. I didn't figure you'd let that happen without a fight, and ..." Graham paused meaningfully. "I'm not willing to let it happen either."

Zach eyed his friend, amazed that he'd given voice to his feelings about a woman. It had only taken a fucking apocalypse. Zach's thoughts went back to Ro. "She looked so ... fragile or something ... when she told us what went down before."

Graham inclined his head. "She didn't look fragile when she devised and executed her escape, did she? And she sure wasn't fragile when she grabbed a backpack and left Chicago by herself." Graham paused. "That girl is gutsy as hell and willing to take a risk. Why shouldn't she take a risk with us?"

Zach exhaled a long breath. "I still think you're an asshole for the way you set this up. Just know that the second she says no, which could be as soon as we walk back in that door, I'm backing off."

"Agreed. Now, this is what I'm thinking ..."

Ro clenched and unclenched her fists while she replayed the conversation in her head. Each time, it seemed like the roar of the blood in her ears got louder and her heart pounded harder. Her initial stunned silence had given way to anger at Graham's highhanded declaration. And then to curiosity. And then to arousal. Apparently Graham and Zach were her one-way ticket on the crazy train.

Zach had promised to come back within the hour. Ro couldn't begin to imagine what she'd be feeling in an hour. At this point, she put fifty-fifty odds on homicidal or horny.

She grabbed the pillow on the end of the couch and hugged it. How the hell was a girl supposed to respond to something like that? Total meltdown? Hunger strike? Strip-tease? Her mind raced with the possibilities. She had options. Hell, she had a *taser*. She could suck it up and mount another escape attempt. Except the scariest thought running through Ro's head was that she didn't want to run from this. She sort of ... wanted to reach out and grab it with both hands. Or she could tell them both to fuck off. It would work. She was confident they'd back off. And then they could refuse to provide the escort Graham had promised.

Dammit. She wanted to smack that "I dare you" look off Graham's face. Cocky asshole. She glanced toward Graham's bedroom. Memories of last night—before she'd had her mini breakdown over Zach's comment—came rushing back. She'd been drowning in the heat from Graham's kiss. Graham had claimed to be up front about what they wanted. Was that what this was? Their declaration of intent? Way to score perfect tens on the shock factor, Conan. He had to be expecting her to balk. Ro thought she'd made it pretty damn obvious that she wasn't down with taking orders from anyone. Exhibit A: her escape attempt this morning. She couldn't really call his bluff, because she didn't think he was bluffing. But she could turn the tables on them—make her own demands. She'd been branded a slut in her past life for something she hadn't done. Why not earn that scarlet letter now? Everything was different. She had nothing to lose. And maybe a hell of an experience to gain ...

Graham. Zach. One hundred percent focused on her. Naked. Ro shivered at the thought. And it wasn't a shiver of disgust.

CHAPTER FIFTEEN

"I have terms." Zach pulled up short as he and Graham entered the cabin. Graham grunted as he rammed into Zach's back. Zach had considered whether they'd need to wear protective cups to confront her. Based on the no-nonsense tone of her voice, he might not have been far off.

"Terms?" Zach responded, glancing to Graham, who'd taken a seat on the couch next to Rowan. Brave man.

"I don't do well with being told what to do. Call it a personality quirk."

"Rowan," Graham started, but Ro cut him off.

"You had your say. Now it's my turn." She shot them both a silencing stare, before muttering to herself, "I can't believe I'm really going to do this."

Graham quirked an eyebrow, and Zach barely restrained his own grin.

"This is how it's going to go down, boys. You called it earlier: I'm in no shape to travel at the moment. I get it, and I see the wisdom in waiting. But I need you both to promise that when *I* say I'm well enough to travel, you *will* get me home."

Graham started to speak, but Ro's gaze hardened, and she continued, "I think what we're about to do requires a hell of a lot of trust, and if you can't trust me to know when I'm fit to travel, we have a serious problem."

Zach and Graham both nodded, albeit Graham more reluctantly.

"Barring any unforeseen circumstances, we'll let you make that call. Within reason. If either of us thinks that you're putting on show to get out of here faster, we will call you on it," Graham said.

"Then I guess you'll just have to give me a reason not to want to get out of here faster," Ro countered.

"Done," Zach said. "You tell us when and where, and we'll—"

She took a deep breath, as if digging up her courage, and interrupted him. "Here. Now."

She glanced at him and then to Graham and seemed to lose a little of her newfound bravado. "But I have to admit, I am completely out of my depth here. Should we … um … flip a coin to see who … um … goes first?"

Zach couldn't hold back a chuckle at her hesitant, yet practical, suggestion.

"Not necessary." He pushed off the wall and rounded the table to stand in front of Rowan. Bracing one hand on the arm of the sofa, he leaned down, invading her personal space. Her pupils dilated and her breathing accelerated. "I get first dibs on fucking that smart little mouth of yours."

Holy shit. This was really happening.

Ro could feel her mouth drop open, liable to catch flies, at Zach's blunt declaration. She'd pegged him as the beta in this triad, but she was wrong. He was just as much of an alpha as Graham.

Zach caught her chin in one hand. "Just like that, doll." He slid his thumb across her bottom lip, and she couldn't stop her tongue from darting out to lick it. Zach slid the digit in her mouth.

Graham slid in next to her, and picked her up, resettling her on his lap. He pulled the hair away from her face and spoke directly into her ear. "Suck him, baby. Show Zach how you're going to suck his cock like a good little girl." Zach groaned at Graham's words. Ro's nipples puckered under the thin material of the t-shirt, and heat gathered between her legs. *They really knew what the hell they were doing.*

A hand slid up and brushed over the hard buds pressing into the cotton. Zach's eye's burned with a predatory light. "You like that idea, don't you? These tight little nipples say you do."

Zach removed his thumb from her mouth with a *pop* and dragged his wet digit down her chin, sweeping down the arch of her neck. Ro moaned, and her head fell back against Graham.

Graham nipped her ear before cupping her breasts and lifting them toward Zach like some sort of pagan offering. One that she hoped Zach accepted. She could feel wetness seep from her center. She heard a rustle of clothing, and her eyes snapped open, hoping Zach was dropping his cargos. No such luck. Zach was now kneeling before her, his look more intense than she'd ever seen it. She looked down to see him gripping the hem of her shirt.

"Look at me," he said.

Almost drowsily, she lifted her eyes and met his gaze.

"Are you sure you're good with this? Everything stops the second you say so."

The offer, although thoughtful, was completely unnecessary. Ro wanted this. *Wanted them.*

She nodded, but Zach didn't move.

"He needs the words, baby. Tell him that you're good with him pulling off your shirt and sucking on your gorgeous tits," Graham said.

Ro swallowed. Moment of truth.

Zach studied her face as she said, "Yes."

"Tell him," Graham demanded softly. "Tell him exactly what you want him to do to you."

Feeling the heat rising in her cheeks, Ro knew she was turning red, in a completely unsexy way.

But Zach just smiled at her embarrassment.

Oh fuck it.

"I'm good with you stripping me naked and sucking my nipples before you fuck my mouth." Her words came out in a rush, like water bursting from a collapsing dam.

Both men groaned at her bold declaration.

"Thank God, doll. Because I've been waiting to get my hands on you," Zach said.

Ro wasn't sure what came over her, because her next words seemed to come out of someone else's mouth. "Big talk. I was hoping for some action."

The gaze that she'd thought of as so friendly and easygoing sharpened with greed.

Oh, hell. Ro was pretty sure she'd just said the exact right thing to unleash a beast she had no idea how to control.

Zach lifted his chin at Graham, and Graham's voice rumbled in her ear, sending chills up her spine. "Now you've done it, babe."

In seconds, her shirt was yanked over her head, leaving her naked from the waist up, sitting on the lap of a man she'd known for less than twenty-four hours, in front of a second man she'd also known for less than twenty-four hours. *Shit just got real.*

Without a bra to corral them, as soon as the t-shirt was gone, Ro's breasts were exposed for only a moment before Graham shifted beneath her and his big, rough palms slid around her ribcage to cup them. His thumbs flicked her puckered nipples, and the shafts of pleasure had Ro going from wet to dripping in the span of a moment.

Zach's tawny head bent, and with his amber eyes on hers, he reached out to gently grasp her left nipple between even white teeth. And tugged. Ro jumped when a finger and thumb pinched her other nipple, and gently rolled it one way, and then the other. Skip dripping, Ro headed straight to drenched. The fingers dropped away, and Zach caught her right nipple and gave it the same attention.

Ro's eyes were starting to drift shut, so she could just focus on the pleasure when she felt a callused hand skim down her ribcage to the waistband of her sweats. *Oh, sweet baby Jesus, this is really happening.*

Rather than freak like her whirring mind told her she should, Ro lifted her hips, pressing against the hand that was now cupping her through the material of her pants.

Graham kissed her shoulder before saying, "Fuck, baby. Your pussy is gonna burn us alive, isn't it?

"Touch me," Ro breathed.

Zach pulled away from her nipples. "You sure you're ready for this?" The hand cupping her mound stilled.

Ro gritted her teeth to stop the moan of frustration. "Please. I need …"

"You need to come, sweetheart?"

"Yes."

"Lift up," Graham ordered.

Ro's hips shifted at his command, pressing into his hand.

Zach wasted no time in dragging the sweats down her legs and tossing them aside.

Hell. Now she was completely naked on the lap of a guy she'd known for less than twenty-four hours, in front of another guy she'd known for less than twenty-four hours. She couldn't even bring herself to care, because the look on Zach's face was one of pure worship.

"Ah, fuck." He looked to Graham. "You didn't tell me she was bare."

Ro felt Graham's answering growl against her shoulder. His hand covered her pussy, and a single finger dragged up her crease toward her engorged clit. He was so, so close.

"Jesus fucking Christ, woman. You're soaked." The fingers disappeared for a moment. "And you taste fucking amazing."

"Spread her open for me, G. I gotta taste that sweet pussy," Zach said.

Thank the Lord, Ro thought, because the pulse thrumming in her clit demanded satisfaction.

"I need—" she started.

"We know, baby. Zach's going to take care of you," Graham assured her.

"But—"

"Hush," he ordered, sucking the lobe of her ear into his mouth as he spread her labia. "If you're good, Zach will get you off faster. If you're not … well, then he might feel the need to make you beg."

Ro's next words, whatever they were going to be, died in her throat as Zach bent his head and dragged his tongue up the middle of her exposed slit. He pulled back and met her eyes. "I'm going to eat this sweet little pussy until you scream."

All coherent thoughts fled as Zach's head bent again and his tongue expertly circled and flicked at her clit, before dragging down to dip into her pussy, fucking her with short thrusts.

Graham's deep voice rumbled in her ear as he said, "Zach loves to eat pussy. He'll fuck you with his tongue until you beg him to stop. And then he'll slip a finger inside you, find your G-spot, and make you scream."

At the word "slip," Ro felt a finger toying with her entrance. She gasped, her hips jerking forward, closer to Zach's face. The digit slid inside her, and she felt Zach groan against her.

"You're so fucking tight, sweetheart. I can't wait to feel you wrapped around my cock."

Ro felt Graham's hands slide back up to cup her breasts and tease her nipples, before he said, "With such a tight pussy, I can only imagine how tight that virgin ass of yours is going to feel when I get inside it." Ro insides clenched, and she felt a second digit sliding inside her.

Zach looked up, his lazy smile beyond sensual. "She likes the thought of that, man. She just squeezed my fingers so hard."

Graham tugged on her nipples, and combined with Zach's continued onslaught of tongue and fingers, Ro was being dragged to the precipice of pleasure. Screw dragged. She was hurtling toward it.

But Graham wasn't done sharing his dirty thoughts. "I think Zach should finger that little asshole while he eats your pussy. You're so dripping wet he won't need any lube … just you."

Ro shivered at the thought, and then froze as the one of the fingers slid out and swirled in her slickness before moving back toward her anus.

"I—" Ro started.

"Hush, baby. We'll take good care of you. Just relax," Graham whispered.

Zach paused in his exploration to glance up at her. Ro didn't know what he saw in her face, but it must've been assent, because he ducked his head and sucked on her clit as his finger dragged over the pucker, spreading her juices. Ro stilled, but the flicks to her clit had her pressing harder against his tongue ... and pressing his finger against the tight whorl of muscle.

"That's it, baby. You push out a little more, and I'm going to be finger fucking that ass of yours."

Ro could feel the climax barreling down on her, and she couldn't hold on to rational thought. She just needed a little more ...

Zach slid his thumb into her pussy and caught her clitoris between his teeth and tongue and tugged. Graham rolled and pulled at her nipples, and Ro let go. The climax broke over her like a twelve-foot swell, crashing through her as she bucked against their hold. Zach continued to suck her clit, and as the orgasm raged on, Ro felt a finger breach her anus and slide inside that dark channel. The invasion was foreign. Dirty. And hot. So hot that she felt a second orgasm rushing on the heels of the first. It slammed into her, weakening her limbs, and she felt her pussy and ass clench around Zach's fingers. Fingers that continued to pump in and out. Fucking her pussy and her ass. *Holy shit.* Ro threw her head back against Graham's shoulder and rode out the orgasm, biting her lip to keep from screaming. The pleasured ebbed, and she wilted, spent from the sensory overload. The fingers slid out of her, and Graham wrapped both arms around her torso.

"That was the most beautiful thing I've ever seen," Graham said. He pressed a gentle kiss against her shoulder, then her neck.

"Think you can handle another?" Zach asked.

CHAPTER SIXTEEN

Shot down by Graham, Zach had grudgingly agreed that Ro needed rest. Dazed from the two most intense orgasms she'd ever experienced, Ro hadn't had the energy to argue. Until they tried to tuck her into bed for the rest of the day and offered to deliver her meals and take turns keeping her company.

Oh hell no.

Ro stood her ground, arguing that although she was injured, she wasn't an invalid. But even with all her snark and attitude, she struggled to meet their gazes. Especially Zach's. The man had devastated her with his tongue while casually slipping a finger into her ass.

Ro knew that anal sex was the new black, but she'd never been tempted to try it. And now, all signs pointed to her losing her last bastion of virginity in short order. With not one, but *two* men. *Holy fucking hell. Go big or go home.*

After what had happened on the couch, neither man could seem to resist the urge to touch her. Their collective hands had carefully redressed her, and Zach had swept her up into his arms and strode out of the cabin. When she'd protested, Graham had smacked her ass. A blond man, who Ro hadn't yet met, had been walking by at that moment. Ro's knee-jerk reaction had been embarrassment, but she quashed it ruthlessly and shot him a look that'd said, *eat your heart out, asshole*. At least she hoped that was what the look had said. Because, dammit, if she was woman enough to participate in a ménage, then she was going to *own* that shit. Graham had caught the look and given her a quick—*approving?*—kiss before striding off.

A few minutes later, she was seated in the mess hall and enduring good-natured ribbing from Alex and Jamie about "The Great Escape." Apparently her stunt had required Alex to dust off his underwater welding skills, because Graham had ordered grates to be welded beneath the wall to block the entrance and exit via the stream. Ro was apologetic, but was assured that it was better to discover any hole in security now rather than finding out about it—potentially with much more dangerous consequences—later.

After lunch, which had consisted of five-alarm chili and jalapeño cornbread made by one of the guys, her next stop —via Zach's piggyback ride—was the central command post, where Graham was taking a shift. Zach was off to take his shift on fire watch, and she was hanging with Graham. It seemed that Graham and Zach had made the decision that she would be with one of them at all times. Before he'd left, Zach had leaned in for a kiss and whispered, "Don't forget, I have first dibs on this sinful mouth of yours later."

Ro had turned crimson. Zach was definitely no beta.

Conversation with Graham had focused on security protocols of the ranch. Now that she wasn't trying to escape, he wanted her to understand all of the systems and procedures keeping her and the other residents safe.

"So, wait, how did you know I was coming?" Ro asked.

"We've got a few different types of perimeter sensors set up. One of which you tripped." Graham pointed to a map on the wall. "This is the wall surrounding the inner compound, and this is the outer fence. Outside the fence we have sensors that are set into the ground and detect vibration." Anticipating her question, he said, "The sensors are set to only go off if the vibration corresponds to a weight that's heavy enough to be a person."

"Did you have those set up before? Or did you set them up after the grid went down?"

"After. All of our electronics, or duplicates in the case of the electronics that we used on a daily basis, were locked down in one of the bunkers. They were protected so that an EMP wouldn't fry them."

Faraday cages, Ro would bet. Her dad had an entire room in their basement at home lined in aluminum that sealed when you shut the door. In the event of an electromagnetic pulse, the metal skin lining the room would shield the contents from the pulse of energy that blew out unprotected electronics. But Faraday cages weren't commonplace.

Ro narrowed her gaze on Graham. "That's not exactly normal, you know. Who got bit with the Doomsday Prepper bug?"

Graham laughed, although it sounded forced. "When you've seen what we've seen and trained for the things we did, you don't think in terms of Plan A and Plan B. We're more into planning for contingencies C-Z." When he didn't elaborate, Ro wanted to push, but a glance at his grim features stopped her.

She looked toward the map.

"You said there was more than one perimeter?"

"Yeah, there's a second perimeter along the outside of

the fence line. Those are your standard run-of-the-mill laser sensors. If the beam is broken, it sounds the alarm in here."

"How do you know where someone broke the beam?"

"We've got each side set up as a series of shorter beams. Each beam corresponds to a section of the map."

"So why bother with fire watch if you've got all of these sensors set up? Isn't that just a waste of manpower?"

"There's no substitute for two eyes and a gun."

"Don't you have a lot of false alarms? Animals breaking the beams?" Ro asked.

"Not as many as you'd think. The beam runs parallel to the fence, only about an inch beyond it. An animal would have to ram the fence to break the beam."

Graham pointed out the gates that had been set into the fence line, as well as routes taken by the guys on fire watch, which differed during a day shift versus a night shift, and the treestands that doubled as watch posts.

Ro was amazed at the system. It seemed damn near impossible to get in without being detected. The thought allayed her lingering concern about the creepy trio finding a way to get to her—or Lia, the woman they'd rescued.

When Travis relieved Graham of his shift, Ro requested that Graham take her to the clinic so she could check on her. While stitching her up earlier in the day, Beau had guardedly answered Ro's questions about her.

All they knew was her name, as the woman hadn't spoken since she'd arrived. No, Ro couldn't try to talk to her, because they were keeping her sedated. When she'd first woken, she'd panicked, and Beau was afraid she'd hurt herself worse. He was planning to reduce the sedative and promised to let Rowan try to talk to her when she woke up. He'd already intended to have Allison present, hoping that seeing a woman, rather than big, hulking men, would help her stay calm this time.

Graham radioed Beau, and Beau said they weren't quite ready. "Give me an hour, and check back."

With an hour to kill, Graham insisted that Ro demonstrate exactly how rusty her skills were with a gun.

CHAPTER SEVENTEEN

"You have a shooting range? Seriously?" Why Ro sounded so shocked, Graham wasn't entirely certain.

"We have to stay sharp, and some of the hunters like to target shoot when they're not out slaying bucks. This building is reinforced and soundproofed. It doubles as a safe room."

"What else are you hiding here? As soon as I think I've got this place figured out, you throw something like this at me." She turned to face him after he settled her on a stool. "You going to share the rest of your secrets?"

Graham smiled at the attitude she couldn't help but radiate. She was a spitfire. And something about her fired his blood like no woman before. He held out the M4 he'd grabbed from the armory.

"You hit the target ... I'll answer a question."

Ro accepted the assault rifle and held out her hand. "Magazine?"

Graham held one out, and she tried to tug it from his grip. "But every time you miss, you owe me something I want."

Ro's gaze narrowed, and she slid the magazine into place without breaking his stare, flipped off the safety, and chambered a round.

Graham glanced to make sure she'd left it on the single-round setting rather than the three-round burst.

"I got this, Conan. I'm not shooting three at a time."

Well, fuck. This might not go as planned, Graham thought.

"And why do you know that?" he asked, grabbing a paper target.

"No answers unless I miss. Target?"

Graham had just clipped the target to the pulley system. He'd initially thought to keep it closer, but instead he cranked it all the way to the end of the lane.

She raised her eyebrows as if to say "Oh, really? This is how we're going to play?"

Graham settled ear protection over her ears and slid safety glasses onto her face before donning his own. She gave him a nod and then raised the rifle. Pausing for only a fraction of a second, she squeezed the trigger.

Graham counted. Fifteen shots. Only one was outside of the red center circle of the target. Graham suspected she'd been trying to eliminate every sliver of red on the paper and gone wide. She lowered the rifle and jerked her head toward the target. "Since I owe you one answer: my dad felt it was important for his daughters to know their way around every gun in his arsenal. The M4 was always my favorite. Erica preferred the bolt action .308."

Graham reached for the crank and pulled the target in. He laid the remains on the counter in front of Rowan, quite sure his cock jerking to life was a completely inappropriate reaction, but he couldn't help it. The woman was sexy as fuck. Casually gripping a rifle perched on a stool in too big sweats and a too big hoody; she was lethal. Graham suppressed his grin and reached for his sidearm. He pulled the M1911 .45 ACP out of its holster and ejected the magazine and the round in the chamber. He slid the extra bullet into his pocket, and held out the unloaded pistol and magazine to her.

"This might be more of a challenge." She reached out to pick them up, and he pulled his hands back. "You sure you can handle it? It's a big gun for a little girl."

"Seriously? Did you just see me kill your little target? I can handle the kick, Conan."

"Okay. Have at it then."

She grasped the pistol and inspected it before checking the clip, sliding it in, flipping off the safety, and chambering a round. She did it all in one smooth, fluid motion. Like her hands had done that very action a thousand times before. Like it was muscle memory. Who the hell was this girl who carried a MOLLE backpack, handled firearms with ease, and responded to him and Zach like she'd been custom made for them? Kryptonite. Fucking kryptonite.

She flipped the safety back on and looked up at him expectantly.

"New target?"

Graham shook himself and pulled a new target from the clipboard attached to the wall and hung it on the clip before starting to crank it out. He looked down at her seated form—her head only came up to his shoulder—even on the tall stool. "How far do you want to go?" Her eyes flared, assuring him the double entendre wasn't lost on her.

"All the way," she replied, smiling a temptress's smile.

Graham ignored his erection, which was now bordering on obscene, and cranked the target out to the end. He stepped back to stand behind her and watched in awe as she raised the .45 and unloaded the seven-round magazine in less than ten seconds. Except for the first shot, which had gone a little high, she'd grouped her shots within a circle the size of a softball. Not bad at all. She re-engaged the safety, ejected the magazine, and handed both back to him with a grin.

"I think that means I get to ask the questions now."

Graham opened his mouth to reply, but was interrupted.

"I think I'm in love with your girl."

Graham and Rowan swung around to see Travis and Jamie standing just inside the closed door.

"I don't know about love, but I've definitely got a boner for her. Damn, woman," Jamie said.

Graham's jaw clenched as annoyance surged through him. He wasn't sure why he cared, but this had been their moment, and the intrusion was decidedly unwelcome.

"What do you need?" Graham bit out.

The grins evaporated, and both men straightened into posture that spoke of years in the military. Travis looked like he was about to salute.

"You weren't answering your radio, G. Ty mentioned you'd headed for some target practice. Two of the perimeter sensors have tripped. Thought you'd want to know."

Graham looked down at the radio strapped to his belt. The green light was off. Fuck. He was so goddamn caught up in Rowan that he didn't even realize the battery was dead. Graham grabbed an extra magazine from his cargo pocket and loaded the M1911 before handing it back to Rowan. Her features screwed up in confusion. He looked to Travis and held out a hand. "Give me your radio."

Travis also looked confused, but complied. Graham turned up the volume before setting it on Rowan's lap. He dragged the stool across the room and pulled her up next to the door and in front of the counter that ran along the back wall of the room.

"Do not move from this stool. Bolt the door behind me. You'll be able to hear everything that's going on, but don't use the radio unless someone speaks to you directly. I'll be back as soon as I can and radio to let you know it's me. Do not open the door until Zach or I come for you." He opened the cabinet on the wall above her head. "There's water, food, blankets, lanterns, and a whole bunch of other crap in here. I shouldn't be long, but if I am, you're well-provisioned."

When she opened her mouth to protest, he kissed her. Hard. "I need you safe, babe." He pulled away and pointed to the section of the floor to the right of the stool. It was covered by worn, gray industrial carpet squares. "If things go bad and someone tries to breach the building, I expect you to carefully hop off this stool, shove the carpet aside, and turn the round metal handle that is recessed in the concrete. It will trigger a hydraulic system, and a small section of the floor will lift like a trap door. You get down the ladder without hurting yourself and hit the red actuator on the wall behind the ladder. It'll release the hydraulics and engage a lock. No one will be able to get in from up here until you hit the actuator again."

Ro's mouth dropped opened, and her eyes widened almost comically.

"With the supplies down there, you'd be set for years."

"Holy shit. Who are you guys?" Ro whispered. She glanced at the contents of the cabinet in front of her. "And you have peanut butter Power Bars ..." Her expression turned blissful before sobering, as if just remembering the seriousness of the situation.

Graham smiled, ducked in for another kiss and turned back to the men.

"Let's go."

CHAPTER EIGHTEEN

Graham stalked across the compound and headed straight for the command post and the armory. He needed another sidearm.

"I'll bring you another .45 and a radio, G," Travis said, reading his mind. "And Jonah already has Allison and Grace in the bunker under the kitchen. Beau's locked down in the clinic." Graham nodded and swung into the command post. Ty was waiting.

"Damn, man, radio broken? Or did you say screw target practice and decide to fuck your girl on that counter in the range? It's the perfect height. I can just imagine. And your girl's got that luscious ass and perfect tits ..."

Graham was across the room before he'd even realized he was moving, shoving Ty against the wall. "You ever talk about her like that again, and you'll never come down from those fucking trees. I'll keep you on fire watch for the rest of the goddamn apocalypse. Get me?"

"Whoa, G-man ... I was just fucking with you."

"Sitrep?" Graham let him go and crossed the room to look at the map showing the area surrounding the property and the sensors glowing red to indicate where the beams had been broken. Graham tried to focus on the situation at hand; otherwise he might strangle one of his best friends.

Ty's attitude did a one-eighty as he straightened. "At fifteen hundred hours, the beam near the southwest corner of the property was tripped. Approximately five minutes later, the next beam was broken. Zach, Alex, and Cam are currently on fire watch and haven't gotten eyes on whatever or whoever it was."

The door opened and Travis entered, holding out both a sidearm and a radio to Graham.

Ty continued, "You want to send out a few more—" A series of three fast beeps sounded and then repeated from the perimeter sensor station. The three men whipped around to look at the map.

Ty got on the radio, "Be advised, we've got another beam tripped on the south side of the fence."

The radio squawked, "Copy that, boys. Still not seeing any movement. I'm coming down the west fence line, but I'm a ways out," Zach reported.

"I'm near the northeast corner, so it'll take me the longest to get over there," Alex added.

"I just finished my loop in the southeast corner. I'm headed west along south fence line," Cam radioed.

Shit. Graham checked the pistol, holstered it, and reached for the radio. "Travis, you're with me. We'll get there just as quick as anyone. Let's figure out what the fuck is going on."

Ty relayed the order into the radio, "Be advised. G-man and T-dog are headed out."

Jamie grabbed body armor from the hooks on the wall and tossed it to Graham and Travis. With efficient movements, the men strapped it on and then loaded up with extra magazines. Graham grabbed the face paint on the shelf by the door more out of habit than anything. He smeared green, gray, and brown paint on his face and jogged out of the building.

Ro was glad that Graham had thought to leave her a radio, so she'd at least have some idea of what the hell was going on. A third sensor being tripped definitely wasn't good. She hoped, maybe naively, that it was just some deer out in the wild trying to get at the lush grass inside the fence.

"Be advised. G-man and T-dog are headed out."

Ro froze; the cards she'd been shuffling fluttering into a rendition of Fifty-two Pick-Up on the counter. "G-man" had to be Graham. And Zach was out there on fire watch, too.

"They'll both be fine. It's not like this is their first rodeo," Rowan said to herself. But still, she didn't like the fear that pooled and clumped in the pit of her stomach like globs of mercury.

How could she be afraid for people that she'd only known for a day? It seemed insane. No, it *was* insane. But she couldn't help it. Hell. She needed to help it. She couldn't afford to get attached. Whatever this was had a definite expiration date. A really short one. Another few days at most. She would not get attached. Because there was no way this ... thing could last any longer.

"This is about sex and making it home safe. That's it. That's all. Then it's over. End of story. Finished," Ro said resolutely.

Stamping out all of the other thoughts in her head like a blanket on fire, Ro gathered up the scattered cards and proceeded to deal a game of solitaire. She tried not to wince at the irony.

CHAPTER NINETEEN

Graham and Zach had both returned for Ro, but their grim expressions didn't bode well for what they had discovered. Footprints all along the fence line. No people spotted. Both men were quiet and contemplative. The banter that Ro had grown used to was absent when Zach gave her a piggyback ride to the mess for dinner. Neither shared their thoughts on the day's events.

The pork chop and mashed potatoes Graham had piled onto her plate smelled delicious, but her twisting gut made them hard to choke down. Unable to stand the silence any longer, Ro said, "You need to put me to work or something. I get that I'm gimpy, but boredom is a dangerous thing for me."

Graham and Zach jerked up from their respective plates to look at her. The smirk she saw easing onto Zach's face helped to soothe the churning in her stomach.

"Don't take this the wrong way and think I'm a misogynistic pig, but ... Allison could use some help with prep and clean up in the kitchen, and maybe even with the laundry and the garden," Zach said, his smirk having reached full power.

Ro held up a hand to stop him. "Hold up. You mean to tell me that poor woman in there does all of that work herself —feeds you, cleans up after you, and grows your food? That just ain't right." Ro couldn't help the country that leaked into her tone as she launched into her mini-rant.

Both men colored slightly. Graham spoke first. "Now wait a minute. It's not like that. We all take turns helping out in the kitchen. The results of which are sometimes more edible than others ... and Beau shoulders most of the load of the garden. And someone always pitches in to help on wash day. But if you're interested, we need to double down on watch, so you'd be freeing up another body to patrol the property."

Ro stowed the mini-rant. "I'm happy to help, but I'm giving you fair warning: my cooking probably isn't much more edible than the worst of you guys. I haven't tried to grow anything in almost ten years, and I've never done laundry by hand. But I'd also rather pull my weight than not, so if that's what you need ... I guess I can start by doing dishes."

Satisfied that she finally had something to contribute to the little society that flourished within the walls, Ro enjoyed the rest of her meal, listening to the guys joke and mock one another. When she was finished, Zach carried her into the kitchen and settled her on a stool in front of the sink. Allison looked at them askance.

Ro rolled up her sleeves. "Put me to work."

Washing dishes turned out to be much more entertaining than Rowan would've guessed. Allison was a veritable font of knowledge when it came to all things related to Castle Creek Whitetail Ranch. She and Jonah and Grace had been living on the property and managing the whitetail breeding and hunting operations. She filled Rowan in as they washed and dried the dishes.

"Do you ever stop working?" Ro asked as Allison hauled out flour, sugar, and butter and began to measure out the ingredients for piecrust.

"Only on Sundays. But honestly, it's what I'm used to." She gestured to her plain blue dress and white apron. "I didn't exactly grow up like you."

Based on Allison's clothes, Ro had assumed as much. "Amish?"

"Mennonite. There's a small community about an hour northeast of here. That's where I'm from."

Ro was familiar with it. She'd grown up seeing the horses and buggies driving alongside the cars, tractors, and giant farm implements that hogged the country roads.

"Then how? I mean, you and Jonah?" Ro didn't want to pry, but she was intensely curious about how a Mennonite woman had ended up with a Marine.

"I married young, and within a year, I was pregnant, and a widow," Allison said. "It was a farming accident."

"Oh God," Ro said, "I'm so sorry. I didn't mean to …"

"It's okay, Rowan. It led me to Jonah, and for that I can be nothing but thankful. But I don't want to bore you with my story," she said, tipping a perfectly measured cup of flour into a huge bowl.

Ro gestured to the sink, which was collecting more dishes as Allison worked. "You see what I've got going on. I'd love to hear your story."

Allison shared about being a young, pregnant widow, and the pressure she'd been under to marry again, even before the baby was born. She'd refused and sworn she'd never marry again for anything but love. Her small and tight-knit community had disapproved and the pressure had mounted until

Allison had to choose: the only life she'd ever known or staying true to herself and her convictions. She'd left the Mennonite community and moved into an apartment in the small town located about fifteen miles away from the ranch. She'd gotten a job, seven months pregnant, working as a cashier at the hardware store. Jonah had come in for paint, and according to him, it had been love at first sight. He'd pestered her until she'd agreed to have dinner with him. She'd thought he was insane, wanting to date a woman who was less than two months from giving birth, but he'd persisted and won her heart. He'd held her hand throughout her delivery and fallen in love with Grace the moment she was born.

"He is the only father she's ever known, and in my opinion, she's the luckiest little girl in the world," Allison said, pressing the crusts into pie plates.

"I can't say I disagree with you. He seems like a great guy," Ro said, remembering the way Jonah had patiently cut Grace's pancakes at breakfast, not complaining when the little sticky fingers left syrup all over his shirtsleeve where Grace kept patting his arm.

"It's funny really," Allison continued, "Now I'm putting to use all of the same skills that I would have in my old life, but it's infinitely better, because I have Jonah, Grace, and the rest of our very masculine family." She smiled. "It is nice to have a woman to talk to finally. The men are like brothers to me, and very sweet, but being the only woman here can be hard sometimes." She poured homemade blueberry pie filling into the crusts before laying the top crusts over and pinching the edges.

"I can't even imagine," Rowan replied. "Although sweet isn't the word I would have picked to describe the guys I've met so far ... More like January through August of the Commando Hotties 'R' Us calendar." Allison laughed.

"How long have you known Graham and Zach?" Ro asked.

"Almost as long as I've known Jonah. They didn't spend as much time here at the beginning. Just on leave, between missions. Jonah was honorably discharged from the service two years before the rest. He'd been thinking of getting out, and meeting me just hurried up that decision."

"So they've all only been here for about two years?"

"Full-time, anyway. They've been coming here for much longer, from what I've been told. Graham always came home at every opportunity to help his uncle, and the rest of them tagged along. When Graham's uncle passed and it became his, he was thinking of separating from the service because he didn't know who he could trust to manage it. It was perfect timing, really, when Jonah decided to get out." Allison smiled. "That first year was a busy one for us. A new baby and a herd of deer. I thought Jonah might lose his mind. But after that last mission, the rest of the men felt like they had no choice but to take the honorable discharges they were offered. It was probably for the best." Allison voice trailed off as she turned to put the pies in the big black wood-fired stove.

"What last mission?" Ro asked.

"It's really not my place to talk about it," she replied, reaching for a dishtowel to dry to the dishes that Rowan had set in the rack next to the sink.

"Did something go wrong?"

"I shouldn't say. It's not something they speak of often."

"Please, I'd like to know."

"I don't know much, honestly. I just know that not all of them made it home, and the mission was under heavy scrutiny by their commanding officer. They all came to live here on the ranch, but about six months later, Nick took his own life."

A stoneware plate slipped from Ro's grasp. The sharp *thunk* it made when it connected with the bottom of the enameled iron sink punctuated Allison's statement. "I had no idea."

"There was no reason you would have known," Allison replied.

"Did you know him?"

"Yes. I knew them all fairly well, except for Tim. He took Jonah's place on the team during the last years, but from what I gather, he never meshed like the rest. He stayed in while the rest opted for discharge."

Allison went on to describe the happy-go-lucky Isaac, who'd been killed in action, and his team leader, Nick, who'd committed suicide, presumably out of guilt and regret. Ro asked about the teams, and Allison explained that they'd made up two separate Force Recon teams, but they'd carried out almost all of their missions and training together. Graham led one team, with Beau, Jonah (and later Tim), Jamie, Ty, and Zach. Nick had led the second team of Isaac, Cam, Travis, Alex, and Ryan.

The information was buzzing through Ro's head. She felt like she'd been given a few pieces to a puzzle she didn't know she was trying to piece together. At least one thing now made sense: why everyone looked to Graham for orders.

They finished the dishes and chatted until the pies were pulled from the oven. Ro learned more about the ranch than she'd even known to ask. How the electricity was generated by three different means: solar, wind, and micro-hydroelectricity from the creek she'd used in her thwarted escape attempt. The garden wasn't just a garden; it was an aquaponic garden system that was used to grow not only plants but also supported several types of fish. And it was sustainable year-round thanks to the insulated and heated greenhouse that ran along one of the compound walls. Ro was about to ask more questions when the screen door swung open on soundless hinges, and Zach walked through.

"Hey there, sweetheart. You 'bout done here? If so, I wondered if you'd like to sit in the clinic for a while?"

"Is she awake?" Ro asked as her heart kicked into a gallop.

"Not yet, but Beau says she should be waking up soon; a few hours at most, he figures. Thought it might help to have a woman there when she comes to."

Ro looked to Allison. "Did you need more help? I can come back after."

Allison smiled sweetly. "It's fine. I've appreciated your help and your company. We'll be along to check in on her later."

Zach swung Ro up into his arms, dropped a quick kiss onto her head, and headed back out the door.

CHAPTER TWENTY

The early evening had passed quickly, and surprisingly, when the woman woke, it wasn't Rowan who seemed to give her the most comfort, but Cam. Realizing quickly that she wasn't needed, Ro had asked to be brought back to the kitchen so she could keep Allison company while she prepped for a second dinner service. Maybe she could even offer to chop something. Or help with whatever menial task Ro could actually complete in a competent fashion.

A crew of the men stomped through the mess hall door as Allison hefted a steaming cast iron stockpot of venison stew onto the counter between the kitchen and the dining area. The late supper was to feed those who'd taken on extra watch shifts after the sensors had triggered. From her perch on the stool by the sink, Ro craned her neck to see if Graham or Zach had returned with the group. She spied Jonah, Beau, and another man she hadn't met. She tried to hide her disappointment behind a sunny smile. She thought at least one of them would be by soon … and give her some sense of whether they'd be collecting on their bargain tonight. The shiver of anticipation coursed through her, dampening her dejection. The tingly feeling in her lady parts wouldn't be denied. She was actually looking forward to paying her dues, so to speak. But she just wanted to *know*, dammit. She needed a sign that tonight was *the night*.

Ro slid off the stool and tested out how it felt to put weight on both of her ankles. The sharp stab of pain had her quickly redistributing her weight onto her good leg.

"Please tell me I didn't just see that," Zach drawled. "And here I thought you were an intelligent woman."

The voice coming from behind her had Ro jerking around instinctively, and she felt the telltale wobble that came right before she lost her balance.

"*Fuck, woman.*" Zach rushed forward, his hands curling around her waist and hoisting her up before she face-planted on the scarred plank floor.

"I gotcha, babe," Zach murmured, face buried in Ro's neck, his arms wrapped tightly around her. "You need to be more careful."

"You startled me. You move like a goddamn ghost. I didn't even know you were there."

"You were trying to walk when you know you shouldn't be," he countered.

Ro pulled back to meet his gaze and was surprised by the sly smile creeping across his face.

"Why do I have the feeling that smile means bad things for me," Ro wondered aloud.

"Because he knows that you just gave us a good excuse to teach you the error of your ways," Graham's low, gravelly voice added.

Ro looked up, shocked to see Graham standing just inside the back screen door that Zach must have entered through. She'd been so wrapped up in Zach that she hadn't even noticed Graham entering. Either that, or he was ninja silent like Zach. Or maybe that was Force Recon silent. Hell.

Living with commandos apparently meant you couldn't get away with anything. Except she wasn't living with them. No. She was just passing some time before she got on her way. She pushed the thought away as Graham's words tumbled through her head.

"Wait, what?"

Graham stalked toward her and simply said, "You'll see. Later." He jerked his chin at Zach. "Let's eat. Gonna need the energy tonight."

Well, that answered her question.

CHAPTER TWENTY-ONE

Ro was sure every eye was on the three of them as they made their way across the compound to Graham and Zach's cabin. Ro remembered the judgmental gazes that had followed her through the hallways of the firm. The difference this time? Ro didn't care. They could all fuck a duck if they had a problem with it. But still, Ro's anxiety increased with every step they took toward the cabin. It wasn't fear of *them*, she instinctively knew. Some of it was fear of the *unknown*. Fear that was colored with the hang-ups she'd been carrying for weeks now. But more than that, it was fear that what she was about to do would change the course of her life irrevocably. Fear that once she'd taken this step, she couldn't take it back. That she wouldn't *want* to take it back. That she'd want to grab it with both hands and let the easy camaraderie and promise of pleasure pull her from her path. But she wouldn't. She *couldn't*. This was a fling. Nothing more. Nothing less. And she was going to start enjoying it. Right. Now.

As Graham carried her up the porch steps, Ro snuggled into the crook of his neck and nipped at his jaw. He slowed before gripping her tighter and shouldering open the door, striding straight to the bedroom. She flicked out her tongue to lick the spot she'd bitten.

Graham tossed her in the middle of the king size bed.

"Hey!" Laughing, Ro flung both arms out to steady herself. "Precious cargo here, boys."

Graham reached down to light the oil lamp and pulled his pistol from its holster on his belt and set it on the nightstand, within easy reach of the bed.

"And don't we know it." Graham looked at her, his chocolate brown eyes blazing.

Zach dropped to his knees on the opposite side of the bed, his playful expression turning uncharacteristically serious for a moment.

"Babe, you sure you're ready for this? Because we're not going to push you if you're not."

Ro responded by sitting up, leaning over, and grabbing a handful of Zach's t-shirt, dragging him closer.

Feeling bold, she said, "I want this. I might be the rookie here, but I want this. Now. With both of you."

Ro saw the flare of lust in Zach's amber gaze at her gutsy declaration. It mirrored the need that she'd seen in Graham's. Zach climbed onto the bed and pushed her back before leaning over her. He braced his arms on either side of Ro's head, caging her upper body beneath him.

"Thank God for whatever we did to deserve you," he breathed, sealing his lips over hers and taking possession of her mouth. Ro moaned at the heat, and his tongue slid inside and tangled with hers.

So caught up in Zach's kiss, she didn't realize Graham had liberated her from her sweatpants until she felt him kissing his way up the inside of her leg. Ro broke the kiss and watched as Graham worked his way up to her inner thigh. He paused.

"I told myself we'd take this slow, but I've got to get my mouth on you. Can't wait."

Zach pulled back. "Spread your legs, baby. Show Graham that pretty pussy. Show him how much you want him to taste you."

Ro bucked her hips at Zach's words and then complied, sliding her legs apart. Zach hitched one of her knees up, spreading her wide to Graham's gaze.

"More," Graham said. "I want you to spread yourself open for me. I want you to slide those fingers down, and I want to watch you fuck yourself. Then, I want you to suck every bit of cream off your fingers so that when Zach takes your mouth, he'll be tasting exactly what I'm tasting."

Ro gulped. And then did as she was told, sliding the fingers of one hand down to spread herself so that she had no secrets from either man. Her other hand joined it, tentatively stroking and bumping her clit. Ro bucked her hips.

A sharp slap landed on her inner thigh.

Ro jerked, meeting Graham's dark gaze.

"I said fuck yourself, not play with your clit."

Ro's mouth formed an O as she slid her fingers lower, dipping into her sheath. She couldn't stop the moan that escaped as she plunged them in and out, assuaging the aching emptiness. Certain that she was about to come, Ro closed her eyes and lifted her hips. But before she could get there, her hand was pulled away.

"You don't listen very well, sweetheart."

Zach's mouth closed over her dripping fingers. He groaned. "Goddamn, you taste good. Sweet and spicy. If I hadn't called dibs on fucking your mouth, I'd have you riding my face."

Ro started to respond with some unintelligible mumble, but Graham's tongue found her center. Her head fell back, and she moaned.

"Damn, baby. So pretty. So soft. So fucking wet."

Zach shifted closer and kissed her. Graham spread her labia apart and teased her clit with his tongue. It was too much. She was going to …

Squeezing her eyes shut, she buried a hand in the dark silk of Graham's hair, unsubtly urging him to let her come.

"Not yet, baby." Graham nipped at her clit with his teeth then backed off.

Teetering on the edge of orgasm, Ro broke away from Zach's kiss. "Don't stop …"

Pushing himself up on his elbows, Graham crawled his way up her body. He leaned down and took her lips. Ro could taste herself on his tongue. Her own flavor stronger on his lips than Zach's.

"You need to be naked for us if you want to come."

Graham propped himself on his elbow next to her as Zach tugged her t-shirt over her head. Graham caught her breasts in his callused palms and tugged at her nipples, hardening them instantly and unleashing another sweet rush of pleasure through her.

Graham reached down to nip at one engorged tip.

"Please …" Ro couldn't stop the plea. Letting her nipple slip through his teeth, Graham backed away, and Zach took his place, pinching her nipples between his thumbs and forefingers.

Frustrated that they'd brought her to the edge without letting her go over, Ro was reduced to begging, "Please … I need to come."

"Patience, baby. You're not in charge here."

When Ro started to protest, Zach's wide hands grasped her hips and flipped her onto her stomach. He maneuvered her easily, positioning her lengthwise across the bed.

Looking up dazedly, she saw Zach unfasten his belt and zipper and shuck off his cargo pants. The rustle of clothes registered behind her, and she knew that Graham was stripping as well. Zach didn't waste time. He had his black boxer briefs shoved down and his erection gripped in his palm. It reared up, almost touching his navel. He gave it a few rough pulls, and Ro watched the clear bead of pre-cum drip over the head. Zach stepped closer, and his erection bobbed in front of her mouth. She couldn't stop herself from licking her lips. He groaned.

"Gotta have that mouth." He braced himself with a knee on the bed, and Ro pushed herself up to her knees. "Open for me, baby."

Ro obeyed, and he painted her bottom lip with the moisture dripping from the tip. Her tongue reached out to taste. Salt and musk.

His balls tightened, bunching up to the base.

"Jesus, baby."

Zach swept Ro's dark hair back so he could watch her tongue the head of his cock.

"I've been picturing what your sweet lips would look like wrapped around my dick since that first night you showed up. I've jacked off with that picture in my head. Let me see it, baby. Suck my cock like a good girl." His words cut off when she took him deep—like she was trying to swallow him whole—stealing his breath.

"Breath through your nose, baby. Swallow me down. That's it," Zach rumbled as he felt the head of his cock slide down Ro's throat as she fought her gag reflex. Her nose was pressing against his stomach as she breathed deep and swallowed him again.

"Jesus fucking Christ. Would you look at that? I knew those pouty lips would look fucking amazing wrapped around my cock." Zach held her hair back so Graham could watch as he fucked her mouth.

"Damn, baby," Zach groaned, reveling in the pleasure. He looked back down at Ro, and saw her hand snaking between her legs to touch herself. Zach couldn't help but thrust harder at the sight, bumping the back of her throat with each flex of his hips. He saw Graham reach out and snatch Ro's hand away from her pussy. Graham sucked her fingers into his mouth.

"I got you, baby." Zach forced the pleasure back, and he watched as Graham knelt behind Ro and cupped her breast in one hand and slid the other down to cup her pussy.

"You want to come when Zach shoots his load down your throat?" Graham asked in a near growl.

Ro pulled away from his cock to answer. "Yes."

Zach cupped her chin. "Then you better get back to sucking my cock." He pushed the head back between her lush lips and pumped in and out, knowing he wouldn't last much longer. The bolts of lust shot down his spine and grabbed him by the balls.

"Get ready, baby." And then he let himself go. Ro swallowed spurt after spurt, the suction of her mouth prolonging his orgasm. She moaned around his cock, and he pulled out and clasped her against his chest as she trembled, coming apart in his arms. Graham's fingers had clearly worked their magic. Her arms wrapped around his hips, and she slumped against him.

CHAPTER TWENTY-TWO

Ro thought she might black out. She wasn't sure if it had been Graham's thumb pressing down with just the right amount of pressure on her clit or the three fingers that had relentlessly plunged in and out of her that had caused her to shatter. Honestly, she didn't care. She fell against Zach and held on. She could feel a bead of sweat dripping down her forehead, unsure if it was from her or from Zach. Again, she didn't care.

She started to pull away, and Graham steadied her from behind. She leaned back, feeling secure in his arms. She turned her head to kiss him. She wasn't sure where her lips landed, but he tasted salty. Unapologetically masculine.

He maneuvered them until they were both propped up on their right sides. With her back to him, Graham's hand smoothed down her hip to cup her center again.

"I gotta get inside you. When you came, you clamped down on my fingers so damn hard. I nearly shot my load when Zach did. That's what you do to me, woman."

He slid his hand down to her left knee, sliding it forward until it touched the bed. His fingers trailed up the back of her thigh and cupped her ass. "I can't stop thinking about how tight you're going to be when Zach and I are both filling you up."

She stilled. *Holy shit. This was really going to happen.* Zach slid onto the bed, and his fingers found her pussy and teased her clit.

When she didn't immediately reply, Graham continued, "You can take us, baby. Don't you want to know what's it's like to be filled up with two cocks? One in your tight little pussy and the other buried deep inside this pretty little ass." She felt his fingers bump Zach's as he gathered up her wetness and swirled his finger around the pucker of her ass. Someone plunged three fingers into her pussy. Zach, she thought.

Graham was relentless in his quest for her assent.

"Tell me that you want this, Ro, or it stops right now. Tell me you want me stretching out your ass while Zach fucks your pussy."

"Yes," she breathed, almost soundlessly.

"Louder, baby."

"Yes," she moaned.

"Yes, what?" Zach prompted.

"Yes, I want you both inside me."

As soon as she said the words, she felt a cold and sticky dribble between her cheeks. When she flinched, Graham murmured, "It's just lube, babe." And then she felt the slippery pressure on her ass before two fingers slid inside. She couldn't hold back the moan.

"Damn, man, she's so fucking wet," Zach said.

"That's because she's a dirty girl and can't wait to be all filled up." The fingers in her ass scissored, stretching the tight channel and firing her nerve endings like synapses.

Clutching handfuls of Graham's blanket, Ro shuddered, the orgasm about to burst within her. Flexing his fingers inside of her, Zach told Graham, "Do that again; her pussy just clenched so hard."

The pressure was exquisite, and the orgasm barreling down on her was even more so.

"Oh my God!" Graham's dick jerked at the sound of Ro's breathy moans. Still working his fingers in and out of her ass, he could feel Zach doing the same in her pussy through the thin membrane that separated them. They drew out her pleasure until she went limp. Goddamn, the sound of this woman coming was the hottest thing he'd ever heard.

Graham slid his fingers out and lubed up his dick.

"I think you're ready, baby."

In response, Ro's ass jerked toward him, as though she was seeking the fingers he'd just removed.

Graham kissed her shoulder and then slid off the bed. Zach rolled to his back and moved toward the edge of the bed. They readjusted Rowan so she was on her knees, straddling Zach. Graham stood between her spread thighs, gripping her hips and smoothing his thumbs up and down her ass before spreading her wide.

"I'm going to push in first, and then you're going to sit on Zach's cock. If it too much, just tell us, and we'll slow down."

Ro whimpered.

"Ro, you with us, baby?" Zach asked.

"Someone better fuck me. Now," she said.

"Since you asked so nicely ..." Graham guided his cock, bumping against the crack of her ass before pressing the head against the tight pucker. "Push out. Let me in," he breathed harshly.

The muscle eased, and Graham felt the head of his cock slide inside the hottest, tightest hole it had ever had the pleasure of knowing. She clenched, nearly pushing him out. "Easy, baby."

"Holy shit, you're in my ass."

"How does it feel?" he and Zach asked in stereo.

"Big."

Graham couldn't stop the chuckle. "That's just the head, sweetheart. But let's fix that."

That's just the head? Oh good Lord, Ro thought. She wasn't sure if she was thrilled or horrified. Hell, she wasn't sure that she could actually accommodate him. She felt Zach's fingers teasing her clit, and she relaxed, letting Graham sink deeper inside. If she'd thought the pressure from his fingers was exquisite, this was … mind-blowingly intense. She arched, and Graham nipped her shoulder before sliding in more.

She couldn't help but ask, "Is it all the way in?" *She really should have gotten a look at his cock before she agreed to let him shove it up her ass. Recon. Or something.*

"Almost. You're doing great."

Almost? Ro couldn't stand the suspense and pushed backward, impaling herself on his dick.

"Fuck! Rowan!" Graham ground out. "Jesus. Zach, you better get in her pussy, because I'm not sure how long I'll be able to make this last."

"Are you okay, baby? You want to take us both?" he asked, looking up at her, his amber gaze burning with obvious hunger.

Graham was holding still, awaiting her decision.

"Yes. Please."

Zach leaned up and placed a kiss on her lips before helping to guide the head of his cock to her entrance.

"And I thought fucking your mouth was amazing," he groaned, as he pushed inside in one smooth, long thrust.

Ro stilled, unable to believe the fullness she felt. It was like every other time she'd had sex, she'd only been doing it halfway. Like she'd spent her whole life waiting for this experience. For these men. For this night.

"Please. Please, move. I need more," she heard herself begging.

And that was when the perfectly timed thrusting began. Graham pulled almost all the way out, and as he started to push back inside her ass, Zach slid out of her pussy. They alternated, pressure and pleasure swamping Ro's senses and rendering her mindless.

"Touch your clit, babe."

Obeying, she slid her hand down to her clit and gasped at the added sensation. Detonation.

Zach felt Ro's pussy flutter, signaling the impending orgasm. He and Graham instinctively picked up the pace of their thrusts, shuttling in and out of her body. Zach reached between their bodies and moved Ro's fingers away from her clit, replacing them with his own. He pressed down, increasing the pressure until he felt her jerk and heard her moan as another orgasm overtook her.

"I'm coming," Graham said, before he roared his release.

Zach felt his own orgasm tear out of his balls, and he tried to pull out, but Ro's clenching sheath imprisoned him. So he just let go.

CHAPTER TWENTY-THREE

Graham shot up in bed as his radio came to life with a crackle of static. He scrubbed his hands from his face and reached out to snag it off the nightstand. Normally he jumped out of bed at every creak. At the moment, he felt like he'd just woken up from a coma. When he looked at the bed and saw Ro curled between Zach and the indent he'd just left on the bed, he remembered the cause of his uncharacteristically deep sleep. Fuck. That woman was something else.

"Be advised, we've got a sensor that just tripped near the main gate. Southeast corner. Alex, what's your twenty?" Cam's voice came through the radio.

"I'm headed in that direction right now, coming down the east fence line. I think I see movement …"

"What's going on man?" Zach asked as he reached for his radio and rolled out of bed.

"Not sure. Let's go check it out," Graham replied, shoving his legs into his cargos and snagging a t-shirt from the floor.

"And here I was hoping for another round—" Zach started to say. But the radio cut him off.

"We got company, boys. Three. Looks like *Duck Dynasty* rejects. You want me to engage or wait on backup? Never mind. Fuck. They've got bolt cutters and are cutting through the fence. I'm going in," Alex finished.

Graham pressed the button his radio. "Do not engage. Wait for backup. You don't know what they're carrying. We're headed your way. Be there ASAP."

"I'm not waiting for them to get in here, G. I can't stand for that," Alex argued.

"Shut the fuck up and stand down."

Graham shot a glance at Ro, who was wide-awake and wide-eyed at the radio chatter. "What's going on?"

"Don't know. Get some clothes on. I'm going to check this shit out. Zach will take you to mess hall and get you locked up tight with Allison."

He gave her a quick kiss and handed her the backup sidearm he kept in the nightstand, and then he was out the door.

As soon a Graham left the cabin, his radio blared to life again.

"They're inside the fence. I can take them out," Alex reported.

"I'm in the southwest corner and coming your way, man," Ty replied.

Shit. Graham was closer. He'd get to Alex way before Ty. It wasn't that Alex couldn't handle himself, but he'd shoot first and ask questions later. And Graham wanted answers more than he wanted dead bodies.

Graham headed to the armory and grabbed an M4. They were all going to have to start carrying them everywhere. Just like they had when they were deployed. He hated that they had to take that kind of precaution in their home, but it was better than the alternative: being caught with their pants down and getting fucked up the ass. Cam was holding down the command post when Graham ducked his head inside.

"Who else is on watch?"

"Travis. But he's way the fuck out on the north edge."

A shotgun blast ripped through the silence of the morning.

Neither Alex nor Ty carried a shotgun.

"Fuck!" Graham yelled. "Alex, sitrep!"

The sharp report of a rifle was the only response. Two shots. Another shotgun blast. And then silence.

It was a bad fucking sign when a Marine didn't keep firing until he emptied his magazine. Unless Alex was taking cover. He might finally be listening to Graham, though he knew it was unlikely.

"Sitrep!" Graham yelled into his radio, and he took off toward the bolt hole. He didn't want the main gate open at a time like this.

No answer.

Fuck.

When he reached the wall to slide the metal bar and swing the door open, Jamie and Beau were right behind him.

Graham led, melting into the woods and moving silently toward the location of the breach. As soon as he heard voices, he halted, holding up a fist.

"He dead, Mel?"

An icy mantle settled over Graham. The one he donned every time he knew he was about to kill.

"I dunno, Len. Dwayne, check and see," a man, presumably Mel, grunted. "That fucker shot me in the goddamn shoulder. Twice. He better be fucking dead. You better fucking shoot him in the goddamn head."

Graham moved soundlessly toward the voices, knowing Beau and Jamie followed directly behind him. He caught sight of three camo-and-flannel-clad figures, one using his shotgun to nudge Alex's prone form. Blood dripped from Alex's head—a small puddle had formed in the dirt. Another man was reaching down to check a pulse. The one with a dark spot expanding on the upper right corner of his flannel shirt pulled out a revolver from his waistband.

"Fuck it. I'm shooting him anyway."

Graham lifted his rifle, and before the man could pull back the hammer, Graham unleashed a spray of bullets. The man dropped where he stood. Another man with scraggily dark hair swung around and lifted the shotgun. Jamie and Graham fired, and he crumpled. The third took off on a dead run, but Graham didn't give chase. He dropped to his knees beside Alex. Beau was checking his carotid for a pulse.

"He's alive."

A burst of rifle fire had Graham whipping his head around, gun at the ready. Nothing. He glanced back to Beau, who was pulling on nitrile gloves and checking for injuries. He unzipped his kit and pulled out a clotting sponge to stop the bleeding from the head wound. Beau carefully lifted Alex's black t-shirt, and Graham could see the divots where the shot pellets had impacted the body armor. Thank fucking Christ.

Graham turned his attention back to the surrounding forest.

"Why is he unconscious? Why the fuck is he bleeding so damn bad from his head? He got shot in the chest. Where else?" Visions of another man lying bloody in the dirt surged to the forefront of Graham's memory.

"No gunshot wounds. And I'm not one hundred percent certain, but he might have been diving to miss the shot and cracked his head on this."

Graham glanced back to see Beau holding up a fist-sized rock. Relief was a tidal wave sweeping through him.

The crunch of boots had the wave evaporating in a millisecond. Graham and Beau raised their M4s. Jamie. The rifles lowered. He was alone. No prisoner in tow.

"Where's the third one?" Graham demanded. "Dead?"

"Gone, G. I don't have a fucking clue how he got away from me. I think I winged him, though. It was crazy; he was there, and then he was just fucking gone. The trail just died out." Jamie shook his head.

"Did you see any signs of anyone else?"

"No, but we need to fix the fence," Jamie replied.

"He okay?" Ty called, hauling ass toward them. Graham lowered the rifle he'd instinctively sighted in on the man.

"Probably," Beau replied. "But he's knocked the fuck out. Let's get him back to the clinic. Be nice to have someone bring a backboard out."

Graham nodded. "Ty, get back to your loop. I'll get Ryan to take Alex's shift. Let Travis know that he needs to stay on his loop." Graham lifted his radio. "Ryan, I need you to get out here and take Alex's shift. And bring a backboard. Zach, give the women the all-clear, but have them stay inside, you copy?"

"Copy that, G. Be there in three with a backboard," Ryan replied.

Then Jamie asked, "What should we do with the bodies?"

As soon as they'd helped Allison, Grace, Ro, and Lia from the bunker beneath the mess hall, Jonah and Zach took off, but not before reinforcing the order that Graham had given over the radio. They were to stay inside, with the doors locked, until further notice. Ro once again sat on a stool in the kitchen, watching as Allison worked on salvaging breakfast, although they weren't certain anyone would actually stop to eat it. Grace played with a doll on the floor. Lia sat on the floor next to her, arms wrapped around her knees. The foray into the bunker had been Lia's first trip out of the infirmary. Cam had broken protocol and left the command post to bundle her up and bring her to the mess hall to be stashed with the other women. Lia was still in rough shape, and shied away from everyone except Grace and Cam. When Jonah had reached a hand out to steady her on the ladder coming out of the bunker, she'd jumped back down to the bunker floor and wouldn't climb a single rung until he'd backed off.

Zach and Jonah had stayed outside to stand guard when the women had been sealed away in the bunker. Ro couldn't help feeling like they'd consigned them to a terrible fate when Allison had hit the actuator and lowered the hydraulic hatch. As Ro hadn't gotten a look at the bunker under the range, she wasn't certain how it compared as far as size. She had been shocked to see a porthole-style door—the type one would see on a Navy ship—at one end of the large room. According to Allison, when unsealed, it led to a tunnel that linked four underground bunkers together—the ones beneath the gun range and the mess hall, and then one beneath the infirmary, and one beneath the command post. Each had a separate door that sealed it off from the tunnels in the event one of the bunkers was breached. It was mind-boggling to Ro, as someone who'd grown up with a father who lived and breathed this type of preparedness. He'd love this place. They'd built an underground community that somewhat mirrored the one above. Kitchen, bathrooms, showers, bunkrooms, medical supplies, communications equipment, and every kind of other supply that Ro could imagine. When she asked Allison how and when this had been set up, Allison informed her that the bunker beneath the mess hall had originally been built as a bomb shelter during World War II, and the others had been added during the '50s. Graham's uncle, a WWII and Korea vet, had stumbled upon them when he'd purchased the camp and modernized them. From what Allison had been told, the man may have had a somewhat irrational fear of a nuclear attack on U.S. soil. But having grown up with Rick Callahan, things like that didn't faze Ro.

The women waited anxiously for a report on Alex. The call for a backboard wasn't good, but that meant he was alive, right?

Waiting gave Ro time to think back on the night before. And what a night it had been. Her mind had been blown— at least for the ninety-some seconds she'd stayed conscious after the most intense sexual experience of her life. Both Graham and Zach had cleaned her up and then cuddled her between them. She'd fallen asleep with Graham wrapped around her from behind and her head resting on Zach's chest.

The rude awakening of the radio left something to be desired, but it also saved Rowan from what she figured could have been an awkwardly embarrassing morning. After all, what exactly was proper etiquette for dealing with the guys who'd double-teamed you the night before? In the real world, pre-grid down scenario, if this had happened (and Ro excluded that time it almost had), Ro would have grabbed her clothes, not bothered to search for her panties, and gotten the hell on to the walk of shame. Hopefully avoiding any awkward conversations. But now, well, hell. She didn't know what this was. It wasn't a relationship, because it wasn't going to last, but she also couldn't just avoid them. The compound was only so big. And she still wasn't supposed to be walking. But she had been—down in the bunker during that excruciating half-hour of radio silence. Ro was a pacer by nature, and she couldn't help herself. On the upside, her ankle felt surprisingly good. By tomorrow morning, she should be good to go. Which was great, but also sucked at the same time. She'd like to blame her damn-near instant and unshakeable attachment on the whole end-of-the-world-as-we-know-it vibe, but she wasn't sure if that was it. She'd never met a guy like Zach or Graham before, and when you put them together, they were unmatched.

If she got them to agree that she was good to travel, she'd be seeing Erica and her dad in two, maybe three, more days. But that also meant she only had two or three days left with Graham and Zach. But it wasn't like there was another choice available to her. She couldn't stay. She knew—*absolutely knew*—that her dad and sister were waiting for her. And she wasn't going to let them down again. This wasn't like last Christmas Eve when she had to pick up the phone to say no, she wasn't coming home for Christmas, because she had to be at the office prepping for a December 27 closing. The worst part about it was they weren't *that* surprised ... because she'd done it on Thanksgiving ... and Erica's birthday ... and her dad's birthday ... and she was a horrible daughter and sister who'd forgotten what was important in life: her family. Had the firm stood behind her when the shit rolled downhill with the Evelyn-Charles incident? Nope. Did she ever have to worry that her family wouldn't stand behind her? Nope. *Would you have to worry about Graham and Zach standing behind you?*

"Irrelevant," Ro said aloud.

"What?" Allison asked.

"Nothing. I'm just going out of my mind not being able to be useful. Please, put me to work."

Allison directed her to crack and scramble eggs, although only a fraction of the amount she normally cooked. The mess hall stayed quiet, so the women helped themselves to breakfast and waited.

And waited.

And waited.

By the time six o'clock had rolled around, Ro was about to lose it. If the mess hall hadn't had its own bathroom, she would've defied their explicit orders long before now. As it was, she couldn't sit around any longer. They were baking a few pies, because they'd keep, and there was a large pot of white chicken chili warming on the stove. None of the men had stopped to eat lunch, and so far, none had shown for dinner. Allison surmised that if they'd eaten at all, it would have been the MREs they had stashed in nearly every building on the property. She opened a cupboard to demonstrate. It was filled with boxes of instant entrees like beef stew, sloppy joes, spaghetti with meat sauce, chili with beans, and more peanut butter Power Bars. Nearly the same selection that Ro's dad had included in her backpack. Probably what she'd be eating starting tomorrow. Hopefully.

Finally, someone banged on the back door. Ro didn't think before she hopped off her stool and rushed toward the door. She didn't make it two steps before Lia grabbed a knife from the counter and held Ro back with an outstretched arm. Graham swung the door open. He froze on the threshold, causing Zach and Jonah to stumble into him.

Graham held both hands up. "Whoa, honey. We're the good guys."

Ro laid a hand over Lia's on the hilt of the butcher knife. "It's okay. They're not going to hurt anyone." She eased the knife out of Lia's grip. "It's okay."

Lia spun, fleeing into the mess hall. They all watched through the serving window as she fumbled with the lock and raced out the front door.

No one spoke for a moment, and Ro laid the knife on the kitchen counter.

"I'll go after her. Jonah, take Grace," Allison said. She pushed the little girl toward her father and bustled toward the front door of the mess hall.

Graham and Zach strode into the kitchen. "You okay?" Zach asked.

"It's been completely uneventful. Well ... until just now."

"Then what the hell are you doing on your feet, woman?" Graham swept her up and carried her into the dining area, settling her into a chair.

"I'm fine, really. I'll be ready to go tomorrow." She pulled up her pant leg—clean jeans that had finally dried—and showed off the barely swollen state of her ankle. "See?"

Graham's gaze flicked to Zach and then back at Rowan. Ro couldn't judge his expression, because it was one she'd never seen before.

"What? Is Alex okay? Is someone else hurt?"

"No, he's fine. Everyone's good," Zach reassured her.

"Then ... what's going on? You want Beau to tell you I'm all better? You just get him in here; he'll agree with me."

And then Graham dropped the bomb.

"It doesn't matter what Beau says. You're not going anywhere. Not anytime soon."

Ro struggled to comprehend the words that were coming out of Graham's mouth.

"I don't understand. You're taking me home as soon as I'm good to go."

Graham paced, and Zach leaned against the counter next to her. Graham spun and trapped her gaze.

"Things change, Ro. It's simple cause and effect. The shit that went down this morning means that you aren't leaving."

"But ..."

"But nothing. We've got a man down, we need to

148

increase our patrols and stay vigilant. One of those assholes got away, and for all we know, there could be more. They're the same guys from yesterday. For some reason, they want in here real bad. And they're not going to be the only ones. So I can't spare anyone, myself included, to escort you home."

Ro felt like a shrink, cataloging her reactions as they bolted through her: surprise, betrayal, anger, understanding, and then ice cold resolve. It was almost like the five stages of grief. Or something.

"I can't risk the safety of everyone I'm responsible for just to take you home." Graham spun away and stalked to the windows, fist clenching by his side.

"Tell me one thing, Graham," Ro started, proud that her voice was even and devoid of emotion. "With the way shit's going down—and we all know it's going to get worse—are you ever going to be able to spare even one person to help me get home?"

Zach answered this time, "Babe, you gotta see where we're coming from …"

"Oh, I see it. But it doesn't change a damn thing for me. I didn't ask for your help in the first place. And I don't *need* it. I feel like I've said this before, but at the risk of repeating myself, I'll say it again: I got myself here, and I will get myself home. And I'll be doing it on the timeline we agreed on. If you can't hold up your end of the bargain, that's on you. But you better not stop me from leaving." Ro could have patted herself on the back for getting it all out without raising her voice.

Graham was across the room in an instant, his callused fingers gripping Ro's chin. "You are not leaving by yourself. No way in hell. Did you miss the part where one of my men was shot today? Are you that naïve that you think you have any chance of safely making it home by yourself?"

Ro jerked her chin from his grip and her previously

detached tone evaporated like water on scorching asphalt. "You already got to fuck me with your buddy. What do you care what I do now?"

Graham gripped her by her shoulders and dragged her against him. "Goddammit, Ro. You are the most stubborn woman I've ever met."

Zach moved in behind her, sandwiching her between them. It was a little too reminiscent of last night for Ro.

"We care. A whole hell of a lot," he said. "Which is why we can't let you go alone. You're too damn important."

Ro slumped back against Zach. This argument was going nowhere. Both sides had gone to the mat, and neither was going to back down. It was time to retreat to their corners and regroup with a new strategy.

Ro exhaled. "Let's just eat dinner and talk about it later. You've got to be starving."

Both men seemed to breathe a sigh of relief. Graham released her to Zach's embrace, but not before dropping a kiss on her forehead.

"We'll figure it out, babe. Just give us some time."

But time was the only thing Ro didn't have to spare.

CHAPTER TWENTY-FOUR

Ro stayed in the mess hall to help Allison wash up after dinner. Zach figured that it was a good thing because it gave him and Graham time to regroup with Ty and arrange the watch schedules for the next week. Adding another man to every shift meant less free time for everyone, but better security. They'd spent the day repairing the fence, burying the bodies, and running drills to prepare for a similar breach situation. It was exhausting, but it was work that needed to be done to be ready for the next time something like this happened. Because there would be a next time. Hell, situations like this were the reason one of the first things they'd done after the grid went down was install the razor wire topping the walls. Over six hundred acres was too much land to protect for a long period of time, especially if a large enough group attacked. But they would defend the inner sanctum to the death. With the lookout perches in the tall oaks and pines within the walls, they could snipe anyone approaching before they could get close enough to do any damage.

Slipping into the command post, Zach held the door

open for Graham and then dragged a chair up to the large wooden table covered in a map of the property. Ty had redrawn the fire watch routes and was waiting for their input on staffing the shifts.

"Did you at least bring me some dinner?" Ty asked.

Zach held out a soup thermos and a spoon. "Straight from Allison herself."

"Damn, that woman is an angel. Not too many women out there like her," Ty said, unscrewing the lid of the thermos and digging in. Between bites and groans of appreciation, he added, "Your woman seems ... unique. She's got guts to spare. You figure out what you're doing with her yet?"

Zach settled into a chair. "Keeping her," he said. Because really, that was the only acceptable answer.

"But somehow we've got to convince her that staying here makes sense," Graham added, scrubbing his hands over his face. "I gotta believe her family would want her to be safe. And the only way we can guarantee her safety is if she stays."

"You think she'll go for it?" Ty asked.

Zach thought back on the conversation they'd just had. "She's not exactly ... seeing things our way yet."

Graham dropped into a chair. "I don't give a damn; I'll tie her to the bed if I have to."

"Good luck with that, man," Ty said. "Because I have a feeling you're going to need it."

CHAPTER TWENTY-FIVE

After wrapping shit up with Ty, and ensuring that neither he nor Zach had a watch shift until the next afternoon, Graham headed back to the mess hall to collect Ro. He was struggling with how to apologize for not living up to the promise he'd made. Especially when she'd lived up to her end of the bargain whole-heartedly. But now that she likely considered their deal to be off, what would happen tonight? Would she demand to sleep on the couch? Graham figured he'd find out as soon as he stopped to get her.

When he entered the mess hall, he was surprised to find the kitchen dark and deserted. Neither Ro nor Allison was anywhere in the building. A cold twinge of unease bloomed in his chest.

He turned and headed for the cabin, catching Zach as he loped up the front steps.

"Did you bring Ro back already?" Graham asked.

"No. Why? What's going on?"

"She wasn't in the mess hall. Neither was Allison."

Zach's eyebrows lifted as he yanked open the door of the cabin. "Honey, I'm home," he called.

Silence.

The icy feeling spread. Graham spun, heading for Jonah's cabin. Allison would have been the last person to see Rowan. But then he caught sight of Jonah leaning up against the wall of the bathhouse. *What the hell?* If Allison were inside giving Grace a bath, Jonah would be inside as well. They usually just left a bright pink puff thing hanging on the door handle. Kind of like the sock on the door handle signal from back in the day. Graham changed direction, heading for the bathhouse. Zach fell into step beside him.

Jonah gave them a nod and jerked a shoulder toward the building. "Your girl wanted a shower. Told her I'd make sure to keep everyone out."

Graham scowled. "Thanks for the update. Feel free to keep keeping everyone *else* out." Graham reached for the handle, but halted when Jonah flattened his palm against the door, holding it shut.

"She's a sweet girl. I hope to hell you know what you're doing, G." Graham met his gaze but said nothing. He didn't know what to say. Because he had no fucking clue what he was doing.

Jonah just nodded and strode away. Back to the cabin where his wife and daughter were waiting for him. Graham didn't like the feeling of envy that crept over him every time he thought about what Jonah had. Shoving the thoughts aside, he silently turned the handle and eased the door open. He gestured for Zach to enter ahead of him and slipped inside, closing the door as silently as he'd opened it.

They both crept across the yellow and white tiled floor toward the steam that was wafting from the shower area. The warmth seemed to melt the chunk of ice that had formed in his chest. Graham froze at the threshold. Ro was sitting sideways on the folding chair, bent over at the waist, reaching for a bottle of Allison's shampoo that sat on the floor. With the back of the chair facing away from the entrance, he and Zach had an unobstructed view of Ro's wet, naked body. As though she'd heard them, her head whipped around, wet ropes of hair swinging.

"You going to stand there and watch, or are you coming in this time?"

Ro couldn't explain it, but she could *feel* them standing there. And she'd made a split second decision. She could be pissed about the change in plans, or she could savor the moments she had left with Graham and Zach.

She'd felt more alive last night than she ever had before. She wanted to feel that way again.

Zach yanked his shirt up over his head and kicked his partially laced boots off before tackling his fly. Graham didn't move. She could tell he was dissecting her reaction. Trying to glean her motivation for the invitation after their words earlier. She decided to save him the trouble.

"I've spent most of my life existing. But last night I felt like I was finally living. I want to feel like that again."

Graham must have decided her explanation was enough because, without breaking eye contact, he reached behind him and grabbed a handful of his shirt and tugged it over his head. His eyes were still on her as he dropped the shirt to the floor and bent over to unlace his boots. The ripple of his abs as he bent down was a feast for her eyes. Distracted, Ro jumped when a hot mouth landed on her shoulder, slowly making its way to her neck. *Zach*. He scraped along the sensitive skin, and Ro leaned back, trying to get closer to him. Hands slid around her to cup her breasts, and fingers toyed with her nipples, bringing them to hard points.

As Graham stepped into the shower, fully nude, Ro

couldn't help but be amazed that, in this moment, they were both hers. She reveled in the thrill. Graham's heavy cock, already stiff and straining toward his navel, bounced as he closed the distance between them stepped under the spray in front of her. His cock was at the perfect level for her mouth. But he had different ideas, because he tilted her chin up with a finger.

"Zach's been kind enough to present those tits so perfectly; I think I have to fuck them," he said. His tone had evolved into a low, gravelly rumble.

Ro swallowed as he came closer, nudging her legs apart with one knee so he could step between them. This position left Ro completely open to them, at their mercy. She shivered at the thought.

"Cold, baby?" Zach asked.

Ro just shook her head and stared up at Graham as he fisted his cock and tugged roughly.

"Arch your back, baby. Stick these gorgeous tits out for Graham," Zach said.

Ro complied, and was rewarded with Graham positioning the head of his cock in the valley of her breasts. Zach squeezed them together and Graham groaned. Her water-slicked skin provided enough lubrication for Graham to slide between them.

Ro couldn't help but watch as the head of his cock appeared. She licked her lips. Graham reached out to grip the base of her neck. She looked up at him.

"Suck the head on the upstroke. You're going to get me off with nothing but your tits and your tongue, and I'm going to give you an honest-to-god pearl necklace."

Ro moaned as he slid his cock back down, and then as he thrust up, she felt his cock tunnel into her mouth. She laved the head with her tongue.

"Fuck, babe. Just like that," he groaned.

His words and their actions had her squirming on her seat. She furtively reached between her legs and found herself soaked—and not from the shower spray. She moaned as she found her clit, and Graham tunneled into her mouth again and again. Zach rolled her nipples, pinching and tugging on them until Ro couldn't hold still. Graham clutched at her shoulders, stilling her movements, and increased his pace. The head of his cock fucking in and out of her mouth was erotic, and she slid two fingers inside herself, spreading her legs wider. Graham stilled, and Ro looked up to see his gaze glued between her legs where she was finger-fucking herself.

He groaned, and said, "You're gonna make yourself come when I say. You got that?"

Ro nodded, and as Graham resumed his thrusts, she timed her movements to his.

"Goddamn, now. Come now."

Ro pressed down hard on her clit, and Zach tugged and twisted her nipples. She unraveled as the climax rushed over her. Hot jets of semen spurted onto her chest as she rode out her orgasm.

Zach could feel his own cock jerk as Ro came apart under their hands. When Graham reached out to rub his come into her skin rather than wipe it away, Zach released her breasts and knew he was seeing a claim. A sign of ownership. She was theirs. Whatever else happened, she was theirs.

Ro slumped back against him, and Graham reached out to shut off the water. Zach felt like he could hammer nails with his cock, it was so goddamn hard. He wasn't leaving this room without getting inside her. And there was still one place he hadn't been.

He looked to Graham, who was gathering Ro up in his arms. Graham met his gaze and jerked his head toward the bench in the locker room. It was great to know that your best friend wasn't about to leave you with a stiff cock and aching balls. It was Zach's turn to be buried inside her. And he wanted that gorgeous ass.

Zach stepped out of the shower area and grabbed a couple towels. One he laid out on the wooden bench, and the other he used to scrub himself dry. Graham sat on the towel, one leg on either side of the bench. He snagged the towel from Zach and dried Ro and himself. He sat her on the bench so she straddled it, facing him. Zach reached into his locker and grabbed the bottle of lube he usually reserved for jacking off in the shower. This was a much better use. Unbelievably better. He straddled the bench and leaned over Ro.

"You ready for more, baby?"

She turned to look at him, noticing the bottle of lube in his hand. Zach smiled as her nipples beaded. She nodded.

"I need words, babe," Zach reminded her.

She swallowed. "Yes. But how exactly ..." She trailed off as Graham gripped her thighs to lift her onto his lap, impaling her on his already hard cock.

"Holy shit!" Ro yelled, her head rolling back. "Warn a girl next time, Conan."

Graham grunted before rolling backward so he was prone and Ro was laid out on top of him, legs spread wide where they were caught over Graham's hips. Zach could see her asshole and where Graham was buried balls-deep in her pussy. The sight of a dude's balls wasn't his favorite, but when he was about to be buried in Ro's tight little ass, he didn't give a fuck.

Zach trailed his finger from the cleft of her ass down to the whorl he was about to slide into. He drizzled lube, and smoothed it around before breaching the tight muscle of her ass with a finger. Her moan was all the incentive he needed to continue. He slid a second finger in, the hole clenching to try to keep him out.

"Relax, babe. Push out. I'm just trying to make sure you're ready for me." He scissored his fingers, trying to stretch the snug passage, which was made even tighter by the fact that her pussy was full of Graham's dick.

He slipped his fingers out and lubed up his cock before pressing the head against her asshole. Gripping the base, he pressed forward until the muscle gave, and the head slid inside.

"Oh God," Ro whispered.

"You good, babe?" Graham asked.

"Mmhmm. It's just … full. The pressure is so … good …"

She trailed off as Zach slid in deeper. Her moan was all the encouragement he needed to continue until he was buried in her ass.

"Goddamn, woman. You're so fucking tight. I don't know how I'm going to last."

Zach felt Graham start to pull out, signaling the start of their alternating thrusts. When Graham started to push back inside her pussy, he pulled out of her ass, reveling in the hot, dark clench of muscle. Zach reached around to toy with Ro's clit, pulling another moan from her.

Ro's mutterings of *oh god, holy shit* and variations of the same kept him pistoning in and out. Her cries got louder right before she clamped down on his cock. Hard. The near stranglehold of her tightening muscle had his orgasm boiling up in his balls and shooting out before he could rein it in. He pinched her clit and felt her bear down again, her cries of pleasure echoing off the tiled walls. A growl from Graham indicated that he'd given in to the hot heaven of this amazing woman.

"Fuck," Graham rumbled in Ro's ear. "That was fucking incredible, babe."

Ro slumped against him, unable to summon the strength to move. She'd lost count of the number of orgasms she'd had. She had no idea her body could do that. *I guess it just takes adding* their *bodies.* Holy hell. Her eyelids drooped with exhaustion. The last thing she'd felt before she gave up the fight against the descending darkness was a kiss to her temple accompanied by a soft, "Most amazing woman I've ever met."

CHAPTER TWENTY-SIX

Ro woke disoriented. She was in Graham's bed, and the sky was still dark, the first hint of gray dawn breaking through the cloak of night. Graham had his arm thrown over her, and Zach's hand cupped her hip. The sheet was thrown back, and she'd been kept warm solely by the heat radiating from their bodies. Ro squeezed her eyes shut to stop the tears from falling. She hated what she had to do, but she didn't see any alternative. Graham was dead set against her leaving alone, and in his dedication to protect the people he'd taken responsibility for, he couldn't spare the bodies, his included, to see that she made it home safely. She bit her lip, and steeled herself against the clawing ache that was shredding her heart. Whether she wanted to leave or not, she couldn't bring herself to stay. She was going to prove to her family that they meant everything to her.

Decision made, Ro paused to make sure both men were sleeping soundly. When all she heard was even breathing, she inched out of their hold and off the end of the bed. Apparently last night's activities, when added to the crazy events of the day, had rendered them dead to the world. Away from their warmth, the shiver that passed through her was a cold reminder of what she was about to do. She smiled sadly, knowing she'd be reliving the events of the last few days for the rest of her life. Shoving aside the urge to crawl back between them, Ro padded silently across Graham's room and picked up her folded clothes off the chair in the corner. She clutched her shirt, picturing Zach stacking them neatly. She took a deep breath, and blinked back the tears. After another deep breath she forced the emotions down. She spotted Graham's M1911 on the nightstand and remembered that he stashed a backup in the drawer. Liberating both guns, she checked to make certain the safeties were engaged. Spying Zach's and Graham's t-shirts on the floor, she picked those up, too. She wanted something to remind her that these men hadn't been just a figment of her imagination. She dressed quickly in the main room of the cabin, stuffing the M1911 in the waistband of her jeans at the small of her back and the other in the pocket of her hoody. She hefted her backpack onto her shoulders from where it sat by the door, and slipped silently out of the cabin.

Ro's first stop was the gun range where she raided the cabinets for MREs, Power Bars, and bottled water to replenish her supply. It felt wrong to take them, but she couldn't believe Graham or Zach would begrudge her the supplies. *No, they'd be too busy wanting to shake some sense into her for leaving.* She crept across the interior of the compound to the bolt hole that she'd seen the men enter and exit when they didn't want to unlock the main gate.

Unlike her last escape attempt, it wasn't her ankle, but her heart that ached. She thought about their reaction to finding her gone. Graham would lose his friggin' mind, and Zach would be so … disappointed in her.

Shoving the thoughts aside, she slid the bolt free, and the door swung open on well-oiled hinges. She stepped through the porthole and carefully closed the door, using a stick to prop it shut from the outside. She didn't like the idea of leaving it unbolted, but from the outside, she had no choice. Ro pulled out her compass, oriented herself, and headed toward the northeast corner of the property. The hidden gate there would be her exit point, and she just needed to avoid whoever was on fire watch. Ro sent thoughts skyward and headed out.

CHAPTER TWENTY-SEVEN

Dodging the roaming patrol had actually been easier than Ro had expected. Finding the hidden gate and sliding under the laser beam that would trip the perimeter alarm hadn't been much more difficult. She couldn't stop looking over her shoulder for the first couple of hours, because she expected Graham and Zach to come rushing out of the woods after her. But that hadn't happened. And the farther away Ro got from the ranch, the more she had to tamp down her mixed up emotions.

It was hard not replay the events of the last few days. *Jesus. Talk about a freaking roller coaster.* Only a week ago, if someone had told Ro that she'd willingly take part in a ménage—and love it—she would've punched him in the throat. Seriously, though. Propositioned for two ménages (okay, surprised with and bargained into) within a few weeks? That had to be some kind of a record. At least among twenty-something professional women with almost no social life to speak of. The craziest part was, while the first one—the Evelyn-Charles incident—had felt so utterly and abhorrently *wrong*, the second one had just felt natural and *right*.

Maybe it was the lack of a silicone strap-on? Whatever the reason, she couldn't regret her decision. In either case. And she was working really, really hard to not regret her decision to sneak out this morning. Maybe someday, like when the power grid came back up, she'd take a drive back to Castle Creek Whitetail Ranch and see if they'd forgiven her for running out on them.

Ro's stomach growled, reminding her that she had missed out on Allison's excellent breakfast. She paused to unzip the side pouch of her pack and pulled out one of the stash of peanut butter Power Bars she'd "borrowed." Tearing the wrapper open with her teeth, Rowan heard a branch snap behind her. Expecting to see Graham and Zach's angry faces, she started to whirl around. But before she caught of a glimpse of whoever was behind her, pain exploded in her skull and everything went black.

Still half asleep, Graham rolled over and reached for Rowan. When his hand found the cold sheet between him and Zach, his eyes flew open. Sunlight filtered through a slit in the blackout curtains covering the cabin's high windows. The morning was still. Zach's even breathing was the only sound interrupting the silence. The icy fingers of dread from yesterday invaded full force, this time gripping his heart and his gut.

Graham glanced toward the closed bathroom door, hoping against hope she was in there. He rolled off the bed and strode to the bathroom, grabbing up his pants from the floor. He jerked the door open.

Empty.

Graham checked the floor for his shirt, but not seeing it, he pulled open his drawer to grab another. He rounded the bed and reached for the gun on his nightstand. It was gone.

Only his radio sat next to the oil lamp.

He pulled open the nightstand drawer and reached in for his backup sidearm. It was also gone.

Yanking his pants on, he said to Zach, "Get the fuck up, man. Ro's gone."

Zach was out of the bed, looking around the room, clearly confused about what the fuck was going on. But Graham wasn't confused. He was absolutely goddamn certain of what the fuck was going on. She'd run. *She'd fucking run.* She'd left him. Because that's what women did. They *fucking left.* Suddenly he was a seven-year-old boy again, waiting in a trashy motel for his mom to come back for him. Except this time he wasn't waiting for shit. He was going after her.

Zach started throwing on clothes as Graham headed into the main room and yanked on his boots. The spot where her backpack had been leaning up against the wall was empty. Further confirmation that she'd run. He strode out of the cabin, slamming the door behind him. First stop, bathhouse. *Empty.* Second stop, mess hall.

Allison looked up from the stove when he banged open the door.

"You seen Ro this morning?" he asked, fighting to keep his tone even.

"No. She hasn't yet been in," Allison replied.

"Fuck!" Graham slammed back out of the kitchen, heading back to the cabin, where Zach was standing on the porch, shoving his feet into boots.

"What do you mean she's gone?" Zach asked.

"She's gone," Graham growled. The pain in his chest intensified as he admitted it. "She fucking left."

"She left," Zach repeated slowly, as if trying to wrap his head around the concept.

"She took my .45 and my back up. Her backpack is gone. The little fool left. And I have no fucking clue how she got off this property without anyone realizing it. Heads will roll if someone was derelict in his duty last night."

"Shit, man. If she's on her own out there …"

"When I find that girl I'm going to beat her ass until she can't sit for a week," Graham bit out.

"So you're going after her?"

Graham shot him an incredulous look. "Of course I am. As soon as I talk to the jackasses on watch last night to see how they could have possibly missed her." Graham thought back to their time in the command post. He might as well have drawn her a fucking map to get out. But she had no idea what kind of danger could be waiting for her out there. *Fuck*.

He headed to the command post. Ryan was seated at the counter fiddling with the ham radio. He spun when the door cracked against the wall.

"Who was on watch last night?"

"Ty, Jamie, and Travis."

"They still out there?"

Ryan looked down at his watch. "Should be back and checking in shortly. They should've swapped with Cam, Beau, and Jonah ten minutes ago."

Jamie stuck his head in the doorway. "I'm right here. What's up? I wanna get some grub and some rack time."

Graham wanted to lunge at him and throw him up against the wall for letting Ro slip out. Because she had to be long gone by now. She was too damn determined not to be.

"You see anything but deer last night?"

"Nah, man. I would have radioed it in, ASAP. The other

guys didn't see anything either," Jamie replied. "Why? What's goin' on?"

Graham opened the door the led to the armory rather than responding.

"Ro's gone," Zach said, answering Jamie's question and watching as Graham grabbed one of their go bags off the shelf and unzipped it. Each backpack was stocked with all of the essentials needed to bug out. Or track down an escaped woman. He grabbed an M4 off the wall, checked the magazine, and leaned it up against the bag. Graham shoved a .45 in the waistband of his pants. Extra magazines and stripper clips of ammo were shoved into the bag, followed by a long-distance radio.

Zach stepped into the armory and mimicked Graham's actions. Go bag. Rifle. Ammo. Radio. His pistol was already tucked into the holster on his belt. Jamie followed him inside.

"Gone, gone?" Jamie inquired. "I don't get it. She should have set off the alarm on the perimeter fence."

"Not if she knew to avoid it," Graham said.

"How …?" Jamie's question trailed off at Graham's glare.

"Look, it doesn't matter how she got out," Zach interrupted. "We just need to get out there and find her. Make sure she's okay."

Jamie paled. "We didn't get that last fucker. He's still out there somewhere, and he's got a hard-on for us."

Graham slung the loaded backpack over his shoulders, and Zach followed suit.

Jamie grabbed a go-bag off the shelf, too, and helped himself to extra magazines and ammo. And the SAW. The M249 Squad Automatic Weapon, which was basically a light machine gun. Then he stuffed a box of linked ammo that fed the SAW into the bag.

Zach paused when he noted Jamie's actions. "What are you doing? You've been up for almost twenty-four hours already."

"Like we haven't gone without sleep for longer, all the fucking time. Plus, I'm the best goddamn tracker on the team, and you know it. And, you might need another gun."

They headed out of the armory to where Graham was standing and speaking with Ryan. "You should take the truck," Ryan was saying.

"Can't," Graham replied. "She's on foot. We'd never find her." He cursed. "And I don't have a fucking clue where she's headed, except northeast."

When Graham caught sight of Jamie, loaded for bear, he nodded approvingly. Zach figured Graham would have already asked Jamie to come along, but he was a little rattled over Ro's abrupt thief in the night disappearing act. "You ready to move?"

"Oorah!"

"Then let's go."

Graham froze when they reached the bolt hole. Zach came up beside him. It was unlocked.

"Well, that solves one mystery."

"She's not going to be able to sit for a week when I'm done with her."

Jamie and Zach followed him through the opening, and Ryan pulled the door shut from the inside and barred it. Jamie paused. "Looks like it was propped shut with a stick from the outside. She's pretty smart, your girl."

"If she was our girl, she wouldn't have left," Graham said.

CHAPTER TWENTY-EIGHT

Once outside the walls, Jamie easily picked up Ro's small tracks. Graham hadn't realized how little her feet were until he was desperately searching the ground for her footprints. *I'm fucking pathetic*, he thought. *Woman walks out on me, and I'm trailing after her like a puppy, looking for scraps of attention. No*, he reminded himself, *I'm just making sure she's safe*. It tore Graham up inside knowing that they could have kept Ro from facing unknown dangers between here and her home if he and Zach had held up their end of the deal.

As Graham had guessed, she'd headed for the hidden gate at the northeast corner of the outer fence. Jamie started to lead them away from the ranch property, still heading northeast. After about fifteen minutes, he stopped.

"I don't like this, man. Not at all."

"What?"

"You see these big boot prints here?" Graham looked at the dirt where Jamie was pointing with a stick.

"Yeah."

"I've been seeing them with pretty alarming regularity. It's like they're trailing your girl." He pointed again. "You can tell that one of them stepped on her print here, so we know they came after her."

Zach looked alarmed. "Wait, you're saying that it looks like someone is following her? Other than us?"

"More than one someone. Looks like two. And men, based on the size of the prints," Jamie replied.

The icy feeling was back. This time it was a fist, clenching his stomach and turning it inside out. It took Graham a few seconds to realize it was absolute gut-wrenching fear. He'd been a team leader. Creeping into the unknown, ready to throw himself in front of a bullet for any one of his men. But he'd rarely ever had time for fear. Even that day he'd watched Isaac, who'd just saved Graham's ass, take a sniper bullet to the back of the head—exploding his skull like a watermelon on the losing end of a sledgehammer; even then, Graham hadn't had time to fear Isaac's fate. He was gone in a flash of a moment. But this, what he was feeling now was real, soul-gripping fear for Rowan. They needed to find her. Now.

"I hate to say this, but … I think I recognize one of the tracks," Jamie tossed over his shoulder, as he charged forward, following the boot prints.

"What the fuck do you mean?" Graham demanded.

"It's the same print as the guy I was tracking yesterday," Jamie answered, not stopping.

"Wait," Zach interrupted. "If it's the same guy from yesterday, why is there more than one set of prints? The other two are dead."

"There had to be more of them than we thought. They're like fucking cockroaches. You kill one, and you turn around to see a dozen more scuttling away," Graham said. "Fuck! Did anyone ever get any answers out of the woman? Did she know how many of them there were?"

"Lia wouldn't talk to anyone but Cam. And as far as I

heard from him, she has almost no memory of what happened after they grabbed her. Beau thinks she's blocking it out because her mind can't handle it right now," Jamie answered.

"So there's at least two of them after Ro." That icy fist sprouted claws and pierced Graham's gut when he thought of the shape the other woman had been in when they'd brought her in. He voiced his earlier thoughts. "We need to find her. Now."

Ro woke to a steady throbbing in her head, a slightly nauseous feeling in her gut, and burning in her wrists. It hadn't been Graham and Zach catching up to her ... unless they'd been really pissed and had taken to hitting women. Given the likelihood of that was the same as her waking up wearing ruby slippers, she was terrified to open her eyes to see who had knocked her out. Opening them slightly, she tried to pretend she was still unconscious, but the squinty vision kicked the nausea up another notch. Ro's eyes snapped open. Chills crawled over her skin.

Dirty blue flannel. Stringy brown hair and scraggly beard. Dark, dead eyes. A shining buck knife flew through the air, end over end, until the fixed blade sank into the trunk of a pine. He tore off a chunk of a Power Bar as he crossed to the tree to yank the knife out. The one who'd wanted to cut Lia for nearly biting his dick off. Son of Red. *Of all the fucking bad luck.* Ro cringed, imaging a similar knife at Lia's throat. She was so unbelievably fucked. A second man was sitting with his back propped against a pine tree. He was equally dirty, but wearing a black long-sleeve t-shirt and a tan Carhartt vest over ripped camo pants and leather boots. He was tracing the wood grain on the butt of a 12-gauge shotgun while he dumped the contents of an MRE into his mouth. Her backpack was lying unzipped at his feet next to another small, dirty canvas rucksack.

Ro was double fucked. And this time the ménage was going to be worse than facing down the strap-on sporting Mistress of Evil. *Think. Think. Think.*

As the Crotch-Cradler released the knife for another throw, he glanced at Ro.

"Finally," Crotch-Cradler grunted. "Thought Ronny mighta killed ya. Not that it fuckin' matters I guess. One bitch is as good as another."

Ro lifted her hands. They were bound by prickly jute rope that dug into her skin and had already started to leave red creases. She didn't say anything. Didn't want to ask, "What are you going to do with me?" because, quite frankly, she didn't want to know the answer.

Ronny stood, gesturing to Ro with the barrel of the shotgun. "So this is the bitch that sent them fucking assholes after us? You sure?"

Crotch-Cradler didn't respond to Ronny, but narrowed his eyes at Rowan. "Because 'a you, I got no pa, no uncle, no cousins, no home, no supplies. Not a goddamn fuckin' thing to my name but this knife, and my gun, the clothes on my back, and the random shit Ronny carries around. The way I figure, you owe me, bitch. And whatever I tell you to do, you're gonna do it. And you're gonna fuckin' love it." His mouth twisted into a cruel smile as he came toward Ro, the blade in his hand catching and reflecting the sun's rays. All Ro could think was, *goddamn, he's like that joke about a country song playing backwards … get your dog back, your house back, your wife back, your truck back.*

"So whatdya say, bitch. You ready to have some fun?" Ro froze, holding her breath as he ran the tip of the blade along her cheek before starting to slice through the neck of her sweatshirt. And then an idea struck. Bargain with them. *Daddy please forgive me.*

Ro swallowed, choosing her words carefully and hoping her movements didn't result in severe lacerations. "How about a trade?"

He paused, drawing back to look her over. "I don't need to trade shit, girl. I'm holdin' all the cards here."

"What if I knew a place where you could resupply every-thing—food, water, gear, clothes, weapons." He stopped slicing mid-chest.

"You talkin' 'bout that ranch? 'Cause I ain't stupid. They'd kill us on sight. Try again, you dumb bitch."

"No. Not the ranch. Somewhere else. My people. They'll help you out. Set you up with everything you need. There are some empty houses near by, and you could set up camp. I … I can't do anything about your family, and I'm sorry," she lied. Because she wasn't the teensiest bit sorry after what they'd done to Lia. "But I'm running from the ranch people, too, and we can help each other out. But they won't help you if you hurt me."

He stepped back, eyes narrowed. "How'd I know you ain't lyin'?"

"I guess you'd have to trust me. I mean, what do you have to lose. If I'm lying, you'll know soon enough. But if you're worried about the ranch guys, you might want to decide quickly, because they're probably coming after me. They were … holding me prisoner. I escaped." Ro did feel bad lying about that particular point, but felt it was completely justified. If these guys were busting ass to get to the farm, they weren't stopping and raping her. It was a win-win in her book.

Then Ronny spoke up. "A place to stay, food, and gear? Come on, Len. That's not a bad deal."

"Shut up, Ronny! I'm thinking," Len snapped, tapping

the blade of the knife on his yellowed and uneven teeth. Then his stomach rumbled. Hunger was a great motivator.

"If you're lying to me, I will make you regret it for the rest of your life. Which won't be fuckin' long." Len's hand whipped out and grabbed the rope, jerking her to her feet. The sharp tug of the jute cut into her wrists. "Let's get the fuck out of here." He shoved her forward. "Lead the way."

Ro looked around, confused and completely disoriented. "Umm … which way is northeast?"

Len grunted and pointed. Ro didn't waste time heading off into the woods. She couldn't believe her crazy ass deal had actually worked. Now she just hoped her dad would read her mind and shoot them on sight.

CHAPTER TWENTY-NINE

"We've got a problem," Jamie said, crouching low and pointing to the dirt.

Graham jerked to a stop, and Zach stumbled into him.

"What do you mean, 'We got a problem'?"

"I think they caught up to your girl."

"What? How?" Graham asked. He bit back the automatic '*She's not our girl*' retort.

Jamie pointed to scuffed dirt. "Someone was dragged." He stood and followed the marks to a stand of trees about twenty feet away.

Zach shoved Graham aside and scouted the area around Jamie. "I've got some wrappers over here. An MRE and a … peanut butter Power Bar?"

Graham pictured the grin on Ro's face when she'd spotted the stash at the gun range, and he swore silently. "It was her. Or at least her backpack. I'd lay money on it."

"Got knife marks in the tree. Like someone was using it for target practice," Jamie said.

Graham hated to ask, but needed to know. "Blood?"

"No. Got tracks leading away from here, though."

"Let's move."

Ro stumbled over a downed sapling trying to keep up with Len as he jogged through the pitch-black woods. After becoming frustrated with her slow pace, Len had taken the lead, tying Ro's bound hands to his belt with another piece of rope. It was like being dragged by a pissed off mule. Despite his appearance as a lazy redneck piece of shit, the man could cover some ground. She'd recognized the last major highway they'd crossed, and estimated they were within fifteen miles of home. *Home*. Knowing she was finally going to make it there was … surreal. Even if it wasn't exactly how she'd planned, Ro was thankful to be making it there alive. *Another stumble. Another bite of pain. Another curse from Len.* Ro hurried to keep up, not wanting to feel the burn of the jute digging deeper into her torn and bleeding skin. Len and Ronny each had a headlamp to guide the way, but Ro's feet were bathed in shadow. *Another yank. Another stumble.* Ro fell to her knees, the rope pulling Len to a halt.

"Get up, bitch." The light blinded her as he turned. A brown stream of tobacco juice spattered the edge of her face.

The exhaustion that had been dogging Ro all day crashed down. She tried, *tried*, to find a second, third, even a fourth wind. But there was just nothing left. She was tapped out. She considered her options. Keep stumbling through the dark and get home, but endure the searing pain in her wrists. Sleep for a few hours and hope like hell they don't rape her. As choices went, they blew, but Ro's screaming muscles wouldn't last another hundred yards, let alone another fifteen miles.

"Look, we're close, okay. Really, really close," she said.

"But it has to be after midnight. Is there any way we can take a break for a couple hours and get some rest? It would be better to show up at dawn rather than in the middle of the night. I'd hate to find myself on the wrong end of my dad's shotgun by accident."

"We stop when I say we stop. You ain't gotta say." Len spun, tightening the rope connecting them.

"Awww, come on. Let's just stop for a few, and then we'll pick it up at daybreak. We been out here for days, and I'm whipped, man. Fuck, I don't think I can even get it up to fuck her." Ronny leered at Rowan. "Tomorrow, sweet thang, you goin' be the meat in a Len and Ronny sandwich."

Len's lip curled in disgust, but before he could speak, Ro said, "Sounds great. I'll even make you dinner first. We'll make a night of it." She figured the Almighty was obligated to forgive her for that revolting lie.

Ronny reached out a perma-dirty hand to touch her face, and Ro forced herself not to flinch. "It's a date, sweet thang."

"Would you mind?" Ro held her fake smile and lifted her wrists up toward Ronny.

"Fuck that, bitch. You stay tied up tonight. Ain't takin' a chance you'll go runnin' off," Len replied.

"Could you at least untie me so I can pee?" Ro asked. "Unless you want to sleep in a puddle ..." Ro could have kicked herself for letting the snark out. She blamed the exhaustion.

Len grunted, but pulled out his buck knife and twisted around to slice the rope off his belt. He yanked her wrists up and sliced between the jute tying them together. He pointed the knife at a bushy evergreen about ten feet away. "You go behind that tree. You got two minutes. Leave the backpack right fuckin' here. You take one step in the wrong direction," he brought the blade to rest against her throat, "and I will gut you."

Ro swallowed, but didn't waste time dropping her pack and hurrying toward the tree. She followed the path lit by the beam of Len's headlamp and ducked behind the thick trunk to take care of business. Peeing in the woods as a woman was more of an art than a science, especially considering Rowan was trying not to flash her ass to her audience. She really needed to *not* be the 'meat in a Len and Ronny sandwich' tonight. Ro lamented her lack of toilet paper for a moment before dragging her clothes back into place. Her wrists burned as the weeping, broken skin rubbed against the cuffs of her filthy sweatshirt. Heading back toward the light, she noticed that Len and Ronny had already helped themselves to the contents of her backpack—including her sleeping bag. She was surprised to see Len toss it to Ronny. They could keep it. No way in hell would she use it after they did. She'd guess that showers had been an every-other-week thing for them, even before the grid went down.

"I'll take the first shift. It's probably about two o'clock. You sleep for an hour and a half, then we'll swap. We're out of here as soon as there's a hint of light. You hear a sound, shoot first, ask questions later," Len ordered. Ro shuddered when he pulled the roll of paracord from her backpack and cut off three lengths. "Get over here, bitch."

With no choice but to comply, Ro went. He yanked her wrists behind her and tied them together, knotting the nylon cord so tightly around her abused wrists that she tasted bile.

"Sit down. I'm doing your feet, too. You ain't goin' nowhere once you're hobbled."

Ro blocked out the pain as she leaned back against the trunk of a tree and inched herself to the ground. Len worked quickly, tying her legs together, just above the tops of her hiking boots. He shoved her to her side, face in the dirt, and looped the last length of cord between her wrists and feet. *Hog-tied*. It wasn't overly tight, but Ro's back still bowed, and she knew the discomfort of the position would make sleep nearly impossible if she wasn't totally exhausted. Ro yawned, tasted dirt, and tried to focus on the positive: she was almost home; she wasn't dead; and she hadn't been raped. Low bar for good things, but she'd take it. She barely had time to dwell on her undignified position before her lids lost the battle and sleep consumed her.

A boot connected with Ro's bound ankles, and she jerked awake. She rubbed her dirt-covered face against her shoulder and struggled to sit up. Pain lanced through her wrists when she accidentally tugged on the cords binding them together.

Len leaned down and sliced through the paracord trapping her legs. Another slice and her wrists were free. Ro brought them forward, needles stabbing her arms as the blood rushed back after hours without movement. Pieces of black paracord stuck to her blood-encrusted wrists. She plucked it off, wincing as fresh blood welled. Ro reached for her backpack, but froze when the knife flashed in her face.

"What the fuck do you think you're doing?" Len asked.

"I … I just wanted a wet wipe, or my first aid kit, something to clean up my wrists," Ro said, eyes riveted to the sliver blade.

"Make it quick. We're moving."

Ro grabbed a wet wipe from the package in her bag and dabbed at the dried blood. It felt like sandpaper against her raw skin. Once her wrists were relatively clean, she dug deeper into her pack and pulled out two folded bandanas and her first aid kit. She smeared on the antibiotic ointment and wrapped the bandanas around her wrists before tying them off. *Apocalypse-chic first aid.* Len gave her a mocking look and ordered her to put on her backpack before he retied her wrists in front of her and fastened them to his belt.

Almost home. Almost home, Ro chanted silently.

The cushion of the bandanas blunted the bite of the narrow cord, and the ever-lightening morning sky allowed Rowan to see where she was walking. Staying just off the county road, the landmarks were all familiar now. There was the crooked silo that had looked like the Leaning Tower of Pisa since Ro was kid. She spotted the obnoxious blue metal roof of the Johnson's house. Above it, the sky was a vibrant work of art, all reds and pinks and oranges smeared like oil paints across the horizon. They turned down an empty dirt road lined with row after row of corn, and Ro finally let herself wonder about Zach and Graham. Were they disappointed to find her gone? Did they even consider coming after her? Or did they just write her off as a failed experiment and move on with their lives? It was hard to swallow the idea that she could be so easily forgotten, especially since she wouldn't be forgetting them anytime soon. If ever.

They made a final turn and a half-mile later, a peeling green and yellow mailbox came into view. Ro wanted to drop to her knees and kiss the ground. She was home. *Finally*.

"It's that one. The driveway on the right." Ro gestured with her bound hands. Len grunted and paused at the end of the gravel drive. Unsheathing his knife, he sliced the paracord off his belt and from between her wrists.

"Don't want your pa gettin' the wrong idea," he said. *Or the right idea*, Ro thought. Looking behind her, she took in Ronny's grinning face.

"Can't wait to get set up with all new shit and a new place. It'll be like fuckin' Christmas. Especially with you under me tonight, sweet thang."

Ro curbed her disgust and faked her smile, looking over his shoulder to avoid meeting his eyes. And that was when she saw it: a flash of light from the cornfield. It reminded Ro of sun reflecting off a mirror … or a riflescope. Ro rubbed her bandana-covered wrists against her jeans and glanced over again. The flash was gone, but she could make out a dark figure crouched low in the yellowing stalks. Her heart pounded. *It was possible. It could be them. But that would mean … they left the ranch—even after Graham told her they couldn't spare the men—and had been trailing her the whole time.* Ro casually turned toward the house, digesting the information and considering what kind of plan they might have. Adopting a normal mien, she took the lead when Len gestured for her to go first. As they headed up the driveway, both men studied everything in front of them and nothing behind. Ro's breathing picked up. *Don't look back. Just pray to God they're really back there and you're not hallucinating.*

Six-foot tall stalks lined both sides of the gravel drive for a quarter-mile before it veered to the right, leading up to a patchy yard dominated by a giant oak with a frayed rope dangling from a thick branch—the remnants of a long ago tire swing. The house was built in the traditional farmhouse style, with white clapboard siding, peeling black shutters, fronted by a wide covered porch held up by spindly columns. The wooden barn, painted red with white trim, sat off to the left of the driveway. A John Deere tractor was parked half-in and half-out of the sliding barn door. Ro could picture her dad, comfortable in the cab with a giant thermos of coffee, getting ready to drive out to the field when the electromagnetic pulse had hit. She hoped like hell her dad and Erica were okay and she wasn't too late. The telltale sound of a pump action shotgun being racked halted their trek toward the house.

"Stop right where you are," a very familiar baritone called out. "Don't take another fucking step and put your hands in the air."

Ro had just started to raise her hands when Len yanked her in front of him. Neither man moved to comply.

"I'm hoping you'll roll out a warm shotgun welcome for these two gentlemen here, Dad," Ro called.

Len jabbed her in the back as the warped front door creaked open and the barrel of the shotgun slid out.

"That really you, Rowan Elizabeth?"

Ro dropped her hands. "In the flesh." She could almost hear her dad repeating the first words she'd spoken. Hell, that was about as clear as she could make it.

"How about you grab my ball cap out of the cab of the tractor, sweetheart."

Ro attempted to sidle away from Len toward the steps leading up to the cab of the tractor, but Len wrapped his arm around her waist.

"I think you should stay right here, bitch," he muttered in her ear, his rancid breath making her gag. He yanked her tighter against him and reached for the gun holstered at his hip when Ro heard the metallic sound of a rifle chambering a round.

"Down!" her dad yelled. She tried to drop to her knees, but Len's arm constricted painfully around her stomach. The report of a rifle cracked through the still morning air. Len swore.

"I'll fucking kill her, I swear," he yelled. And then to Ronny he said, "Fucking shoot 'em."

Ronny snapped into action, yanking his shotgun out and unloading shell after shell in the direction of the front door before ducking behind the tractor. *Rat-a-tat-tat*. A burst of automatic weapon fire exploded, and holes punched into the metal panels of the tractor. Ronny pin-wheeled toward the tire. Len swung around, dragging Ro with him, and shot wildly in the opposite direction of the house. Ro couldn't focus to count the shots as someone unloaded serious firepower in Ronny's direction. *Rat-a-tat-tat. Rat-a-tat-tat. Rat-a-tat-tat.* Ronny wasn't moving.

"Fucking shoot me, motherfuckers! I'll take her out with me!" The hot barrel of Len's revolver jammed into her temple. "I will fucking blow her brains out if you take one more shot." For once, Ro thanked her shorter-than-average stature and shrank down. She'd seen enough movies; someone could totally go for the headshot. For a moment, the sounds of the gunfight quieted. Ro slammed her heavy hiking boot backward into Len's shin. She jabbed her elbow into his gut and the arm bracketing her body loosened. Ro dove toward the rows of corn and covered her head. The crack of a rifle sounded, and Len's body landed on the gravel drive with a thud.

"He's down. Go, go, go!" Graham yelled. "Jamie, check the other one."

"Get the fuck away from my sister!" Erica's scream was earsplitting. "Back off, or I will shoot you."

Ro started to rise, but instead found herself caught up against a hard chest. "Jesus, babe, don't fucking scare me like that again. I will tan your ass until you can't sit for a week," Zach breathed, pressing a hard kiss to her temple.

"Are you deaf, asshole? Don't you fucking touch her!"

Ro turned in the safety of Zach's arms and beamed when she saw her sister, dressed in camo, armed to the teeth and ready to start shooting. Again. "It's okay, E. They're okay. Weapons down."

"Then you better get your ass in here, because we've got a big fucking problem." At her words, Ro noted Erica's deathly pale face. Her sister disappeared back into the house, leaving what remained of the door open. Ronny's shotgun had obliterated over half the wooden panel. Ro pushed away from Zach and headed toward the house.

"Whoa, sweetheart, I'm not letting you get out of arm's

reach for a long fucking time," Zach said as he snagged her arm. "We go together."

"This one's dead," Jamie called from the vicinity of the tractor. Ro didn't need anyone to tell her that Len, who was missing most of his head, was also dead. Graham flanked her other side and they headed to the house as a unit.

"What happened?" Ro asked as they climbed the wooden stairs to the covered front porch. Erica didn't have to answer, because Rowan caught sight of their dad. The right shoulder of his black t-shirt was shredded and blood pooled on the worn hickory floor. Erica looked up, tears streaming down her face. "Do I put pressure on it? There's wood stuck in it. *Shit.* I don't know what to do."

Graham knelt next to her father's unconscious body and yanked open his pack, pulling out a black plastic package. He tore it open with his teeth and extracted what looked like a white gauzy sponge. He applied the sponge directly to the wound. "Zach, give me yours and some bandages." Zach was already digging through his bag and tearing open a similar package, which Graham pressed to the exit wound. Pads of gauze followed as Ro realized the sponges had to contain clotting agents, because the flow of blood was already slowing. Graham looked up, his dark gaze trapping Ro's. "We need to get your dad back to Beau. ASAP."

Ro's heart dropped as she considered the trip back to the ranch on foot. He'd never make it. Her heart clenched to think she might've spoken her last words to her father. *It wasn't supposed to happen like this. And it was her fault.*

"You got a doctor?" Erica demanded.

"Yeah, but he's over a day out on foot."

"We've got wheels. We've just been waiting for Ro to get home so we could bug out. We're all packed and ready," Erica said. "So let's go."

Graham nodded to Jamie. "Go with her, check it out,

and see if you can bring the vehicle around so we can load him."

Jamie followed Erica as she led him toward the door that opened into the garage. Ro looked to Graham, his hands still pressing the bandages against the wound, and then to Zach, who knelt beside her.

"Thank you. For coming after me. I know …" Ro's words trailed off as Graham flashed her an intimidating look.

"Now's neither the time nor the place. We'll discuss it later." He shifted his attention to Ro's dad, effectively ending the conversation.

Zach looped an arm around her shoulders and pulled her against him. He whispered in her ear, "It'll all work out, babe." He paused before adding, "Anything you need to get out of the house before we head out? Because I don't think you're coming back."

CHAPTER THIRTY

Graham had to admit that he was be impressed by the level of Mr. Callahan's preparedness. His vehicle of choice was a 1965 Ford diesel crew-cab pick-up truck. It was plenty old enough not to use electronics that could be affected by an EMP and could also run on biodiesel. A steel topper that Mr. Callahan had hand-fabricated covered the bed of the truck. It added a ton of weight, but it provided cover for the supplies in the back and featured small gun ports that could easily slide open and shut. Graham, Zach, Ro, and Erica crammed into the front bench seat, and Jamie sat in the back, where Mr. Callahan was laid out. He tried to keep the unconscious man as still as possible as they followed Erica's directions down every back road and two-track to make their way southwest. It would have been faster to travel the main roads, but any road worth traveling was largely impassible. Cars, which may never run again, were lined up as if stuck in a perpetual traffic jam. The dirt roads and two-tracks were bumpy, but trying to dodge the cars would be worse. Jamie had wrapped pressure bandages around Mr. Callahan's shoulder and upper torso to keep the bleeding under control and the clotting sponges in place, but with every rut, Graham feared the bleeding would start again. He carefully hauled ass while following Erica's uncanny sense of direction. The two-track spilled out onto a gravel road, and Graham eased off the gas and waited for Erica's next direction.

"Shit. I don't know which way we should go," Erica said, craning her head right and left before studying the compass bobbing on the dash. "Chances are there are more cars if we head west down this road, but I don't like the idea of going east because we'll end up backtracking." She looked to Graham, chewing her lip. "Ideas, big man?"

The corners of Graham's mouth twitched. Little Rambo Girl, as Jamie had taken to calling her, was one-of-a-kind. *Just like her sister.* Graham shut the thought down as soon as it entered his head. He reminded himself that she'd walked out on them, and it didn't fucking matter if she was one-of-a-kind or one-in-a-million. She'd made her choice. Although, watching her clutch her sister's hand and shoot worried looks at her father, he was starting to see things more clearly. You don't back a desperate woman into a corner and expect her not to react. Graham couldn't help but think about the night his mother had walked out of their shitty motel room in Cincinnati. He wished she'd had a more compelling reason than just looking for her next fix. Hell, Graham wished she'd thought her son was a compelling reason to stay. The old bitterness was unshakeable. And Zach wondered why Graham had never been in a hurry to find a long-term woman to tuck into bed between them. He pushed the thought aside and focused on the task at hand. "We need to make time. Let's head west and take our chances. We can't be too far from the ranch."

Erica's expression was determined as she nodded, reaching for the map on the dash. "Show me again exactly where we're headed. I'll get us there."

Ro forced herself to release the death grip she had on Erica's hand. It was like her subconscious was telling her not to let go or else she might lose her sister forever. They'd finally made it. Travis swung one of the main gates open as they approached. As soon as they were in range Zach had radioed the command post to advise Ty of the situation. Graham increased the speed as they headed toward the steel walls that had meant both safety and captivity to Ro. Right now, those walls looked like her father's salvation … and maybe, her future? The possibility was hard to believe given that Graham had barely spoken a word to her since he, Zach, and Jamie had shown up in all of their commando-glory to take down Len and Ronny in her dad's driveway. A section of the steel wall slid open revealing the compound that Ro had snuck out of only the morning before. It seemed like a lifetime ago.

Ty had promised that Beau would be ready and waiting. Ro hoped like hell that the ornery bastard would be able to help her dad. He'd woken a few times during the ride, which hadn't been nearly as long as Ro feared. Even with the painfully slow pace, it had only taken a little over an hour.

Graham drove straight through the center of the compound and pulled up along the front of the clinic. Beau was standing in the doorway, hands already gloved. Jonah stood next to him holding a backboard. Erica and Graham shoved open the front doors of the cab, and they all climbed out. Erica opened the rear passenger side door and waved Jonah over. Jamie, Graham, and Jonah worked seamlessly as Beau directed them to move her dad into the clinic. When Ro tried to follow, Zach stopped her at the door.

"You should wait out here. Your sister, too. You need to let Beau work and not get in his way."

Ro pushed against Zach's outstretched arm. "I need to be in there."

Jamie was dragging a screeching Erica from the clinic. "Let me go! You can't keep me out."

Jamie closed the clinic door with his free hand, leaving Jonah, Beau, and Graham inside.

"He'll be fine. They've got it covered. Just give them some space," Jamie said.

Ro hoped he was right, because she really, really needed her dad to be okay. The alternative was unacceptable. Every girl needed her daddy when the world fell apart. Especially since the last time she'd seen him, she'd been distracted, worrying about work and counting down the hours until she could safely sneak away to put out all the fires that had sprung up in her absence. *And where had that gotten her?* Ro tamped down the resentment. She needed to let it go. But it was hard when she looked at what she'd sacrificed for the sake of her ambition: time with her family, the people who mattered.

Ro sagged against Zach's hold, and he maneuvered them until she sat in his lap, leaning against the side of the clinic. Instinctively, she curled into his big frame. Erica's temper had calmed marginally, and she paced back and forth in front of the building. Jamie watched her intently.

Erica paused in her pacing and faced Ro. "So you and him, huh? Does that mean the big, grumpy one who drove us back is available?"

Ro knew her sister was only trying to take her mind off what might be happening inside the clinic, but she still wanted to snap out an unequivocal "no." Except she didn't have the right to make that statement.

Zach's arm tightened around her as though he could read her thoughts. "Graham's pretty hung up on someone, and it might be a long wait if you're trying to get his attention," Zach said.

Ro swiveled in his lap so she could see his face. "He barely looked at me ..." She trailed off when Erica cocked her head.

"Wait ... what? I was joking, but now I'm just confused. If you and him ... and you and the other one ..." The door to the clinic opened as Erica said, "You're doing them both?"

Ro was paying diligent attention to the ground and mentally kicking herself for the rush of hope that flooded her at Zach's words. She didn't want to explain the situation to her sister, and she really didn't want to look up at the doorway, because she knew, *just knew*, that Graham was standing there, probably trying to process the snippet of conversation he'd overheard. Then again, he'd have an update on her dad, and that was more important than dodging the awkward situation. Face burning with embarrassment, she met Graham's appraising gaze reluctantly. "How is he?"

"He lost a lot of blood before we got it controlled, so Beau is giving him some. He's working on cleaning the wood splinters out of the wound, and hopefully he'll finish that up before your dad comes around. Beau thinks he should pull through just fine. You can go in and sit with him after Beau's done. It'll be about a half hour or so."

Ro sagged against Zach, overwhelmed by relief. But Erica wasn't satisfied.

"You have a blood supply?"

"We've got two universal donors. So we donate and rotate it out. Shit happens. Never know when you might need it."

Erica sized up Graham. "Who the hell are you people?"

"Nobody special."

Erica's expression turned thoughtful. "If you somehow

talked my sister into sleeping with you *and* him, I'd have to say there's something special there. I mean ..."

Ro closed her eyes and prayed that a sinkhole would miraculously develop beneath her.

When no sinkhole appeared, she settled for saying, "Can we not have this conversation right now?"

"I just wanted to know why the guy looks so pissed, when he's got a hot piece like you doing the ménage thing. Is it because the other guy missed the hole and accidentally ..."

"Oh my God." Mortification flamed through Ro as she buried her face in her hands. "I swear to Christ, I should have muzzled you freshman year when you told Mitch Hopper I was masturbating to his yearbook picture and you heard me moaning his name through my bedroom door." She looked up to see Erica's grinning face and pushed to her feet. She threw herself at her sister in a full body hug. "I missed you so much."

"Missed you, too, big sis. And you really should have thanked me for that. After all, the hottest guy in school ended up asking you to the senior prom, and I'm pretty sure you lost your v-card that night."

Ro slapped her hand over Erica's mouth. "Seriously, no more."

But they could all hear Erica's garbled, "So what gives? Ro not putting out?"

Ro chanced a glance at Graham and straightened when she met his penetrating stare. Ro expected him to ignore Erica's question like he had so many others. But he didn't.

"You want to know what happened? Your sister dropped into our world like a stun grenade. Looks harmless and then, *bam*, it detonates, and you're fucking blinded to anything but the flash. That's why they call it a flash bang. Then she walked out before we could find our bearings. Took my goddamn heart with her."

Ro stumbled back from the intensity of his words. Zach caught her and wrapped an arm around her. Erica's mouth had dropped into an O, but she didn't respond. Ro was too shocked to appreciate that Graham had finally figured out how to shut up her lovable, mouthy sister. But hell, Ro was speechless. What did you say to something like that? *I'm sorry* seemed so trite. And how did you sincerely apologize for hurting someone when you knew you'd make the same choice again?

Ro took the coward's way out. She shoved away from Zach, disentangling herself from his arms. "I … I have to go. I need a shower." And then she ran.

What a fucking mess, Graham thought. He wanted to punch through the wall of the clinic. With the way he was feeling, he'd probably break his goddamn hand. *I'm a fucking moron*, he castigated himself. The first time in his entire adult life he'd tried to tell a woman how he felt about her and he completely fucked it up. He scrubbed both hands over his face.

"Are you in love with my sister?" Erica twisted to look at Zach, and then added, "Both of you?"

Zach laughed, though it sounded forced. "You really go for the balls with every question, don't you?"

"I'm just trying to figure out what's going on here." She stared Zach down with narrowed eyes. "Because that," she pointed in the direction of the bathhouse, "is not normal Rowan Callahan behavior."

"What's your point?" Graham asked, wanting to go shoot something until he no longer felt like the world's most pathetic asshole.

"*My point* is that you just verbally bitch slapped her and

then alluded to the fact that you might be in love with her. That's bad form, my friend. Bad form." She tapped a finger against her lips and mumbled, "Especially if she feels the same way."

"You don't know that," Graham said, crushing the surge of optimism at her words.

"Maybe not. But what I do know is that nothing could have stopped her from coming home after the shit hit the fan. Not 200 miles. And sure as hell not love. But if she's in love with you—both of you—then walking away was probably one of the hardest things she's ever done. My sister," Erica pointed toward the bathhouse again, "fights tooth and nail for what she wants and doesn't give up. Not unless there's a pretty fucking compelling reason. You know, like her family waiting on her to bug out and survive the apocalypse."

Graham's earlier thought about Ro being backed into a corner resurfaced. *Fuck.* He'd really fucked up.

CHAPTER THIRTY-ONE

Ro slammed the bathhouse door shut and was relieved to find it empty. No one needed to see tears streaming down her face. The indignity might be more than she could bear. She dropped onto the bench and started to wipe the tears away, but the fabric of the bandanas against her face distracted her from the mess of roiling emotions. She grabbed one corner with her teeth and awkwardly untied the knot. She gingerly unwrapped the fabric from her left wrist. The tears that came next were a direct result of the broken and oozing skin peeling away with the cotton. *Holy balls that hurt.* The ropes had gouged trenches into her wrist. She bit her lip as she repeated the process with her right wrist. It was going to hurt like hell to wash them, but she couldn't risk infection. The first aid kit in the red and white metal box attached to the wall would at least have gauze and antibiotic ointment, so she'd be able to wrap them up afterward. She might look like she'd botched a suicide attempt, but it was better than the alternative.

Ro worked quickly, washing her hair and cleaning her injuries under the warm spray. She attempted to remove the remaining jute fibers, but it was a losing proposition. Gritting her teeth through the pain, she scrubbed. Trying to distract herself, she let her mind wander. The first place it went was to the words Graham had spoken. What was she supposed to do with that? Was he telling her what she'd lost, or was he saying he still wanted her? And what about Zach? He hadn't been moody or brooding like Graham, but had seemed to welcome her back with open arms. How was he not crazy pissed too?

Ro shut off the water and blindly reached for her towel.

"Here you go, babe," a voice said as a towel was pressed into her grasping hand.

Ro slapped a palm over her chest, as if holding in her scream. He hadn't thought she'd heard him come in, and he was right.

"What the hell! Give me a heart attack, why don't you? *Jesus*, Zach."

"Wanted to make sure you were okay."

"I'm fine. Just needed to clean up." Zach tried not to stare as she rubbed herself down with efficient strokes. She wrapped the towel around her torso and tucked the corner between her breasts. Before he could enjoy her cleavage, his attention snagged on the ugly red marks ringing her wrists. He pulled her hands away from her body.

"What the fuck did they do to you?" he said, flipping her palms up and surveying the lacerations. Ro's hands shook slightly when she answered.

"They didn't want to take the chance that I'd run off. So they made sure I couldn't."

Zach thought back to the gut-wrenching minutes they'd sat in the cornfield. They'd spotted the trio turning down the dirt road, so they'd headed into the rows to try to gain a tactical advantage and flank them. He knew she'd been tied man in the lead, but through his binoculars he'd seen the bandanas beneath the rope and figured they would have blunted any rope burn, but they must have come after the damage had already been done. He lifted her hands to his lips and kissed each palm. When he looked up at Ro, her expression was teary and confused.

Her words were barely audible when she asked, "Why are you being so nice to me? Why aren't you pissed?"

Zach knew he should've anticipated the question, and now he had to decide if he was going to answer her honestly or give her some bullshit reason. He looked at the dripping curls falling over her slumped shoulders. He couldn't help but draw her into his arms, the water droplets still clinging to her skin, her hair soaking his shirt. Zach backed up to the bench and sat, pulling her down and positioning her across his lap.

Zach kissed her forehead. "Sweetheart, I'm not pissed. I'm proud of what you did." Her brow furrowed, and Zach could almost picture a conversation bubble appearing in the vicinity of her head that said, *'What the fuck?'*

"That's not to say I wasn't scared shitless for you and didn't want to spank your ass for putting yourself in danger."

"But ..."

"We've all got our stories, Ro, and one thing that Graham and I have always had in common is that ours aren't the prettiest." Zach took a deep breath, psyching himself up to lay it all out there. "I'm from a small town in Kentucky. My old man was a mean drunk who liked to beat on my mom, and then when I got big enough to stop him, he turned on me. I guess it was more sporting, because I wasn't afraid to fight back. No matter how hard I begged her to leave him, she wouldn't do it. She was too damn worried about what her church friends and the neighbors would think."

"Oh, God. Zach …" Ro's arms snaked around him and squeezed. Zach dropped another kiss on the top of her head.

"I didn't care that he took it out on me; it was better than having him hit Mom. The day after I graduated, she told me to get in the car, and she drove us straight to the Marine Corps recruiting office. My old man wouldn't hear of me going to college, because that was for pussies and rich kids. He expected me to go work in the factory, just like him. But Mom wasn't having that, and unbeknownst to me, she'd been talking to the local recruiter since I took the ASVAB in school. She must have told him enough of what was happening, because once it was clear that I was interested, he made things happen. Two days later, I was on a bus to Parris Island for boot camp. I knew the old man would hit the roof when he realized I was gone. He worked third shift, so he wouldn't figure it out until the weekend when he went looking for a punching bag. I tried to get her to pack her bags and go to stay with my grandma, a friend, or anyone, but she wouldn't do it. Said everything would be fine, and it was her duty to stay with her husband. I was too young and excited to be getting out of that hellhole to realize she was just paralyzed by fear."

Zach's gut knotted as he got to the part he hated to remember. He felt Ro tense as she asked, "What happened after you left?"

"Three days into boot camp, a chaplain showed up at the barracks to tell me that my old man shot and killed my mom, then ate the barrel of the gun himself. They were both gone."

Ro's horrified gasp and painfully tight grip eased some of the pain that still clutched at his heart when he thought about the chaplain's words. *"Son, I'm sorry to tell you that your parents are dead ...*" Zach could still see his apologetic expression as he'd relayed the grisly tale.

"I knew, I just *knew* that he wouldn't take my leaving lying down. And I knew he'd blame her. I was only seventeen, and I couldn't enlist without a parent's consent. Hell, I can't help but blame myself, *and her*, for not doing more to prevent what happened. She didn't have to die. All she had to do was choose the life she wanted instead of being afraid to leave the lot she was dealt." He took a deep breath and started to pack the memories away again. He lifted Ro's chin so he could look her in the eyes. "So you see, I can't be anything but proud that you made the hard choice and took action when it would have been easier to do nothing. You did what you had to do, and I can't hold it against you. Hell, Ro, your guts and determination just make me love you more."

Ro held on to Zach and struggled to keep from sobbing for the boy he'd been and everything he'd endured. Her chest ached at the regret and guilt and soul-deep pain etched on his face as he told his story. She started to form words over and over, but they all seemed inadequate. Instead, she squeezed tighter and pressed a kiss over his heart.

Zach hugged her back before disentangling her arms and studying her wrists. *Sharing time was over.* "We need to have Beau take a look at these. Can't take any chances. Not with you."

"He's busy with my dad. I can wait."

"That's the other reason I came to get you. Your dad's awake and is demanding to see his first born."

Ro smiled and her eyes mist with tears. *Again.* The rollercoaster of emotions over the past two days had taken a toll. "Can I borrow some clothes?"

Outfitted, once again, in baggy sweatpants and a giant hooded sweatshirt, Ro walked hand-in-hand with Zach across the interior of the compound toward the clinic. He'd tried to carry her, but she'd argued that she was fully capable of using her own two feet. Graham was nowhere in sight, and Ro was grateful for the reprieve. She had no idea how respond to the bomb he'd dropped. He thought *she* was the grenade in this situation? She'd just been minding her own business when they'd shattered her preconceived notions about relationships and sex and *everything*. And now her sister knew that she had been with them both. Ro wouldn't let the fear of her dad finding out change anything. When she'd first embarked on this … relationship … with Graham and Zach, she'd decided she was going to own it. She couldn't do any less now. If there was even a relationship to own. But that didn't change the fact that her dad was probably going to lose his ever-loving mind. So she'd just hope that his discovery would come later. *Much, much later*.

She tugged at Zach's hand, pulling him toward the clinic. Her excitement to see her dad had her breaking into a jog. Ro pushed the door open and smiled widely when she saw her dad sitting propped up against a stack of pillows.

"There's my girl," he said, grinning broadly. "You're a sight for sore eyes, honey."

"How are you feeling?" She surveyed the bandages that wrapped from the upper right section of his chest over his shoulder.

"Just fine. Only a few scratches. Nothing to worry about."

Ro arched a brow. "A few scratches?" Typical Dad response. He'd label anything as 'just a scratch' unless it involved losing a limb.

"I'll be good as new by tomorrow."

"I've heard that before," Beau interrupted. "And I'll say

the same thing to you as I did to her: you need to take it easy
for a while. You just had minor, non-anesthetized surgery,
and I'm gonna be pissed if you start bleeding again. The
painkillers are making you feel like Superman now, but
you're going to feel it when they wear off."

"Okay, okay." Her dad held out his hands in a placatory
gesture. "Doctor's orders, I get it. Now come here, Ro. Your
old man needs a hug."

Ro settled herself on the left side of the bed and carefully
squeezed her father's uninjured side. "Missed you, Dad.
Thanks for waiting for me."

He rubbed a few tears off her cheek. "None of that now,
honey. We're all fine. And you know I'd wait on you as long
as it took." Ro reached up to dash the rest of the tears away,
and the sleeve of the sweatshirt slid down to expose her wrist.
Her dad snatched it up. "What the hell happened to you?
Did they do this?" His features turned feral as he looked
from Zach to Beau and then to Graham, who'd just entered
the clinic.

"No, but it's … a long story. None of them had anything
to do with it," Ro reassured him. Her dad pulled her other
hand up and surveyed it.

"Jesus, Ro. What the fuck?" Graham bit out. He was
across the room and kneeling at her side before Ro even realized he was moving. Before she could respond, Beau was
rolling toward her on his stool and shoving Graham out of
the way to inspect her injuries.

"I guess you're up next. And let's hope this is the last time
you need first aid for a while. The antibiotic shot I gave you
with your stitches should be sufficient."

"Stitches?" Her dad was frowning at her. "What the hell
did you need stitches for?"

Ro sighed. "Like I said, it's a long story."

"Then you're lucky I've got plenty of time on my hands."

CHAPTER THIRTY-TWO

Graham was impressed with the rather edited version of events that Ro shared with her father. She'd managed to omit the fact that she had slept with him and Zach, not that he expected her to share that particular detail, but she also glossed over the part about how she ended up leaving the ranch by herself. Graham suspected that had Rick Callahan not been doped up on painkillers, he would have noticed the holes in her story and demanded answers. It was easy to see where Ro had gotten her bulldogged determination. She and Erica had spent the remainder of the day at their father's bedside. After they'd eaten the fried catfish Travis made for dinner, Beau had shooed them away with orders that Rick needed to rest.

Graham sat on the couch in the dark, alone with his thoughts and one of the several bottles of Jack they'd stored. One question had been plaguing him since the sun had set: where was Rowan going to sleep tonight? He'd been informed that Allison had set Erica up in the cabin that Lia was using. Graham couldn't picture the ultra-timid woman getting along with the rough-edged country girl, but reports indicated they'd clicked nicely. It was a small cabin with two sets of bunk beds, so there was certainly room for Ro, if she chose. And that was the problem: Graham didn't want her to choose to sleep there. He still wanted her in his bed. He'd just taken a swig of whiskey and was thinking about Erica's words outside the clinic when the door opened on silent hinges.

Ro tried not to appear nervous as she cut behind the mess hall to head to Graham and Zach's cabin. But her palms were sweaty and her heart raced, so she figured she probably looked just as nervous as she felt. She was going so far out on a limb, and the only assurance she had that it wouldn't break off beneath her was Zach's declaration. Graham was the wildcard, and she didn't know how he'd react to her presence. The cabin was dark as she eased the door open and crept inside. It was the opposite of the move she'd made thirty-six hours before, and the irony wasn't lost on her. She shut the door behind her and tiptoed to Graham's bedroom. *Empty.* She padded across the living room and stuck her head in Zach's room. *Empty.* Where the hell were they?

"Looking for someone?" Graham's voice came out of the dark.

"Jesus, fuck, you scared me!"

"Why are you sneaking around in the dark in my cabin? Or is that just your M.O.?"

Bravado flaring to life for the first time since she'd returned, Ro asked, "Are you going to hold that over me for the rest of my life?"

Light flickered from the oil lamp on the table as Graham lit it. "You could have been killed. If we hadn't been there ... Hell, I don't even want to think about it."

"Why did you come after me? You told me you couldn't spare anyone. What made you change your mind?"

"Why are in you in my cabin?" He lifted a bottle and swigged, ignoring her question.

"This conversation is going nowhere." Frustration gripped her. The spark of optimism she'd felt on her trek to the cabin was doused. "I'll go find somewhere else to bunk, and you won't have to worry about where I am." She pivoted toward the door and took two steps before she was yanked off her feet and tossed over Graham's shoulder. She barely comprehended what was happening when she landed with a hard bounce on the mattress.

"Good Lord, you are a such a caveman. What the hell are you doing? You don't want me here, so just let me leave." Ro was proud that her voice didn't break when she spoke.

"Don't tell me what I want. Because it's fucking clear you don't know a goddamned thing about it." The oil lamp on the nightstand blazed to life.

Ro scooted up the bed until she was leaning against the headboard. "Of course I don't know what you want. You grunt more than you use actual words, and when you do say something, it's so fucked up, I can't even figure out how to respond. This," she gestured between them, "is a total disaster."

"How hard is it to understand that it gutted me to wake up to an empty spot where you were supposed to be? How hard is it to understand that you were supposed to pick me—us—and when you didn't, it stirred up some bad shit for me?" Graham's jaw clenched and the lines bracketing his eyes deepened.

"What are you even talking about?" Ro buried her hands in her hair and dug her nails into her scalp. "You've got to decode this shit for me, Conan, because I don't read minds. I might be multi-talented, but mind reading is beyond me."

Graham's laugh came out as choked huff. He rubbed his face roughly. "Could you just shut up for a minute? Another talent you haven't quite conquered is recognizing when a guy is trying to lay it on the line."

Ro shut her mouth so quickly her teeth clacked together. Graham was silent for more than a minute. Ro knew this for a fact because she counted, waiting for him to speak.

"I don't … do well with … desertion," he said, the words sounding as if they'd been dragged from his throat with rusty pliers. His gaze pinned her, daring her to comment on his raw statement. Ro stayed quiet. After Zach's revelations earlier, she wasn't sure she could handle whatever it was that Graham had to say. He stalked across the room to shove open the blackout curtain and peer into the dark night. He rested a forearm on the high windowsill, head dropping forward. "Fuck, I can't do this."

He spun and started for the doorway when Zach stepped into the room. "Come on, man. Just tell her." Ro jumped, surprised once again by Zach's stealthy entry.

Graham attempted to shove Zach out of the way, but Zach continued to block the doorway. "What the fuck does it matter anyway?"

Ro decided it was time to bare a piece of her soul. "I left because I've put my family last in every decision I've made for the past ten years. This was my chance to finally put them first, and I was doing it, without regret, until I met you." She paused and took a deep breath. "I wasn't deserting you. I was *choosing* them. For once. But you had to go and make me fall in love with you. *Both of you*. I couldn't let that matter, even if it ripped me apart. Don't you see? How do you not choose your family?"

Graham swung around, his movements almost violent. "My mother managed it when she left me in a shithole motel room when I was seven years old. It was three days before housekeeping caught me trying to steal Cheetos out of the fucking vending machine because I was starving. They found her a week later, floating in the Ohio River. The kicker—she'd been dead for less than twenty-four hours."

"Oh my God, Graham …" Ro said, mouth hanging open in disbelief. Apparently her childhood, even with a mother dying of cancer, had been all rainbows and unicorns compared to both of theirs.

"I don't want your pity. Social services got in touch with my uncle, and I moved up here. It was probably the best thing that'd ever happened to me up to that point. This place is the only real home I've ever had. It's easy to take for granted … but when you've never had one …" He cleared his throat. "My uncle put me in school—first grade, even though I'd never seen the inside of a classroom in my life. My mom had been too busy moving us from fleabag motel to fleabag motel to put me in school. She'd disappear for hours every night. It didn't occur to me until I was older that she was a junkie, turning tricks to feed her habit."

"I … I don't know what to say," was all Ro could get out.

"You don't need to say anything. You just need to know that when I woke up to find you gone, I thought I'd never see you alive again. All I could picture was you, dead in the woods somewhere. And all because you were too damn stubborn to let us protect you."

"I'm fine."

"You almost weren't," Zach said.

"So what we do now?" Ro asked.

Graham felt hollowed out. Drained. Like he'd just confessed his sins and wasn't certain whether he'd be granted absolution.

"I guess that depends on you," he said.

"What do you mean?" Ro asked.

"You're the one driving this train, sweetheart," Zach said. "If you hadn't noticed, we've both laid our hearts at your feet. What you do with them is your choice."

"Way to put the hard decision on me," she said, her tone a weak attempt at humor.

"You're the only one who can make it," Zach replied. Graham stayed silent, studying her features for any indication of her decision.

When finally Ro spoke, her words came easily, as if the choice was obvious. "Everyone who matters to me is inside these walls. There's nothing that could make me leave again." She looked at each of them before saying, "If it's truly my choice, then I choose this. Both of you. Us." Graham exhaled a harsh breath. *She. Was. Theirs.*

"You sure, darlin'?" Zach asked. "Because you make that choice and there's no going back. We'll be keeping you, come hell or high water." Graham could've snapped Zach's neck for giving her the option to change her mind. *She was theirs.* The decision had been made.

"I'm sure." She reached for the hem of her sweatshirt, and Graham's eyes widened.

"Whoa, baby. It's been a hell of a long day, and all that's on the menu tonight is sleep," Graham said.

"But I thought … You don't want me?"

Zach sat on one edge of the bed, and Graham crossed the room to sit on the other. "You know that's not the case. But, we're wiped. I think I speak for both of us when I say, we just want to hold you tonight and wake up with you tomorrow morning," Zach said, trying to reassure her.

"Huh," Ro said, continuing to pull her sweatshirt over her head, exposing naked skin beneath. She tossed it to the floor. "I've got to admit, that doesn't really work for me." She leaned back to rest on her elbows. Her lusciously rounded breasts swayed dangerously close to Graham's hands, and an impish smile curled on her lips. "I'm actually pretty disappointed with that decision." Her nipples were already pebbled, and Graham remembered how they'd felt against his tongue. His cock jerked to life.

"You're not playing fair," he murmured, mesmerized by the rise and fall of her breasts in time with her increasingly rapid breaths.

"I don't care," Ro replied, her gaze daring them to resist her. It was a losing battle.

"Fuck. You win. Zach, might as well help her lose the pants."

"Happy to," Zach said, tugging them down her legs, revealing bare, smooth skin. Graham swore the woman owned zero pairs of underwear. And thank God for that.

"Forget something, babe?" Graham asked, reaching over to skim his fingers up the inside of her naked thigh, not stopping until he reached her plump lower lips that were already slick with need. Graham dragged a finger up her slit, feeling his cock flex against his zipper when Ro moaned.

Zach knelt between Rowan's spread legs, and Graham watched as he dragged his tongue from ankle to knee, nipping at Ro's sensitive spots. Graham slid a finger through her wet heat as Zach approached her inner thigh. He trailed his finger up, circling her clit while Zach tongued her entrance. Graham brought his finger to Rowan's mouth, and interrupted her moan to paint her lips with her wetness.

"Taste yourself."

Graham held back his own groan as Ro's tongue circled his finger. When she sucked, all Graham could think was how much he wished it was his cock instead. *Fuck.*

She started to buck her hips against Zach's mouth, and all thoughts of his own pleasure fled as Graham realized she was about to come. In that moment, there was nothing he wanted to see more than her eyes glazed over with passion. He withdrew his finger and slanted his mouth over hers, catching a hint of her sweet and spicy flavor. He inhaled her whimpers as Zach worked her toward orgasm. He rolled her puckered nipples between his thumb and index finger, pinching and tugging until she bucked harder. Her elbows collapsed, and her body tensed. Graham bent to tug a peak between his teeth, and Ro buried her fingers in his hair. Graham loved the sharp tugs that signaled her impending orgasm. She stilled. And then her whole body tensed and writhed as she rode out the pleasure.

Graham pulled back. *There... that* was the look he needed to see. She was so goddamn beautiful and open in that moment that he knew he would never deserve her.

CHAPTER THIRTY-THREE

Ro jerked awake at the sound of a shotgun being racked. The heaviness of exhaustion-induced sleep made it hard to focus. Graham bolted out of bed, reaching for his sidearm and pointing at the intruder in one smooth, instinctive motion. Zach shoved her behind him, but not before she saw her dad standing in the doorway. A shaft of light cutting through the gap in the blackout curtains highlighted the twelve-gauge pump-action that normally rested in the gun rack of his truck.

"What the fuck, Callahan?" Graham yelled, reaching for a pillow to cover the impressive morning wood he was sporting.

"No one could tell me where my daughter was this morning, but that sweet little girl in the mess hall thought for some reason she might be in 'Mr. Graham and Mr. Zach's cabin.' Helpful little thing. And astute."

Ro pushed Zach's big body aside and yanked the covers up to her chest. "Was the shotgun really necessary?"

His jaw was set, eyes appraising them. "You tell me. Because I can't unsee what I just saw. Which was my first-born snuggled up between two men." He looked from Graham to Zach. "Naked men."

"I'm twenty-eight years old, not sixteen. I think it's a little late to be outraged to find out that I have sex."

"Good God, Rowan. I don't need to hear that."

"Seriously, Dad. What are you doing out of bed, anyway? You could've died yesterday. You need to rest. Beau is going to kill you if you tear open your stitches and start bleeding again."

Graham and Zach both looked at her, as if to say, *Really? You're giving* that *lecture?* She ignored them both.

Her dad leaned against the doorframe, balancing the shotgun barrel on his good shoulder. "I'm going. But before I do, I've got something to say." His gaze sharpened. "What you do and who you do it with is your business."

"Thank you very much," Ro said.

"But I'm not planning on sticking around here for too long. We've got our own place to get to, and I was assuming you'd be coming with us."

Ro's stomach dropped. *Not again.*

Rick Callahan's words were an uppercut to Graham's gut. The icy cold dread he'd felt two mornings ago returned, ten-fold. He ran through the irrefutable facts in his mind: Rowan had already chosen her family over them once. She'd told them last night that it was the only choice she could make in that situation. Faced with the same options, she'd make the same choice again.

"But sir, you and your daughters are all more than welcome to stay here for as long as you'd like. Hell, you can stay forever," Zach said. "We'd be happy to have you."

"Well, you may understand this and you may not, but

sometimes a man has to have his own place, follow his own path. And staying here would not be that place or that path for me and mine."

"With all due respect, sir, shouldn't your family's safety be your first priority? And they're safe here," Zach said, trying a different angle.

"Son, if I wanted you dead, you would never have woken up this morning. I learned a thing or two in the jungle. I can keep my girls safe."

"But, sir—"

"Let me lay it out for you. If you don't think Uncle Sam is gonna come knocking on your door sooner rather than later, you boys are crazy. This place is too well prepared not to be on someone's radar. I don't plan to be here when that happens, and I don't want my girls to be here either. When that time comes, if you resist, it'll be a blood bath. If you don't, they'll confiscate your ranch and everything on it under the authority of the National Defense Authorization Act and round you up and take you to some goddamn FEMA camp. It'll be the same as a concentration camp, complete with a stock of body bags and easy access to mass graves. I've been a POW once, and I'm not about to repeat the experience or anything like it. I got a place tucked away where the feds and the military will never think to look."

Graham watched the color leech from Ro's face and took in the unnatural stillness with which she held her body. It was all the answer he needed. Sometimes you had to be cruel to be kind. Graham smoothed his features into an expression-less mask before speaking the words he'd never be able to take back.

"We understand your concerns, sir, and respect your decision. We're happy to have you rest up here until you're ready to travel, and we'll supply you and both of your daughters with any additional provisions you need when you all leave." His stomach twisted as he emphasized the words *both* and *all*.

If it was possible, Ro paled further at his words. It occurred to him that they were probably the words she'd wished he'd said when she'd first stumbled into their lives. Hearing them now would crush anything she might feel for him, but he wasn't going to force her to choose again. This time, he'd take her pain and bear it himself.

Ro wrapped the sheet carefully around herself and slid to the end of the bed. She stared at the wall as she gathered her clothes, not sparing a glance at either him or Zach.

She cleared her throat. "I think we should head to breakfast, Dad. I'll get dressed and follow you in a minute." Her words were toneless, robotic.

Rick narrowed his eyes at him and Zach and then nodded and backed out of the room, shotgun in hand. Ro followed closely after him, leaving the bedroom with her clothes clutched to her sheet-covered chest.

"I'll see you in a few, sweetheart."

As soon as they heard the front door shut, Zach shoved on his pants and raced to the front room. Graham picked his clothes up off the floor and dressed slowly.

"Don't think for a second you're going anywhere, Ro," Graham heard Zach say resolutely.

"I can't talk about this right now," Ro said. "I have to go." The hitch in her voice was a razor blade to his skin—a self-inflicted slash.

"Baby—"

"Back off, Zach. Your team leader has spoken. It's done. If you don't like it, I suggest you take it up with him."

The front door slammed. Graham heard a *crunch* as Zach punched through the cheap wooden paneling that lined the front room.

"What the fuck, man?" Zach exploded as he burst into

213

the bedroom. "Just … What. The. Fuck? If you weren't my best friend … I would kill you right now. Please tell me this is another elaborate plan to get her to stay."

Graham remained mute as he sat on the bed and pulled on his boots.

"You gotta talk to me, man. Because you just fucked up the best thing that ever happened to us. We just got it all figured out." Zach raked his hands through his already disheveled hair and yanked.

Graham tucked his sidearm into his holster and hooked the radio onto his belt. He chose his words carefully before he faced Zach.

"What exactly do you think we had figured out? Because her dad just turned the clock back by two days, and if you think for a minute that she wasn't going to make the same choice she made before, then you're a fucking idiot." Graham swallowed, proud his voice didn't shake.

"So what? You decided to make the choice for her? 'Here's some supplies, don't let the door hit your ass on the way out.' That's your answer? Because it's a piss poor one, and you should be fucking ashamed of yourself."

"What I did was save her from having to tear herself apart trying to choose between us and her family again. It was the *right thing to do.*" Zach shrank back as Graham roared the last words.

"Making her think she meant nothing to you was the right thing to do? You might as well have slapped her across the face. And in front of her dad? The fact that he didn't unload that shotgun shows that he's a better man than me, because you just tossed his daughter out of your bed like she was garbage. I feel like I don't even fucking know you." Zach spun and left the room. Graham flinched as the cabin shuddered with the force of the slamming door.

CHAPTER THIRTY-FOUR

Ro was thankful for the numbness that settled over her. It was like her body and mind had gotten together and decided she didn't need to process whatever the hell had just happened. It was certainly better than feeling like Graham had ripped several vital organs from her body and ground them beneath the heel of his combat boot. In front of her father, no less. That was a humiliation she'd rather not relive.

Her reeling mind said she probably wouldn't have to worry about the possibility of a repeat while locked in whatever bunker her father had provisioned. After this morning, the lack of men in their party might merit a solid check in the 'pro' column if she was weighing her alternatives.

Her dad sat on one of the picnic table benches on the covered patio outside the mess hall. She cynically supposed she probably owed him a thank you for bringing Graham's true colors to light sooner rather than later. Although, after last night, that thought rang false. The declarations of love and then making love ... It had been more than just sex. It had been ... reverent. She'd felt worshipped when they'd taken her together. It had seemed like they'd finally figured out how to move forward as a unit. But now, in the light of day, it was like Graham would rather push her away than risk deepening their connection and eventually losing her. Ro stumbled. Was that his motive? Or did he really not care? The latter was hard to swallow, but Ro's confidence in her ability to discern a person's motives was still too tattered after the Evelyn-Charles incident. People made declarations of love all the time without meaning them, and apparently Graham was no different. Her dad stood, interrupting her musings.

"Now, sweetheart, before you get upset …" he started.

"I'm not upset with you," she said, cutting him—and the conversation—off. "But why are you up and around already? Shouldn't Beau have you chained to a cot in the clinic?"

"You know me, broke my leg and the next day I was harvesting the west field, using my crutches to help me steer. Life doesn't stop just because it'd be more convenient for you."

Ro smiled weakly as her father dished out his own brand of wisdom. For a paranoid country bumpkin, he was a pretty smart man. One who'd never waivered in his support of her, her sister, or their dreams. Graham and Zach had been dealt piles of shit when it came to their childhoods; she'd gotten so lucky, but hadn't appreciated what she had. A rush of emotion pummeled the wall of numbness. She dropped onto the bench next to him and rested her head on his uninjured shoulder. If there were a 'Worst Daughter of the Year' award, it would go to Rowan Callahan.

"I'm sorry, Dad. I'm sorry I made excuses and didn't spend more time with you. I'm sorry I didn't come home more. I'm sorry it took *this* to make me realize I was terrible daughter."

He slid his arm around her and pulled her close. She breathed in the familiar spice of his bay rum aftershave; it was a scent she'd forever associate with him. "What's this nonsense? A bad daughter? I don't know why you'd think that, Ro. I'm so damn proud of you; there are days I think my chest might explode from preening like a peacock."

"But I was never home, and I ..."

"You were chasing your dream. There's no harm in that. No apologies necessary. You were living your life and going after your goals with the same single-minded focus that your mama applied to hunting me down and bagging me like a dog."

Ro couldn't help but smile. "Is that how it went? She chased you?"

"She sure did. Haven't I ever told you that you get your drive and your guts from her? I was just a simple country boy, but your mama, before she was sick, was a sight to behold. There was nothing she couldn't accomplish if she put her mind to it. Smartest woman I ever met."

Ro couldn't help but wonder how her mother would have tackled the situation she faced. "What would she have done in my shoes?"

"She would've found a way to have her cake and eat it too. And your mama liked her cake."

"I don't see how that's possible. You won't stay, and they won't go. They're mutually exclusive options." Ro looked up at him. "Please explain to me again why you won't stay. This place is perfect. They've got everything."

He pulled away and turned to face her. "Well, sweetheart, that's the problem. It's too perfect, and that means there's a giant red bull's-eye painted on this place. It's obvious these boys are former military. Which means they still know people in the military. Which means people in the military know them, know where they live, and probably know what kind of preps they've made. It all comes down to how loyal those people are and how long that loyalty will last when things start to get real tough out there and they've got orders to carry out."

He had a point, and it was one Rowan couldn't refute. And even if she could, once his mind was made up, there was little to no chance of changing it. Ro sighed, the impossible nature of the situation weighing her down until the welcome numbness returned.

He picked up the shotgun from the picnic table. "You want me to go back and shoot 'em? Or maybe just one? It's not like you really need 'em both, right?"

Ro covered her face with both hands. "We are never talking about this again."

Now, if only she could train her mind not to think about them again. She forced a fake smile and went into the mess hall for breakfast.

CHAPTER THIRTY-FIVE

The last seven days had followed the same pattern: Graham woke up, worked for eighteen hours, pulling double or triple fire watch shifts or manning the command post, before falling back into bed. *Alone.* From what he'd gathered, Rowan and Erica had ganged up on Rick and persuaded him that his health required he stay more than the one day that Callahan would have preferred. No one had told Graham, and he'd refused to ask, exactly when the Callahans were planning to leave. Every day he dreaded getting the radio call announcing their truck was exiting the main gate. Every day the announcement didn't come, he didn't know whether he was relieved or disappointed. It was like drawing out the days on death row; at some point you had to give up hope of a pardon and welcome the needle that would end you.

Zach was still avoiding him … and their cabin. Graham wasn't sure where he'd been sleeping, but his mind conjured images of Zach and Rowan curled up together in one of the vacant guest cabins. He crushed those thoughts. Sitting at the desk in the command post, chuckling half-heartedly at the good-natured barbs being thrown back and forth on the radio, he tried not to think about spending another night alone. About spending the rest of his nights alone.

The door banged open, and Zach stalked into the room. He paced the small space before slamming both hands on the desk. His gaze burned into Graham. "They're leaving tomorrow."

The words were as devastating as Graham had predicted. There'd be no pardon for him. Not that he expected or deserved one. He stayed silent.

"Are you really going to let her walk out of here? Without even trying to change Callahan's mind?"

"I assume you've probably wasted enough breath on that for both of us."

Zach's glare was vicious as he yanked one of the chairs from beneath the low counter and threw himself into it. He scrubbed his hands across his face, chest rising and falling rapidly.

"How is she?" Graham asked, his tone casual, but the question had been plaguing him all week.

Zach thumped his palm down on the counter, making the radio equipment jump. "You have the balls to ask me that? After you've been like a fucking hermit? You don't deserve to know. This is your fault."

Graham exhaled slowly and swallowed. "It was the only choice—"

"I'm going with them," Zach said.

Zach waited for the explosion that he expected to follow his announcement. But Graham only stiffened, his mouth dropping open. His stunned gaze met Zach's. Graham looked like he might speak, but he closed his mouth without saying a word. *Yeah*, Zach thought, *Graham hadn't seen that one coming.*

But Zach hadn't been able to come up with another alternative that he could live with. He finally understood why Graham had preempted Rowan's decision. He'd wanted to spare her the agonizing pain of choosing between her family and them—again. What Graham hadn't realized was that, given the circumstances, none of them could escape that pain. Rowan sure hadn't. She looked pale and drawn, as if she hadn't slept in days. Her sassy walk had lost its bounce.

Zach didn't break Graham's stare, and he wasn't changing his mind. The Callahans might not be aware of his decision yet, but he'd follow them like a pathetic, lost pup if they tried to leave without him. Zach knew he owed Graham an explanation, but how did you explain to your best friend, your *brother*, that you'd weighed the options and, like his mother, you hadn't chosen him. Zach's stomach twisted like a washrag wrung dry. He went with the truth.

"You've been my best friend since I was seventeen years old. I'd never have survived all the shit we've been through over the last fifteen years without you either watching my back or leading the charge." Zach looked up at the ceiling and squeezed his eyes shut. "But I'm in love with her, and I'm not going to let her walk out of my life. Not willingly. I might've thought this ranch was my home and my life, but I was wrong, man. It's her. She's everything. I love you like a brother, but she's my future, even if you've decided she isn't yours."

"Get out," Graham said, his tone low and menacing.

"Graham—"

Graham shoved the chair back and took a fighting stance, the vein in his forehead visibly bulging. "Get the fuck out," he snarled. "Get the fuck off my ranch."

Zach unfolded himself from the chair and stared at Graham, who was clenching his fists reflexively, and looked to be barely restraining himself from taking his head off. "I'll be gone in the morning."

Zach turned and walked away from his best friend, closing the door on his past. Now, he just had to tell his future about his decision. And hope that her response was worth the friendship he'd just destroyed.

Graham embraced the rage and let it build until it drowned out the pain and betrayal that had swamped him at Zach's announcement. *This was her fault.* She was the reason that the one living person he thought he'd always be able to count on —the one person who'd always had his back—was walking away. Graham had once again been judged and found wanting. He had to vent his pain on someone, and it might as well be the source. He couldn't help but think, if she'd never stumbled into his crosshairs, then he wouldn't be losing his best friend and feel like he'd been through an emotional meat grinder over the last couple weeks. Graham knew his thoughts weren't rational, or hell, even sane, but he had to grasp onto something or he felt like he might break. And breaking wasn't an option.

He threw open the door that Zach had shut with such finality and stormed across the inner compound, desperate to find Rowan and unleash his temper. His search didn't take long; he found her in the mess hall, sitting at the dining table with Grace and Lia, watching the little girl color. He needed them gone. Because he sure as hell didn't want an audience for this. He'd probably end up on his knees begging her to stay. No one needed to see that.

"Everyone out," he said. "I need to talk to Rowan. Alone."

"Graham?" Allison called from the kitchen. "Is something wrong?"

"Just need a minute," he replied, his tone sharp and unyielding.

Allison bustled through the door from the kitchen; she tilted her head, studying his combative posture. She said nothing as she tugged Grace by the hand and backtracked into the kitchen.

"We'll go check on the garden and pick some veggies for dinner," she said. Lia trailed after them. She paused at the doorway, looking at Graham for a long moment and then back at Rowan. Graham saw Ro give her a nod, and only then did the woman cross into the kitchen.

"You've been avoiding me for a week, and now you can't wait sixty seconds to clear the room?" Ro thrust away from the table and stood, wobbling slightly. "You've got to scare a five year old girl and a woman who is trying to claw her way back from being terrified of men? Smooth, Conan. Real smooth."

Graham paced, gripping the back of his neck with both hands. "How did you convince him? That's all I want to know. How in the fuck did you convince a man you've known for a goddamn second to desert everything that matters to him? To turn his back on his home and the men who've fought beside him—bled for him? That's all I want to know. Then I'll let you go on your merry way to live happily fucking ever after together."

"What are you talking about?" Graham dismissed Ro's confused tone.

"Don't pretend you don't know. You're better than that. You're so fucking good that you forced my best friend to choose, and let me tell you, he didn't fucking choose me."

"You're speaking English, but I don't have a clue what you're saying."

"Don't you fucking lie to me, woman!" Graham roared, and he thought he heard a whimper.

Rowan backed up toward the wall, and Graham scarcely noticed her unsteadiness and rapid, shallow breaths.

He crossed the room and got in her face, gripping her by the upper arms and pressing her against the wall. She flinched, and he barely restrained himself from shaking her. "Tell me what you said to him," he demanded. "And why the hell didn't you say it to me? Am I just not good enough for you either?" His voice broke on the last words.

The metallic sound of a round being chambered accompanied the quiet voice that said, "Let go of her and step away, or I swear to God this bullet will end you."

Graham jerked his gaze over his shoulder to see Lia leveling a shaking M1911 at him. "Do it now," she said.

Graham released Rowan's shoulders and stepped away, lifting his hands in the universal gesture for "Don't shoot." With the shape they'd found her in, and her habit of pulling weapons on him, Graham figured Lia had to be at least a little, if not a lot, unstable. With the torment he was feeling at that moment, he didn't particularly care if she decided to pull the trigger, but there was no way he'd trust her not to shoot Rowan by accident. Even if Graham wanted to shake the living crap out of her, he'd never willingly expose Ro to danger. He might be able to live knowing that she and Zach were happy and making a life together without him, but he didn't think he could live in a world where she didn't exist.

Beside him, Rowan trembled and slumped against the wall. Her knees gave way, and she dropped, landing in a heap on the floor. Lia's eyes went wide, and her finger moved to the trigger.

Torn between grabbing Rowan and neutralizing the threat, he hesitated. His training took over, and he surged toward Lia, intent on knocking the barrel of the gun away from its aim at Rowan and twisting her wrist to force her to drop it. But his split second of indecision meant that Lia was pulling the trigger just as he rushed her. The explosion of the shot at close range was deafening. Graham felt a sickening punch to his left oblique.

Fuck, that hurt.

He dragged Lia down and dropped to his knees, the gun thudding to the floor beside them. A scream pierced through the low buzz in his ears as Graham shoved the gun behind away, and Lia scuttled backward toward the kitchen. He touched his burning lower left side, and his hand came away red. He covered the wound with both hands, trying to staunch the steady flow of blood. He stumbled to his feet, heading for Rowan and praying to God she hadn't been hit.

CHAPTER THIRTY-SIX

Ro's brain had been moving at turtle speed all day. She attributed it to the pounding in her temples that made it nearly impossible to concentrate, even on something as simple as coloring with Grace. And then Graham launched into a tirade that was beyond Ro's current capacity for comprehension. When he'd pushed her against the wall, he hadn't gripped her arms tightly, despite the anger that had been emanating from him. She'd started to feel woozy, and her knees had gone weak, and she hadn't been able to stop her ungraceful slide down the wall. Lia had looked like a virago, bent on protecting her, even though Ro didn't need protection from Graham. Even in his pissed off state, Ro had no fear that he'd hurt her. And then it had all unraveled, each motion seemingly exaggerated as Ro took them in: Graham's lunge, the flash of fear in Lia's eyes, Graham's swipe to the barrel of the gun, the muscles in Lia's hand flexing, and then the discharge of the pistol. Ro screamed when Graham fell to his knees.

"Graham!"

"Oh God. Oh God. Oh God," Lia chanted, awkwardly crawling backward away from Graham and the gun.

Ro snapped out of her haze long enough to croak, "Get Beau. Go."

Lia disappeared into the kitchen, and Ro heard the back door slam shut behind her. Graham was coming toward her. The red trail in his wake reminded her of watching her dad almost bleed out days before.

"Are you okay?" he asked, kneeling beside her.

"Me? Are you serious?" Ro pressed her hand over his, trying to help stop the bleeding. Graham flinched. "I'm sorry." She started to pull her hand away, but Graham shifted, covering her hand with his big, bloody one.

"It's okay. As long as you're okay. We're good." Ro nodded, but his next words were drowned out as the front door to the mess hall crashed open, and Zach and Beau flew into the room. Beau ripped his kit open, and carefully removed Ro and Graham's layered hands from the wound. He shredded Graham's shirt and tossed it aside. A deep, bleeding furrow, edged with torn flesh, was exposed.

"Oh my God," Ro breathed, falling back against the wall. Her vision swam, and her eyelids fluttered.

"Ro—. *Fuck*. Someone grab her …"

The rest of the words were lost as the blackness descended.

Ro woke disoriented. Her head throbbed, and her entire body ached. She surveyed her surroundings in the dim glow of the light and deduced she was flat on her back on a cot in the clinic. A noise to her right had her cautiously turning her head toward the sound. Zach was passed out on the cot next to her. *What the hell is going on? Why am I so damn tired?* Moving her head took so much energy. Ro groaned, and Zach jolted up, as if he'd been sleeping with one eye open. He rolled out of his cot and was at her side.

"Hey, baby. You joining the land of the living again?"

Ro started to respond, but her tongue stuck to the roof of her mouth. "Water?"

"Just a second." Zach stood and crossed to the sink, filling a small paper cup and returning to her side. Ro reached for the cup and realized she had an IV attached to the top of her hand.

"What happened?"

Zach sat on the edge of her cot and helped her sit up. She accepted the cup and sipped, as Zach pointed to her bandaged wrists. "Infection—from one of your wrists. It was bad, babe. Beau's pretty sure it was antibiotic resistant. He had to get creative. We weren't sure his treatment would work. You're lucky."

"I don't understand ..." When she'd asked what happened, she'd meant what had happened to Graham.

"I'm not going to pretend to have the answers to that. You'd have to ask Beau. I'm just fucking happy you're finally awake. You scared ten years off my life."

"But—" He pressed a finger to her lips.

"Important things first: how do you feel?"

"Tired. Achy. Like I got hit by a bus."

"I should get Beau." He started to rise.

"No, wait." She was almost afraid to ask. "Is Graham okay?"

Zach gave her a small smile. "Yeah, babe. He's going to be okay."

"Going to be?" Ro frowned. That didn't sound good at all.

"He's moving a little slow, but he's damn lucky that bullet

just grazed him. Another inch, and he'd have been missing a chunk of his side."

Ro shivered at the thought, and then wondered why he wasn't in the clinic with her. *Probably would've needed to sedate him to get him within ten feet of me.* She mentally cringed when she remembered the barely-leashed rage in his grip when he'd pushed her up against the wall. She was still confused about what had set him off. All she knew for sure was that it had something to do with the man sitting next to her.

"What happened? He avoided me for days, and then he was furious and spoiling for a fight. I just … don't get it."

"That's my fault. Not yours."

Maybe her head was still too fuzzy to follow logical reasoning, but Ro wasn't getting it. "I'm missing something here."

Zach started to respond, but the door to the clinic creaked open, and her dad stuck his head inside. "She awake yet?"

"Yes, sir. I'll give you two some privacy. And, I'm already late for fire watch." Zach kissed her forehead. "We still have a lot to talk about. Soon. I'll let Beau know you're up so he can fill you in."

Ro didn't have a chance to answer before he stood and headed for the door. He exchanged nods with her dad and exited.

"Well, girl, you scared the life out of me."

"Now you know how I felt."

"How about we don't do that again."

"That's a deal."

"How're you feeling?"

"Not too bad."

"Truth, Ro."

"A little bit like I wandered into oncoming traffic. But it's nothing I can't handle. I'm ready to go whenever you are."

"I have a feeling that boy of yours isn't going to want to leave until you're back to full steam."

Ro started to reply, but stopped when she replayed his words in her head. "You mean *let me leave*."

Her dad tilted his head and smiled slyly. "He didn't tell you?"

"Tell me what?" Ro asked, again doubting her capacity to follow a rational conversation.

Her dad jerked his head toward the door. "That man of yours told me, bold as brass balls on a bull, that you weren't leaving this place without him, and if I didn't like it, that was too damn bad."

Ro's jaw slackened. "What?"

"Good thing the bunker is big enough to fit at least a dozen comfortably, because our party just grew by one."

Ro's thoughts were whirling, rerunning the conversation she'd just had with Zach, and then Graham's tirade in the mess hall. *"You forced my best friend to choose, and let me tell you, he didn't fucking choose me."* It was all starting to come together. Holy shit. Zach was going to leave the ranch—and everyone on it—to be with her.

Her heart clenched when she remembered what else Graham had said. *"Tell me what you said to him, and why the hell didn't you say it to me? Am I not good enough for you either?"* Graham thought she'd talked Zach into leaving. Thought somehow she'd made a choice and it wasn't him. *Just like his mother.* Ro started to rub her eyes, but paused when the IV tugged at her hand. What to do now? Could she let Zach follow through? It tore at her to think that she'd come between the two men when the bond of their friendship had seemed wholly unbreakable. They were a team. A unit. *I suppose this is why normal people don't attempt permanent ménages,* Ro thought absently. *Someone probably always ends up being the odd man, or woman, out.*

"Ro? Are you okay?"

Ro slumped against the pillow. "I'm fine. Just tired, I guess," she said, not wanting to share her realization. "Are you sure you're okay with that? With him coming, I mean?"

"I don't think I have a choice; that man loves you, and it's not my place to stand in the way of that."

Ro tried to smile, but her happiness at Zach's decision was tainted by everything he would be giving up. She untangled the IV before pressing the heel of her hand to her forehead. *Why did everything have to be so goddamn complicated?*

"You should get some rest, sweetheart. I want to make sure you're good and healthy before we head out. You still look much too pale for my liking. We'll get Doc Beau in here to check you out, and when he gives us the all clear, I'd like to get on the road. No real hurry, but the sooner the better."

Ro's smile felt forced, but she just nodded and said, "Sounds good."

He kissed her forehead. "I love you, Ro."

Tears burned her eyes as she watched him leave. To the empty room she said, "What the hell am I going to do now?"

CHAPTER THIRTY-SEVEN

Beau had returned within minutes after her dad's departure. He'd explained that he'd prefer she stay in the clinic and on the IV fluids for a few more hours. He wanted her laying low as much as possible and not expending too much energy. And then he'd blindsided her with a question.

"I don't usually have to ask this, because generally my patients are men, but when was the first day of your last period?"

"Ummm … hell … let me think." Ro had switched from the shot to the pill a few months before because she kept missing her three-month appointments due to her insane work schedule. Her doctor had gotten pissed when she'd cancelled her appointment for her IUD twice. The pill had made sense because she could have the prescription mailed directly to her office, and it kept her period like clockwork. Except … when she'd made her mad dash out of her condo she hadn't grabbed any toiletries … and with everything that had happened, she hadn't even considered …

Ro stilled. *Oh, fuck.*

"Problem?" Beau asked, and Ro realized she'd spoken aloud.

Ro squeezed her eyes shut and clasped her fingers in front of her face and nodded. "I'm not on anything right now ... I haven't been since the day I left Chicago."

"It's not really any of my business, but have you been ..."

"Fucking two different guys repeatedly without protection? That'd be a yes," Ro quipped. "I'm such an idiot. What the fuck was I thinking? How did I let this happen?" Her face burned. She hadn't thought about the possibility of pregnancy or STDs. At her age, she should be backhanded for being such a moron. *How do you forget something like that?* Her only excuse, and it was a tenuous one, was that she was still trying to get back into the habit of taking her pill every night. Without the alarm on her phone ... *fuck.*

"Okay. Don't panic. Do you remember when your last period started?"

Ro took a few deep breaths, thinking back. She laughed humorlessly. "Yeah. It started and ended not too long before I left the city." It started the morning after the Evelyn-Charles incident. Ro remembered thinking that if it had started just one day earlier, she wouldn't have been in that situation.

"Well, I'm going to suggest you take a pregnancy test, just in case, even though it's probably too early to tell."

"What about STDs? Do you have any way to test for those, too?"

Beau hesitated before replying. "Ro, I'll be straight with you on that—as far as I know, Graham and Zach have never been with a woman without wrapping their shit up. It's standard operating procedure for all of us, and quite frankly, I'm pretty fucking surprised they weren't doing the same with you. It's not like there's a shortage of condoms here to be concerned about. We prepared a little ... over-zealously on that score. Even so, I hit you pretty hard with broad-spectrum antibiotics, so I'd say you're probably good. If you notice anything, let me know, and we'll figure it out."

Ro laughed maniacally. "How did pregnancy tests make the list of necessary supplies?"

Beau smiled, his eyes sympathetic. "Allison and Jonah were trying to get pregnant before everything happened, so I stocked up just in case." He stood and headed to the cupboard and pulled out a plain white rectangular box. He nodded toward the tiny bathroom. "I'll help you move the IV pole."

"If I'm pregnant, would the infection ... hurt the baby?" she asked, starting to freak herself out.

Another sympathetic smile. Which, coming from Beau, just added to her freak out. "It shouldn't have any effect, especially not this early."

Ro took the test, trying to ignore the fact that Beau was in the next room. He helped her maneuver the IV pole back to the cot and tried to distract her with funny stories about the team while Ro sweated through the next three minutes.

It was negative.

"That's what I expected, given the timing we're talking about, but you should really take another one in a week or so," Beau said.

"I'm not going to be here in another week," Ro replied, her words quiet and directed at her lap.

"Zach told me he's going with you."

Ro looked up, meeting his blue gaze. "Does everyone know?" How would they react? Would they be pissed? The thoughts only added to her fatigue.

Beau shook his head, one side of his mouth quirking. "I think he was waiting to tell you first." He rolled his stool to the desk and pulled open the skinny center drawer and held up a deck of cards.

"Would you like to play?"

"Why are you being so nice to me?"

Beau frowned. "Why wouldn't I be?"

"One, you were kind of prick to me before, and two, I've done nothing but cause trouble since I got here."

He grinned, and they both turned as Erica opened the door.

"Hey, sister, how're you feeling?" Her focus shifted to Beau. "Damn, you *do* know how to smile." She plopped onto the edge of Ro's cot. "So, when you going to spring her?"

Rowan had been wondering the same thing.

"Will it matter what I tell you this time? Or are you going to ignore everything I say?"

Ro squirmed. "I'll take it under advisement. How about that?"

"Good enough, I suppose. I'd like to see you stick around the clinic with the IV for another night, and not head out for at least a few more days, although a week would be better. You need some good home cooking from Allison and a shit ton of rest. You have to take every injury more seriously when you don't have a trauma center a few minutes away."

Erica pointed to the deck of cards. "We playing, or what?"

Beau nodded, and Ro settled in as he dealt. Then she proceeded to watch Erica hustle them both at five-card draw.

The next morning she awoke to find a note from Zach crumpled under her face on her pillow. It was a little drool-smeared, but it said he'd slept in the cot next to hers, but had to take a shift in the command post and would be back as soon as he could. Beau had shown up shortly after, removing her IV and unwrapping the gauze from her wrists. He commented that the red streaks that were the telltale sign of infection had already receded, and the wounds were starting to scab over again. He started to apply a new dressing, and all Ro wanted to do was go back to sleep. As he worked, her thoughts wandered. Other than the cot in the clinic and the bunk in Erica and Lia's cabin, she'd only slept in one other bed at the ranch. And that bed might as well have a giant "Do Not Enter—Trespassers Will Be Shot" sign above it. Even if it didn't, she wouldn't be too eager to crawl into it; she hadn't forgotten how easily Graham had ejected her from it. Her next option: Zach's bed, which wasn't a viable choice. Ro couldn't imagine laying there, knowing that Graham was sleeping a wall away. It would be cruel and unusual punishment. Erica helped her make a decision when she'd brought Ro some freshly laundered clothes.

"Your stuff is still in my cabin. You cool with staying there? You're more than welcome. But, as much as I'm sure you'd like someone to cuddle with, I don't think having a guy in the cabin is that great of an idea. Lia … well, it's just not a good idea."

Ro carefully pulled on jeans and a long-sleeve t-shirt. "How is she doing?"

"Honestly, I think she's got a long way to go before she'll be able to be around a guy without looking like she's going to crawl out of her skin. Except for Cam. He doesn't seem to make her as nervous as everyone else."

"Has she … said anything to you?"

Erica shook her head. "Not really. But I'd love to kill the guys who hurt her."

"You already helped. One of the two guys I came to the farm with … he was one of them."

"Are you serious? What the hell were you doing with them?"

"Long story …"

"Well, that's the price you're going to pay to stay in our cabin again. Because you must have had a hell of a good reason to be with a piece of shit like that."

"Does it help to know that all of the others are dead, too?"

"Marginally. Now spill."

So Ro spilled.

———————

The next three days were awkward, to say the least. Graham was firmly back to avoiding her, but the inner compound of the ranch wasn't so big that he was completely successful at it. Each time she saw him, her heart clenched before she could harden it. He made his choice. And hers. But she still wanted to know why he'd done it. Why he hadn't even consulted her—or waited thirty seconds—before shutting out the possibility of a future together. She hadn't yet gathered the courage to demand answers from him.

And then there was Zach. He was attentive as could be, but he was pulling far more than his fair share of fire watch and command post shifts. Ro wasn't one hundred percent certain, but she assumed it was because he felt guilty about leaving his team short-handed and wanted to contribute as much as he could before they left. It could have been Graham's revenge, but she didn't think he'd be that petty. Graham's actions were more of someone who had systematically cut them out of his life. At least he'd cut Ro out. Zach hadn't mentioned any encounters with Graham, but Ro assumed they had to have spoken. She hadn't found the right moment to ask. The rest of the time, Zach picked her up at the door of her cabin and walked her to the mess hall to eat. It was almost like they were dating, middle-school-style. Considering the man had had his dick in her ass, it was a

237

little strange. They'd kiss, they'd cuddle, and they'd share heated looks, but that was it. The one time they'd attacked each other and started to get naked in the bathhouse, Ty had barreled in. His "nice tits" remark had Ro scrambling to throw her shirt back on, and the mood had been ruined. Which was just as well, because Ty had started stripping, intent on taking a shower.

Ro had been disappointed, but a little niggling part of her was concerned about being with Zach without Graham. She told herself that it would be fine. Hell, every sexual encounter she'd had before Graham and Zach, except for the Evelyn-Charles incident—which she didn't count—had been one-on-one. A few two-on-one experiences and now she was worried about not having them both? *Spoiled, Ro?* She had to believe that if they'd continued on with their ménage, she would have been with each of them separately, probably sooner rather than later, so now shouldn't be any different. *But it was.*

When Ro wasn't contemplating that, she was trying to avoid thinking about the possibility of being pregnant. She told herself that it wasn't likely. Weren't there only like three days in any given month you could possibly get pregnant? Didn't lots of women try for years to get pregnant without luck? What were the odds? They couldn't be *that* good. And then she thought about that show, *16 and Pregnant*. She bet those girls had thought the same damn thing. So, what if she was? The baby could be either Graham's or Zach's. It wasn't like a paternity test was a possibility. She never thought she would ever be in a position where she didn't know who her baby daddy was. Might as well move into the redneck trailer park in the woods. *Oh wait, they'd firebombed it.*

And now, Ro was heading back to the clinic to meet Beau and get his all clear on leaving tomorrow morning. Only one more day at the ranch, and Allison had declared that a farewell dinner was required. She'd already started cooking up the feast. Ro pushed open the door, wondering if Beau would suggest another pregnancy test. Mind drifting, she stumbled when she saw Graham seated on the middle cot, Beau changing his bandages. Her gaze was drawn to the red and angry-looking wound that interrupted Graham's heavily muscled frame. She could see what Zach meant, another inch and Graham could have died. Ro shivered at the thought. A throat clearing made Ro tear her gaze away from his side.

"I … I'll come back. Didn't realize you were busy."

Beau looked at Graham, eyebrow raised. Ro couldn't interpret their silent conversation.

"It's fine. I'm almost done with him. Have a seat. The doctor will be with you shortly."

Unsure of what else to do, Ro sat at the desk chair Beau had gestured to. The silence was heavy with unspoken words. Graham felt like a stranger. And dammit, it *hurt* not being able to go to him and press into his uninjured side and have him hold her close. She'd thought his words that morning were simply his defense mechanism. Like he'd decided if he didn't give her the chance to reject him, it wouldn't hurt. If that had been his plan, did he regret it? Especially after Zach had decided to leave? It was too much to expect that Graham would follow his lead and decide to come with them. This was the only real home he'd ever had. How could she expect him give it up for her? She couldn't. She would never ask him to.

Graham broke the silence first. "So you're leaving tomorrow."

It wasn't a question, but Ro answered anyway.

"Yes."

She thought that not being able to touch him was painful? This *conversation*—if you could even call it that—was painful. Where was the heat and passion he'd radiated when he'd stormed into the mess hall? Where was that Graham? The one who had tossed her over his shoulder and carted her around and ignored her protests? *Oh wait, that Graham only came out when he cared about someone.* Someone he hadn't ruthlessly shoved out of his life. *Bastard.* Ro could feel her ire building. She dug her fingernails into the padding of the armrests, but couldn't stop her words.

"Don't forget your party hat tonight. I'm sure you'll be first in line to wish us farewell. Hell, I bet I'll have to watch the bumper of our truck to make sure the gate doesn't hit it on our way out."

Beau finished taping up Graham's dressing and rolled away from the cot.

"How about I give you two some time—"

"No need," Ro said, cutting him off and standing. "I think we've said all there is to say."

"Oh, look at that, I need more gauze. Better go find some." Beau rushed to the door and was gone before she could protest.

"How are you feeling?" Graham asked, his words wooden.

Ro lost the flimsy grip she had on her temper. "Seriously, that's what you have to say to me? After everything, that's what you've got? Jesus, Graham. You—"

"You're leaving tomorrow morning … with my best friend. What am I supposed to say? You tell me. Because I don't have the slightest idea of how I'm supposed to feel right now, let alone what I'm supposed to say."

"I didn't ask him to go!"

"Trust me, I know all about it. It was his choice. And he picked you."

"It's not always a matter of someone not choosing you. You're a grown man. You make your own goddamn choices.

240

Clearly, because you chose to cut me loose the second things got hard."

"It wasn't like that," he protested.

"No? Then what was it like?"

"I wasn't going to let you tear yourself apart over this. I was trying to make it easier for you."

"Don't do me any favors."

"Jesus, Ro. No matter what I do, I can't do right by you."

"You didn't even try."

Head and heart pounding relentlessly, Ro couldn't handle another minute of this conversation. She didn't want it to deteriorate into saying hurtful things she didn't mean. And she would *not* let him see her cry. She pushed away from the chair and didn't look back when she said, "Have a nice life, Graham."

Graham clenched his fists and fought the urge to explode. The woman was infuriating. She tossed off words without thought, not realizing they ripped through him like the bullet that had creased his side. What was he supposed to do? Turn his back on the home he'd been given and all of the people who counted on him? The fact that Zach had been able to do it still stunned him. It was inconceivable. Impossible. Out of the question.

She hadn't even asked him to leave with them.

That was the harshest truth to face. His split second decision to spare her emotional turmoil had spiraled out of control, wreaking havoc on his carefully ordered life. She'd leave, and everything would go back to normal. Except Zach would be gone. And Graham was pretty sure he'd have missed out on his one shot at happiness. After all this, he couldn't figure any way that he deserved a second shot.

CHAPTER THIRTY-EIGHT

The food Allison prepared for the farewell dinner was excellent, Ro thought, if you could chew through the thick layer of awkwardness that pervaded the whole affair. Even the five year old picked up on the tension. "Mommy, why is everyone so quiet? I thought this was a party?"

Graham was a no-show. He'd volunteered to take a command post shift instead, freeing up Jonah to attend. Ro didn't hear what Allison said to Grace, but the little girl didn't ask any more questions that highlighted the too-sober nature of the evening. Ro wanted to hide under the table, or better yet, run away. The self-doubt was beating her down, and she couldn't manage to do more than push her food around on her plate. The barbecued pulled pork should have smelled delicious, but Ro's stomach was churning too much to eat more than a few tiny forkfuls. She didn't even bother picking up the sandwich.

"Babe, aren't you hungry?" Zach's expression was concerned. He offered her a homemade French fry from his plate. "Want one?"

Ro smiled weakly and wanted to kick her own ass for

being so obviously miserable. But she couldn't fake happiness. Being disingenuous … wasn't her forte.

"I'm just tired," she said, not mentioning that her boobs hurt, and she was starting to freak the fuck out about what that might mean.

Jonah stood, drawing the attention of all in the room. He raised his water glass and said, "I want to propose a toast. To the Callahan family: it's been a pleasure to know all of you, and I hope you'll always feel like you have a place here, if you need it. And if you don't, may your stores be bountiful, your ammo dry and plentiful, and your lives happy. Take care of our boy; he's one of the best of us."

Everyone clinked their water glasses and finished dinner without further fanfare. The guys each stopped to slap Zach on the back and give her a hug. None of them said much more than, "Take care of yourselves." Ro's guilt grew exponentially.

"All right, see you bright and early," her dad called, heading for the door. "This train is leaving at oh-six-hundred."

Erica grumbled about getting up so early, but moved to the kitchen to help Allison and Lia clean up. Ro didn't have the energy to offer, even for politeness sake. She wanted her bed and for the next twenty-four hours to be over.

Zach walked her back to her cabin and kissed her softly on the forehead. "I'll be by in the morning to get you." He plucked a peanut butter Power Bar from his pocket. "Just in case you get hungry. Don't think I didn't notice you didn't eat a damn thing for dinner."

She buried her head in his chest. "I'm sorry I've been such a drag, I just …"

He kissed her forehead again. "I know, babe. This isn't easy for me either."

"Then why are you doing it?" she whispered.

"Sometimes you have to make the hard choice, because it's the right choice." He stepped away. "Now get some sleep. I love you."

The door cracked against the wall, and Graham instinctively reached for his gun. Seeing Zach stalk into the command post brought on a sick feeling of déjà vu. The last conversation that had started this way hadn't ended well. He forced himself to relax and reached for the half-empty bottle of Jack on the desk. Zach studied him as he poured the shot and tossed it back. Graham welcomed the burn of the whiskey streaking from his throat to his gut. He'd never been drunk while on duty, but this seemed like an appropriate occasion. He flicked a glance at Zach's aggressive posture.

"She's miserable. And it's your fault."

"That so?" Graham decided the mention of Rowan merited another generous shot. He sloshed the amber liquid into the glass and lifted it to Zach in a toast before downing it. The *crack* of the shot glass connecting with the table echoed like a gunshot in the small room. "Pull up a chair. I'll even find you a fucking glass. We can toast your new future." Graham had tried to avoid watching them celebrate tonight. Tried to stay out of the way and not color it with his bitterness, but he should've known Zach wouldn't let it go.

Zach paced.

"Cut the shit, Graham. I know you, and this has to be ripping you up. But you walk around like it's just another fucking day. We're *leaving*. Tomorrow. There's a chance you'll never see Ro or me again. How can you fucking act like it doesn't matter?"

Graham jolted up. The screech of the metal on concrete was as discordant as his thoughts. *Fuck this shit.* He grabbed the shot glass from the desk and hurled it at the wall. "You see that?" He pointed to the shattered glass. "That's how I fucking feel about this. But what the hell am I supposed to do? Beg her to stay? Because I'm not going to put her through that."

Zach reached for the whiskey. "Did you ever think about coming with us?" He paused to take a swig from the bottle before looking at Graham. "Did the possibility ever even occur to you?"

Graham yanked the bottle out of Zach's grip and barely held back from heaving it at the wall. "Of course it fucking occurred to me. But you tell me how the hell I'm supposed to turn my back on everything and everyone here? How do I do that? Because I sure as shit don't know how."

Zach stood, face lined with strain and shoulders slumped in defeat. He walked to the door and paused at the threshold. "You just choose her." He met Graham's gaze. "I'm gonna miss you, brother."

Graham was left alone, clutching the whiskey bottle with Zach's words ricocheting through his brain.

CHAPTER THIRTY-NINE

Ro watched as her dad rearranged the gear in the bed of the truck before stowing her own backpack in the cab. The truck was parked alongside the armory for easy loading. Apparently, Graham had offered her father more firepower to ensure they had a safe trip to their undisclosed location. The gesture was a little too much, "Here's your hat, what's your hurry?" to Ro.

"You coming to get some grub?" her dad asked.

Allison had cooked up an extra-early breakfast, but Ro's stomach was too knotted up to consider eating.

"I'm good."

"I'll be back in a few, and then we're heading out." Her dad sauntered off to what was likely their last home-cooked meal for a while, and Ro caught sight of Zach. He was weighed down with two sea bags and a backpack. He dropped them to the ground near the tailgate with a thump. Ro pushed off the side of the truck, gathered her courage, and intercepted him as he started to shove them inside.

She laid a shaky hand on his arm. "I can't let you do this."

Zach jerked backward like he'd been slapped. "Please tell me you're talking about my packing skills. Tell me you're not saying what I think you're saying."

Ro squeezed her eyes shut, trying to stop the tears that were poised to fall. "I can't be the reason you throw away a friendship that means everything to you. I can't be the reason that you turn your back on everything that matters to you."

"Ro—"

"No, listen to me." Ro forced back the sob that was trying to claw its way out of her throat. "This is a mistake, and you know it. You're going to resent the hell out of me as soon as we drive out those gates, and it's going to kill anything we could have together. Graham may not be with us, but he would be hanging between us at every moment. Some part of you has to know I'm right." She lost the battle with her tears, and they streamed down her face.

Before she could swipe them away, Zach cradled her face with his big hand. "Why are you doing this?" His thumb skimmed across her cheek, catching her tears.

"Because I'm making the hard choice. *The right choice.* The only choice I can live with."

"Don't I get a say?"

She just shook her head.

"Don't do this, Ro. I love you." It broke her to see tears gathering in his eyes.

"I know," she said, barely able to get out the words. "I love you, and I love Graham, too. But it's all or nothing for us. Anything less is going to destroy at least one of us, and I can't let that happen. Not if I can stop it."

"Rowan, I swear to God, woman," Zach started, his features twisted with anguish.

"Please," she whispered. "Don't make this harder than it already is." She leaned up on her tiptoes to press one last kiss to his cheek. She pulled away from his grip and lunged into the backseat, shutting and locking the door. Burying her face in the arms her bulky gray sweatshirt, she sobbed.

From his position inside the doorway of the command post, Graham could hear and see everything that was taking place next to the Callahan truck. And what he was hearing and seeing gutted him. *Why would she do it?*

Rick Callahan's rangy stride carried him out of the mess hall. His youngest daughter followed, dressed in camo pants and a black sweatshirt, her trademark dew rag covering the top of her head. Rick paused as they neared the truck, spying Zach bent at the waist as if he'd just been sucker punched. Zach straightened slowly before shouldering his bags. They exchanged a few words, but Graham couldn't hear them. By the look on Erica's face, it was safe to say Zach had just informed them of Rowan's unilateral change in plans. Rick shook his hand and slipped him a piece of paper. Zach walked away, staring down at the scrap of paper in his hand. Rick tapped on the window, and after a beat, Rick and Erica climbed into the cab of the truck, and the engine roared to life. The truck shifted into gear and started to pull away, circling the armory and command post to head for the gate.

Graham jerked away from the door, as if shocked from his stupor by the growl of the diesel engine. He jogged toward Zach, cutting him off and stopping directly in his path.

"What the fuck, man?"

"I was wrong. I thought I could watch her leave, but this shit isn't working for me. You were right—she's it. She's everything. And we can't let her leave. Not without us." He held out his radio. "Tell Ty to stall them at the gate. I need to grab my stuff."

Zach looked incredulous. "Are you fucking kidding me? Now? You decide *now* that you can't live without her? You wait until she breaks my fucking heart? What the hell is wrong with you?" Graham didn't even try to dodge Zach's fist as it connected with his jaw. He staggered back a step and stared at his friend.

"You done? Or you need another?"

"You're such a prick, G. If I had more time, I'd beat you into the fucking ground."

"So, we good?" Graham held out a hand.

Zach clasped it. "Yeah, fucker. We're good. Now get your shit so we can go get our girl. I'm not letting her get away. No matter what she thinks is the right choice."

Graham took off running toward their cabin as Zach radioed Ty with instructions to stall the Callahans. He spotted Beau leaving the clinic, a black civilian backpack slung over one shoulder.

"Where you headed?"

"Going after our girl."

"Shit. They already leave?"

"Yeah, but we're holding them up at the gate. They're missing a couple passengers."

Beau looked confused. "Little Rambo Girl miss the train?"

"No, man. Me and Zach."

"But I thought—"

"Can't explain. Gotta hurry."

"Well, then just give this to Ro." Beau tossed him backpack. Graham slipped it over his shoulder without asking about the contents. He was already running down the list of things he needed.

Ro stared out the window. The farther away they got from the walls, the harder the tears fell. Her fingers tangled her in hair as she silently promised herself that once they'd crossed through the gate, she'd stop crying. It made her feel better to believe her own lie.

The main gate was in sight, and Ty appeared to be fiddling with the lock. Her dad braked and cranked down the window.

"What's the problem, son?"

Ty rounded the hood and poked his head in the window. "Grabbed the wrong set of keys for the padlock. But don't you worry, one of the guys is bringing 'em out. It'll just be a few minutes."

They waited. And waited. Ten minutes later, Ro's dad said, "We'll just go back and get the keys."

"No need," replied Ty. "Here they come."

They? Ro's head snapped around, and she saw Graham and Zach stalking toward the truck, loaded down with gear, determined looks on their faces.

What the hell?

"Now what's this about?"

"Not my place to say."

As if synchronized, Graham and Zach threw open the back doors of the cab. Ro looked from one man to the other, dumbfounded.

Zach leaned on the doorframe closest to Ro, and said, "Move over, babe. You ain't leavin' without me. No way, no how. Don't care what you say."

Mouth hanging open, Ro looked to where Graham was shoving gear under the bench seat.

"What … what are you doing?" Ro asked him.

Graham looked up. "You were right. It's all or nothing

for us. And nothing isn't something we can live with." *He'd heard that?*

"But the ranch … your team … I thought—"

"I was dead wrong to think I could let you go. You're more important than the ranch. They'll be fine. It's Zach and me who won't be fine if we let you leave without us."

Ro was still processing his statement when he tossed her an unfamiliar black backpack. "That's from Beau."

"What is it?"

"No clue, babe. Didn't take the time to check. Was in a little bit of a hurry."

Erica leaned over the seat and snatched the bag from Ro before she could unzip it. Rowan didn't argue, because Graham and Zach had finished stowing their gear and were climbing into the back seat, sandwiching her between them. *Where she belonged.* The warmth of that thought chased away any lingering confusion.

Ty smiled. "Sorry for the hold up, folks. It turns out I do have the right key. It'll be just a minute."

"What the hell is all this?" Erica said. She held up two white rectangular boxes and a fat pill bottle. "Is there something you aren't telling us?"

CHAPTER FORTY

The main gate swung open, but Rick didn't put the truck in gear. He was staring at the bottle and whatever else Erica was holding. Graham nabbed the bottle just as Rick grabbed one of the boxes and opened it.

"Rowan Elizabeth Callahan, why am I holding a pregnancy test?"

"Umm …" Ro mumbled.

Graham read the label on the bottle out loud. "Prenatal vitamins." He turned and stared at Ro and then met Zach's gaze over her shoulder. "You know about this?"

"One of them knocked you up?" Erica asked.

"No! I mean, I don't know. Nothing's for sure. The last test was negative. Beau is just being overly cautious."

"You were going to leave and not say anything about the fact that you could be carrying our baby?" Graham demanded.

Ty, sensing something was wrong, closed the main gate.

An uneasy silence settled over the inhabitants of the truck. Graham figured they were all waiting for Rowan to speak. He sure as hell was. Her dad broke the silence first.

"This changes things."

"Fucking changes everything," Zach said. "I can't ... I don't even ... Why didn't you tell us?"

"There's nothing to tell!"

"Yet," Zach challenged.

"When will you know for sure?" Graham asked.

"I don't know, another few days. Maybe a week?"

Rick put the truck in reverse and then proceeded to make a three-point turn and started driving back in the direction of the walls.

"What are you doing?"

"Rowan, your mother almost died giving birth to both of you girls. There's no way I'm taking you away from the only doctor we have available if you're pregnant."

"And if I'm not? What then? We're packing back up and leaving because you're so damn sure this place has a target on it?"

"If you're not, well, I guess we'll see then. But after this morning, I can't imagine trying to separate you from these two boys. They're willing to give up everything for you, and a man doesn't do that unless he's either crazy or in love. But you better believe, if you're pregnant, I will stand by with a shotgun until one of them marries you."

"I don't care if she's not pregnant," Graham said. "We're marrying her anyway."

Ro stared at him. "You are?"

"We are."

"Wait, you lost me," Erica interjected. "How can you both marry her?"

"You let us worry about that," Graham said, rolling the window down to yell orders to Ty about the change in plans.

"And that was the worst proposal ever, by the way," Erica added.

"That's because it wasn't a proposal," Graham replied. "It's a done deal."

The Great Rowan Callahan Period Watch lasted almost four days. Rowan refused to take a pregnancy test during those four days because it seemed indulgent when she could just wait it out. She'd finally been able to talk Graham, Zach, and her dad out of a wedding. It wasn't that she didn't want to marry them, but Ro didn't see any point. First, it wouldn't be legal, because they couldn't exactly go apply for a marriage license for three. Second, the county clerk wasn't exactly issuing marriage licenses *at all*. People had more important things to worry about—like surviving. And third, leaving the ranch to find an officiant would put everyone's safety in jeopardy, and that wasn't a risk Ro was willing to take just to placate the men in her life. She was still struggling to process the fact that Graham and Zach had both been willing to give up everything to be with her. A commitment like that didn't get stronger because of some piece of paper or a ceremony. Ro liked to think that she'd demonstrated her commitment to them in the privacy of their cabin. Multiple times. After she'd atoned for not telling them she might be pregnant.

Graham and Zach finally lost their collective patience on the morning of day four and cornered her in the bathroom. Wordlessly, Zach held out the test and gave her the sternest look she'd ever seen on his face. After she'd peed on the stick, Ro sat on the bed trying to play out the scenario both ways. Heads, she, Zach, and Graham left with her dad and Erica to live for an indefinite period of time in an undisclosed location. Tails, they stayed. Her dad hadn't said he and Erica would still leave, but Rowan couldn't picture him willingly being separated from his only grandchild.

Zach sat next to her, fingers tangled with hers. Graham paced the bedroom. Rowan had a strong suspicion that he was counting to one hundred eighty very slowly in his head, because he spun and said, "It's time."

"Who wants to do the honors?" Zach asked.

"All of us," Rowan said, voice hoarse with strain.

They crowded into the tiny bathroom—Rowan first and the two men just behind her, one on each side. Rowan looked down at the test on the counter and saw … a little blue plus sign.

"Holy shit." She stumbled back into two sets of strong arms. She felt lips on her hair and her cheek.

"Let's move this party out of the bathroom," Zach said, ushering them back into the bedroom.

"No. We need to double check." Now that the preliminary verdict was in, Ro's concern about wasting pregnancy tests went out the window. She had to know for sure.

Graham went rigid. She hurried to explain, "I mean, it could be a false positive, right?"

"Do you want it to be a false positive?"

Ro shook her head. "I just need to be sure."

Zach grasped her shoulders. "We've been dancing around the subject for days, but I have to know, are you regretting this? Do you want this baby or not?"

Ro stared at the floor, thoughts chaotic and approaching the thousand miles per hour mark. She forced herself to form words into a coherent sentence. "I … I'm. Shit." She rubbed her face. "Does it matter that I don't know whose baby it is?" she asked.

Zach maneuvered her backward, until she could feel the mattress against the backs of her knees. He gently pressed her shoulders until she sat. Both men crouched in front of her, and Graham spoke first. "This baby is *ours*. All of ours.

Doesn't matter at all whether I'm the father or Zach is the father. This baby is *ours*."

"Do you care whose baby it is?" Zach asked.

"No," Ro whispered. "But I don't want either of you to be disappointed in eight months when this baby doesn't look like you."

Graham's lips quirked into a smile as he smoothed her hair away from her face. "If the baby comes out looking like Zach, I'll be sure to knock you up the next time."

Ro could feel her eyes go big and her mouth drop open. "You're going to want more?"

"Is that a problem?"

"I … hell. Let's just make sure this one comes out okay first."

Graham handed her another test. "Go make sure, babe."

Ro took it, and then looked at them both carefully. "What if it's negative?"

"Then you take another?"

"No. I mean, what if I'm not pregnant?"

"Doesn't matter one goddamn bit. You're ours, too."

Ro stood, kissed Zach, and then Graham, and went to take the second test.

The plus sign was still there.

CHAPTER FORTY-ONE

Holy shit, I'm going to be a dad, Graham marveled as he followed Ro and Zach across the compound to the mess hall. He'd never considered the possibility before meeting Ro. Quite frankly, it still scared the living hell out of him to be bringing a child into the world when nothing was certain, and there was no hospital to run to if something went wrong. He had faith in Beau, but nothing was more important than protecting Ro and their baby. He still needed to convince Rick that the ranch was the safest place for them to be after the baby was born. He didn't want Ro worrying for the next eight months about what might happen and whether she'd be faced with another devastating choice. She didn't need that kind of stress, and he was going to make sure she didn't have to deal with it. It was time to pull out the big guns. He was going to show Rick the bunkers and make whatever promises the man needed to hear in order to convince him to stay.

They filed into the mess hall. Erica, Rick, Grace, and Beau were seated around the scarred wooden table. Their heads popped up like meerkats when Ro walked into the room. He figured the shit-eating grin Zach had been sporting since they'd seen that second positive test gave away the results.

"So?" Rick asked.

Graham put his hand on Ro's shoulder. Her eyes misted as she nodded. Erica was out of her chair and across the room before anyone could respond to Ro's silent confirmation. She flung herself at Ro.

"I'm going to be an aunt!"

Graham studied Rick, thankful the man's shotgun was nowhere in sight. His weathered face transformed into a wide smile as he rose.

"Come here, Rowan. Give this grandpa-to-be a hug."

Erica squealed as Ro extricated herself from her sister's embrace. When she stepped away from him, Graham realized that he was going to have a hard time letting Ro out of his sight—or hell, out of his reach—for the next eight months. The woman was his heart, his soul, and every other damn thing that mattered.

She hugged her father, and tears dotted her lashes.

"Don't cry. Not unless those are happy tears." Ro nodded, and her father wiped them away. "Everything's going to be fine, Ro. We'll figure it all out."

That was his cue.

"I wanted to talk to you about that, Rick. There's one more part of the inner compound here you haven't seen yet, and I think it might change your mind about a few things."

Rick released Ro from the hug. "What are you talking about? I've been over every inch of this place."

"No, sir. You haven't. But if you come with me, I'll show you the rest." Graham started for the kitchen. "Ro, baby, why don't you stay up here and eat breakfast with your sister? Let Beau tell you all the stuff you're not supposed to do for the next eight months."

Her eyes sparkled with tears as she whispered, "Thank you."

Zach followed Graham and Rick into the kitchen, and squatted to roll up the colorful rag rug that lay in the center of the floor. Graham knelt beside him and lifted a loose plank. Rick cocked his head to the side as Zach turned the recessed metal handle and a section of the wooden floor and a slab of eighteen-inch thick concrete lifted.

"What the hell?"

"Come on down," Graham said as he climbed down the ladder. Zach waited until Rick had made his way into the bunker before following. Graham stood next to the red dome mounted on the wall.

"This actuator releases the hydraulic system so the floor drops back into place. Once the system is engaged from below, this bunker is inaccessible from above."

"Well, I'll be damned …" Rick's look of wonder gave Zach hope that Graham's revelation might actually change the man's mind.

"That's eighteen inches of poured concrete, reinforced with twice the amount of rebar normally used. That construction carries through to the rest of the bunker." Graham pointed toward the porthole-style door across the room. "That steel door is a foot thick and, when it's locked, it isolates this section from the rest of the tunnel and bunker system."

"Rest of the system?"

"There are four bunkers, each provisioned and equipped with independent air filtration systems and stand-alone wells. If one section is compromised, the rest are still safe. This was originally built as a bomb shelter, and then upgraded to a

259

fallout shelter. We've added our own touches over the past few years."

"Well, shit. This place might just be built better than my little hidey-hole. It's certainly bigger, especially if the other rooms are this big."

"They're near the same size."

Zach was about to release a breath when Rick said, "I still think you're going to have a problem with the feds beating down your door."

"Then we fall back in here. We've got enough supplies to last us for years."

"But what kind of life is that? Living underground?"

"The same kind of life you've got to offer. Isn't your 'hidey-hole' underground? What makes it safer than this?" Zach could tell Graham's patience was wearing thin as the muscles of his jaw tensed.

"It's not the same. The main living quarters might be underground, but it's far enough out of the way that it would be safe to come up during the day. There'd be fresh vegetables once the garden was established."

Well, fuck. This is going nowhere fast, Zach thought. Time to put a stop to the pissing match.

"Just … stop. This isn't about what you've got or what we've got. The only thing that matters is keeping your daughters and the baby safe. We're on the same side. At least for now, anyway." Zach met Rick's stare. "We can't let Ro wonder for the next eight months whether you're going to walk out those gates with or without her and us as soon as she gives birth."

"Now wait a minute—I'm not going to try to separate her from either of you." Rick blew out a rush of air. "Look, as far as I'm concerned, the window for safe travel is closing pretty damn quick. I can't say what this world is going to be like eight months from now, but I will swear to you that I will not do anything to make Rowan unhappy, as long as she and Erica and the baby are safe."

Zach felt the tension in the room drain away. *That's good enough for now.*

Allison insisted on another celebratory dinner—one that actually involved celebrating. Ro laughed as Ty and Travis toasted Graham and Zach repeatedly, urging them to take shot after shot of whiskey. Neither of them would be worth a damn if they kept going at this pace. Which was too bad, because she was ready to drag the pair back to their cabin and do very dirty things to them.

Grace giggled as Ro's dad stole her nose and pretended to forget where he'd hidden it. Cam sat midway down the table, shielding Lia from the boisterous noise of the room. Erica cleared dishes and carried them to the kitchen. Ro pushed away her plate. The only evidence of her dinner was the bare rib bones and a smear of mashed potatoes. Full, she laid a hand on her stomach and marveled that there was a person growing inside her. A little bean that would be an amazing combination of her and one of the men accepting congratulations for 'knocking up the little woman.' She leaned back in her chair. The warm glow that settled over her had nothing to do with pregnancy and everything to do with the fact that somehow, despite everything that had happened in the last month, she had found a new home and was surrounded by the people she loved. Ro fingered the dog tags hanging from the chain she wore. One was Graham's, and one was Zach's. They'd dropped it over her head uncer-emoniously before dinner, explaining that if she wouldn't relent on her no-wedding stance, she was damn well going to wear some sign of their commitment. In Ro's mind, they were better than any ring.

She'd gone from a strap-on induced pity party to celebrating the news of her pregnancy with her two men and her family. And all it had taken was a damn apocalypse. Go figure.

A girl really couldn't ask for more.

Well … maybe she could.

She covered her mouth with her palm and faked a yawn. "I'm feeling a little … tired."

Her hand hid a wide smile when Graham and Zach stood in tandem. Zach swung her up in his arms.

"Let's get you to bed, baby." Graham smoothed a wisp of hair away from her face. Ro grinned. She was getting lucky tonight.

EPILOGUE

"I swear to God, I'm going to neuter you both! You're never fucking touching me again!"

Graham flinched as Rowan's grip approached finger-breaking strength. He looked over at Zach and noted the pained expression on his face. After delivering the baby, Beau might be setting and taping fingers.

"I see the head," said Beau. "Give me another push, Ro. You can do it."

"Come on, baby. You've got this." Graham adjusted the pillows behind her with his free hand.

"Fuck you, you don't know what I've got. Holy shit, that hurts!"

"Breathe, baby. Just breathe," Zach said.

Ro breathed, and Graham's stomach knotted at the agony twisting her features.

A cry cut through the sound of Ro's panting breaths, and Graham's zeroed in on Beau ... who was holding a white-faced infant streaked with blood. *Holy shit. We have a baby.*

"Congratulations. It's a girl."

Beau immediately moved to lay the baby on Ro's bare stomach, drying her off and covering her with a blanket.

Graham marveled at their tiny, squirming daughter. *Holy shit. We have a daughter.* He leaned down to kiss Ro's hair as Zach kissed her cheek. Graham focused on the baby and her thick black hair. *Holy shit. That's my daughter. Our daughter.*

Beau clamped the umbilical cord and cut it. Ro moved the baby up to find the nipple she was already rooting for.

"Wow," Zach said. "Just … wow."

"What are we going to name her?" Graham asked.

They'd been arguing for months, but had narrowed it down to two girl names and two boy names.

Ro glanced up, eyes bright with tears. "Mira. I want to name her Mira."

It wasn't a name that Ro had ever mentioned. Zach shrugged. After watching her go through labor … "Whatever you want, Ro. I think it's perfect." Graham leaned closer. "Welcome to the world, Mira."

They watched their tiny daughter until Beau eased her from Ro's chest and sponged her clean. After she was dried and swaddled, he asked, "Which of her daddies wants to hold her first?"

Zach reached out, and Beau settled the baby—*Mira*—into his arms. "Holy shit, she's so little."

A light tap on the door stole Graham's attention. He walked over and opened it a crack, revealing a concerned Jonah. "We're a little busy at the moment."

"I know, I know. I'm so sorry, man. The timing sucks, but the sensors triggered about ten minutes ago, and now we've got someone at the gate wearing a uniform. Travis seems to think you might know him from your last tour. We haven't engaged. Wanted your input first."

Graham glanced at Ro, Zach, and Mira. Keeping them safe was his first priority, regardless of the shitty timing.

Rumors had been swirling over the ham radio waves. The military was reportedly out rounding up every able-bodied person to work as a laborer in the New Hope For America Work Corps camps. Small militia groups had formed and were engaged in guerrilla warfare, ambushing them repeatedly. Whichever way Graham figured it, someone showing up at their gate in a uniform could only mean bad things.

"Give me a minute. I'll be right there."

Graham returned to Ro's side, leaning down to kiss her forehead. "I'll be right back."

"What's going on?"

"Don't worry. I've got to go check on something. I'll be back to hold my baby girl in a little bit. I love you." He nodded to Zach before grabbing the M4 propped next to the door and heading out to deal with whoever was interrupting the most important moment of his life. Friend or enemy, the first thing they'd be getting was a fist to the jaw.

The End

ACKNOWLEDGMENTS

I'm not sure whether most readers read this part of the book, but I always do. So my first thank you goes to the readers. Without you, I'd just be writing for myself. And while that'd be entertaining, it wouldn't be nearly as much fun. To my betas: AJS and CNS. You told me what sucked and what worked, and your feedback made this book so much better than I could have ever made it by myself. You have my eternal gratitude for taking the time to read everything I threw at you. To Madison Seidler: Thank you for taking a chance on me and giving me the confidence to hit publish. Your editing skills are truly an asset to the indie author.

And last, but certainly not least, thank you to my entire family for everything you are and everything you do. Without you, I wouldn't be me. For Dad, I miss you more than you'll ever know. Thank you for teaching me that no goal is ever too big to pursue. Consider this writing gig my BHAG. Although, I will say, I hope you're not reading this up there. I'm pretty sure you'd ground me for the rest of my life, regardless of the fact that I'm 30 years old.

DON'T MISS OUT!

Visit www.meghanmarch.com/subscribe to subscribe for my newsletter and receive exclusive content that I save for my subscribers.

ALSO BY MEGHAN MARCH

Magnolia Duet:

Creole Kingpin

Madam Temptress

Legend Trilogy:

The Fall of Legend

House of Scarlett

The Fight for Forever

Dirty Mafia Duet:

Black Sheep

White Knight

Forge Trilogy:

Deal with the Devil

Luck of the Devil

Heart of the Devil

Sin Trilogy:

Richer Than Sin

Guilty as Sin

Reveling in Sin

Mount Trilogy:

Ruthless King

Defiant Queen

Real Dirty

Real Sexy

Flash Bang Series:

Flash Bang

Hard Charger

Standalones:

Take Me Back

Bad Judgment

ABOUT THE AUTHOR

Making the jump from corporate lawyer to romance author was a leap of faith that *New York Times*, #1 *Wall Street Journal*, and *USA Today* bestselling author Meghan March will never regret. With over thirty titles published, she has sold millions of books in nearly a dozen languages to fellow romance-lovers around the world. A nomad at heart, she can currently be found in the woods of the Pacific Northwest, living her happily ever after with her real-life alpha hero.

She would love to hear from you.
Connect with her at:
www.meghanmarch.com

Made in United States
Orlando, FL
18 August 2024

50494657R00171